THE DEMON ABRAXAS

BY

RACHEL CALISH

Bella
BOOKS

2013

Bella Books, Inc.
P.O. Box 10543
Tallahassee, FL 32302

Printed in the United States of America on acid-free paper.

First Bella Books Edition 2013

Editor: Katherine V. Forrest
Cover Designed by: Kristin Smith
Photograph Credit: Elena Koulik and Aldra

ISBN: 978-1-59493-379-0

About the Author

Rachel Calish lives on the Internet, but frequently downloads herself into real-time so she can play with her pup and two cats. She's a fan of Border Collie mixes, because any dog blends well with Border Collie, and stays in shape by trying to keep up with one. Rachel grew up on mythology and fairy tales, to which she has added a deep love for fantasy stories and gaming. These days, you can often find her in the company of literary werewolves and entrepreneurial elves. As her staid, grown-up personality, Rachel Gold, she is the author of the young adult novel *Being Emily*.

Visit her on the web at rachelcalish.com and bengemily.com

For Kim Albee, who is good with all sorts of beings.

Acknowledgments

I'd like to thank Professor Larry Sutin who went through many edits with me back when this was my Master's thesis. (Yes, you can get a Master's degree writing fantasy!)

Many thanks to Katherine V. Forrest for her edits and humor—and to Linda Hill and Karin Kallmaker at Bella Books for their encouragement.

I can't thank enough my astounding beta readers (especially those who read two or more drafts) and early editors including Wendy Nemitz, Sara Bracewell and Lyda Morehouse, and my cherished alpha reader Alia Whipple.

I also want to thank Jane Wisdom, for her significant help with the early drafts, and Allison Moon, for invaluable brainstorming and other inspirations.

And this book wouldn't be complete without expressing my deep gratitude to Reggie Ray and Craig Lindahl-Urben for being embodiments of wisdom—they get the credit for all the wise things Abraxas says and I'll take credit for any of it that I messed up in translation.

"This name occurs in connection with Greek magical formulas and is frequently considered the name of some magician's helper such as certain uncivilized tribes believe in even at present. But it appears that Abraxas has a much deeper significance. We may conceive of the name as that of a godhead whose symbolic task is the uniting of godly and devilish elements."

— Hermann Hesse, *Demian*

CHAPTER ONE

"We could be out dancing," Ruben said and rattled the ice in his glass impatiently.

He looked like a Titan standing in the same room as the men Ana worked with. Most of them were short and skinny or short and potbellied, plus they'd given the casual, thirty-second attention to their clothes that most straight guys did. In his short-sleeved designer shirt, Ruben looked like a movie star—even though he was only a semi-employed character actor.

"You invited yourself to this party, remember?" Ana told him and tried to keep from smiling. She wanted him there with her just in case that last-minute invitation she'd fired off actually bore fruit.

"I forgot what a straight wasteland you work in," he said. His beautiful mouth sulked, but his eyes were bright with teasing.

"Bear that in mind the next time you suggest I find a girlfriend at work," Ana told him.

She set her empty glass down on a table and peeked into her purse to check the clock on her cell phone. In another half-hour they could make a graceful exit. She could send Ruben off to the bars and…do what? She was all gussied up in a Donna Karan silk dress she'd picked up crazy on sale, maybe she should try wearing it out on the town. It wasn't like she could do any worse.

"I should go talk to my boss," she said.

"I thought she wasn't here."

"Not Helen, my other boss. The boss of both of us. Can you stay out of trouble?"

"No."

"Try?"

He pouted and she rolled her eyes at him. At least flamboyantly gay didn't stand out in San Francisco the way it would have in South Dakota. Ruben could butch it up for events like tonight, but his bearing still screamed "Queer!"

Ana turned away to look for Stephen Detlefsen, but he was already headed her way. His massive shoulders, the remnant of youthful athleticism, were now entirely dwarfed by an expansive belly so large he could have been carrying two children full term.

"Great work on the anniversary announcement," he said and clapped one heavy hand on Ana's shoulder. Ana was taller than Detlefsen, even when she didn't have heels on, but that never seemed to faze him.

"That was mostly Helen," Ana admitted.

"Where is she?" he asked. At the same time, Ruben said, "Holy shit, is that HER?"

Ana turned in the direction Ruben faced. In a room full of men wearing khakis and ill-fitting jackets, the woman in the ivory suit looked like a swan landing in a junkyard. Dr. Sabel Young, professor and occasional corporate diversity trainer, stepped into the crowd easily, greeting people as she passed, lightly pressing hands offered to her. Ana didn't know if Sabel remembered everyone who turned to say hello to her, but they certainly remembered her. She wasn't tall, maybe two inches short of Ana's five-foot-nine frame, but her body moved with a composed elegance that made her seem taller—or maybe it was the heels. Ana couldn't see her feet and even if they were visible, she wouldn't waste her time looking there.

The ivory jacket was gorgeous with a single button below the delicate V of the deep collar and a subtle empire waist. Sabel had paired it with a black shirt open at the throat and showing just the top rise of her breasts. Her straight black hair matched the shirt and the contrasting black and ivory highlighted her pale skin.

Ana felt too tall, too awkward, too heavy, too much shoulder and angle, bone and weight and muscle. She was as uncoordinated as a kid who'd happened into her mother's closet. Her purse didn't match her dress, the shoes weren't right at all, she should have worn the pearls...oh, that's right, she didn't own pearls. But of course Sabel did—a tiny strand of pearls strung on white gold that looked almost as fiercely expensive as that jacket. Did she moonlight as a corporate trainer just for the outfits? Ana wondered as Sabel headed for them.

Sabel had worked with Roth Software to deliver two trainings to their nearly four hundred employees and Ana had been the one assigned to help set up the rooms and coordinate the events. At first she believed the frivolous assignment was a hint that the company thought she had too much free time. By the time they were setting up the second training Ana began to wonder if Sabel had asked for her specifically. She couldn't tell if Sabel was flirting with her in a subtle and completely corporate-appropriate way or if it was only her wishful thinking.

Ana had already spent the whole three hours of the first training mentally undressing Sabel, assuming she was safely inaccessible. But then something she said in their last meeting stuck with her and inspired Ana to forward the invitation. After hitting send, she'd realized that she should have just added Sabel to the batch email list and not waited days and sent the invite personally.

Ana picked Ruben's glass up off the bar and took a long drink from it. The alcohol burned her back to the present.

"Dr. Young," Detlefsen said, boomingly because he never said anything quietly. "Are you checking up on us?"

She smiled and inclined her head as she shook the hand he held out to her. He spared her his usual bone-grinding grip.

"You remember Ana?" he asked.

"Yes, she took wonderful care of me."

"Thank you," Ana managed through dry lips. "And this is my roommate Ruben."

"My *pleasure*," Ruben said with too much emphasis. He held out his hand but when she reached to shake it, he turned her hand and bowed his head to kiss her knuckles.

Sabel bent with him so that her head remained lower than his throughout the gesture.

"I'm utterly charmed. Is that Armani?" Ruben said. Ana wanted to kick him.

"You have a discerning eye," Sabel told him and gently reclaimed her hand from his fingers. She turned back to Detlefsen. "I wanted to congratulate you, and everyone, on your fifth anniversary. That's a landmark for so many companies. I hear you started with four people."

"And now we're nearly four hundred," he said proudly. "Let me introduce you to the founders."

The two of them went off toward the center of the party and Ana stared after them.

"Yes, you should," Ruben said.

He caught the bartender's eye and ordered a fresh drink while pushing the half-empty glass back toward Ana. She sighed and took another sip of the fruity vodka thing.

"Do you really think she plays for our team?" Ana asked.

"You said she was flirting with you."

"What if I was reading into it?" Ana watched the moonbeam brightness of Sabel's suit move through the room away from her.

"A diversity trainer? Honestly? Honey, that's a synonym for queer."

"I thought you told me to stop chasing ice queens."

"That was so last week," he declared. "I'm making an exception. I'll take your car, you tell her I was a shit that forgot about you and you ask for a ride."

"Like hell you will. I was thinking I should go by Helen's place. It's not like her to miss this event."

"This thrilling party of the century?" Ruben asked.

He waved his hand around in an arc to indicate the vast room filled with people talking quietly to each other.

"She practically helped found the company," Ana told him, but the words sounded thin.

"And that's a reason to go by her place in the middle of the night? Oh, wait, she lives near that gal you hooked up with a few months back, the swimmer?"

"Marine biologist," Ana said.

"And you're trying to tell me that an advanced degree beats an Armani suit?"

Ana glanced across the room and got a beautiful view of the way the short jacket ended just above Sabel's shapely backside. "She has a Ph.D. too," she said, her voice sounding plaintive to her own ears.

"That's it, I'm catching a cab to the bars—you're not allowed home until you have her number."

"I don't think the security system has a 'dateless and denied' setting," Ana told him.

"It does now."

He kissed the side of her head and headed for the door. She could tell the sexual orientation of every man in the room based on whose eyes followed Ruben as he left.

She leaned her elbow on the bar and sipped her way through the rest of Ruben's drink. Then she fished her phone out of her purse and texted the marine biologist to see if she was home, awake, and interested. She could just swing by Helen's apartment building and see if the light was on, maybe call up and ask if Helen needed anything and then, having discharged her good Samaritan duty, swing a few blocks over and take care of some other pressing needs.

"Ana," Sabel's voice said next to her ear and she jumped. "Hold still."

A warm touch brushed the back of her neck, sending a shiver down the length of her body. She felt a feathered kiss of fabric as well and then Sabel ran her silken fingertips along the neckline of Ana's dress.

"There you go. Your tag was sticking up."

Ana stared at her. Was she serious? Was she flirting? Was she somehow both flirting and serious?

"Thanks." She was overly conscious of her elbow on the bar and straightened up. Not a single intelligent word came to mind. This close, Sabel smelled like fresh mint and wildflowers and apricot musk.

"Is Helen here?" Sabel asked. "I wanted to congratulate her."

"No, she, um, emailed me earlier that she wasn't feeling well. It is her kind of event. I thought I might go check on her, though I suppose it's late." Ana clamped her mouth shut. She sounded like an idiot.

"I think that's thoughtful," Sabel said. "Are you two friends?"

"We've worked together for a few years. She's taught me a lot about public relations. I was just in marketing before." Ana stopped but Sabel didn't say anything else so she tried to come up with something to get her talking, "You're a professor when you're not training corporate geeks like us?"

"Religious studies with a focus on social psychology; diversity training gives me a practical application for it," Sabel said and looked like she would say more, but Detlefsen called to her to come meet someone else and she apologized to Ana and slipped back into the crowd.

Ana waited, but the group of people standing around Sabel talking kept growing. Would all ninety percent of the men in the room, the straight ones who hadn't watched Ruben's exit, eventually magnetize to Sabel? I should go over there, Ana thought, just push into the group and talk about something meaningless for an hour.

But she didn't know how to do that. She wasn't used to feeling this flummoxed in a work setting. If only she hadn't considered in detail how she wanted to get Sabel out of the charcoal gray suit she'd worn to the second training, then she might be able to carry on some sufficiently mundane conversation.

Ruben was going to kill her for leaving. She picked her purse up off the bar and headed for the door. Helen lived in Ashbury Heights in an old Victorian that had been cut up into large apartments. Of course there was no parking anywhere near it, even for the little silver and white Mini Cooper Ana had bought to navigate the horrible parking in San Francisco. She had to park two blocks away in a space that was marginally legal. Only after she locked the car and started walking in her heels did it occur to her that it was ten at night and she was trooping the streets in an evening dress and heels to intrude on her boss at home.

On the bright side, after she checked on Helen it was just another mile to the apartment of that tall and charmingly awkward marine biologist she'd hooked up with off and on for the last six months. Ruben was right, she had a thing for smart, inaccessible women, but tonight that could work to her advantage.

Helen's building was in the middle of the street and when Ana rounded the corner, a BMW sat double-parked in front of it, lights out. She ducked into a doorway and peered around the corner. Could this be Helen's mystery lover? Ana knew she had someone, but Helen never talked about him. It was a nice car: a 5-series. A man came out of the front door and motioned to someone in the car. Two more men got out, dressed entirely in black. Ana opened her purse and pulled out her phone and can of pepper spray.

The two men hauled something out of the backseat, long and heavy, wrapped in a blanket. Ana's heart hammered before she fully realized why. This was the kind of scene she expected to see on television, not from twenty feet away. She wanted to believe it was a rolled rug, but the contours of hip and shoulder were too clear: they carried a body between them. They were carrying a body into Helen's building and there were only three apartments they could be going into.

There was a chance, her rational mind suggested, that it was Helen and she was unconscious for some good reason, like having passed out at a party or...or... Perhaps if Ana meddled she would only embarrass herself and everyone involved.

Her gut told her to call the cops now. She ducked back into the darkness of the doorway and dialed 911.

"Please state the nature of your emergency," the operator said.

Ana whispered the address and told her, "There are three men in black here, they're carrying a body into the building. It's Helen Reed's apartment, I'm afraid she's in danger."

"Are you in danger?" the operator asked.

"I don't think they saw me."

"Can you stay where you are?"

"Yes."

"All right, I have police and ambulance on the way. Can you stay on the line? I only want you to keep talking to me if it's safe for you to do so."

"Let me look," Ana whispered. She turned, crept to the edge of the doorway again and looked.

A man stared at her from two feet away. "There you are," he said as if he'd found a lost pet.

Ana pepper-sprayed him in the eyes, then ran. A heavy weight, much too large to be a fist, hit her in the head and knocked her into darkness.

* * *

Sabel stood in the doorway to the bedroom and stared at the unmoving figure on the bed. She couldn't risk touching her and leaving fingerprints, but she knelt by the bed, held her own hair up and back, and leaned an ear over Helen's mouth. Yes, she was dead and no more than a few hours gone based on the warmth still radiating from her skin.

Her instructions were to watch and inform—and not get involved. She still felt like she'd failed. She hadn't been able to figure out what Helen was mixed up in and now the woman was dead.

She straightened up and went back to the doorway. Then down the hall, across the living room and out the front door. She used a soft cloth to pull the door shut and then a touch of magic to remind the door that it had been locked before she went in. The bolt clicked back into place.

Had Ana come by to check on Helen? Had she rung the bell or just seen the lights off and assumed Helen was sleeping off an illness? Sabel stepped out of the front door into the cool air. There were sirens in the distance coming closer. Were they for Helen? If so, who had called the police?

She started walking quickly back toward her car, but the glint of a streetlight against a piece of metal on the sidewalk caught her eye. It was a cell phone. She picked it up and walked around the corner where she could look at it without being spotted by the police.

Last number dialed: 911.

The number before that: Helen Reed.

And there was a received text message from a woman named Shery: "I'd love to see you, come by any time tonight."

Sabel smiled at that, but the other two were troubling. She navigated to the email app for confirmation and, as she'd anticipated, the emails were all addressed to Ana Khoury. So Ana was here, called 911 and then dropped her phone?

She opened her mouth and took a long inhale of the evening air. The taste of power prickled between her tongue and palate. Magic recently used left this trace in the air like the charged ions before a storm. Ana didn't have magic, so someone had used it on her.

Sabel hurried back to her car where she could focus. In the driver's seat, she opened her purse and pulled out the short golden hair she'd taken from the back of Ana's dress earlier in the evening. She'd taken it to use in case she needed to follow Ana to Helen—if Helen wasn't really at her apartment—but now she could use it to find Ana herself. She wrapped the hair around her fingers doubling and tripling its potency, then she brought her hand close to her mouth and breathed over it the words, "Lead me."

The hair tugged her hand toward the north. She started the car and drove, feeling the pull of the hair around her fingers. She'd just crossed the Golden Gate Bridge when the sensation cut off abruptly.

"Shit!" she said, "shit, shit shit," and hit her fist against the steering wheel with each repeat of the word.

If they had killed Ana too, the hair would still tug for hours. No tug meant Ana was deep inside someone else's magic. For that to happen to a woman with no magic of her own... Sabel had no way to know exactly how bad that could be, but it was very bad.

CHAPTER TWO

Ana opened her eyes on the dark blur of a moving road. She was slumped in the passenger seat of a car—from the look of the hood it was the BMW she'd been watching—and she couldn't move. *I've been drugged*, she thought in some far corner of her mind. Through force of will, she made her head roll left enough to see the man driving.

Pay attention, she told herself, *you have to stay awake and find a way out of this*.

He was extraordinarily beautiful, in a rugged, thick-featured way. In profile a brutally strong cheekbone framed a darkly-lashed eye and thin, sculpted lips. At least he wouldn't be hard to describe to the police, even if she only saw one side of his face. The fingers of her right hand twitched and then crept together into a fist.

"What did you do to me?" she asked, slurring and stumbling through the words.

His visible eyebrow lifted. "You can still talk? Delightful. Too bad I can't keep you around." The way he sighed at those last words made her cold inside.

Her fear came with a bottomless grief. There had been kids in her hometown, the well-dressed ones with good colleges in their futures, who had expected her to die young and would be surprised to know she'd made it to thirty. She'd promised herself she'd outlive all of them and she had a long way to go yet to pull that off.

"Where are you taking me?" Ana asked. Her mind seemed blessedly clear in contrast to her uncooperative body.

He laughed and the rich baritone sound was bitterly silky in Ana's ears. "I'm not going to tell you," he said. "You're a gift for some friends."

"You must not like those friends very much."

He didn't reply and they drove into Marin, winding into a neighborhood of well-kept houses with large yards. Soon he would stop the car and she was going to fight her way out. The old familiar adrenaline of anticipated pain flared inside her, burning off the remaining sluggishness in her limbs. She hated men who thought a busty blond woman like herself could neither think nor fight, and she aimed to make this one pay for his mistake.

He pulled up a long driveway lined with young sycamores, their leaves yellow-gray in the moonlight. As the car slowed, Ana clicked open the door and threw herself out. Her body hit the ground at an angle and she tumbled. The ridiculous part of her mind swore about the dirt grinding into the silk dress as she scrambled up, her muscles still slow and clumsy.

"Grab her!" a new voice shouted from behind. Molasses seemed to encase her, like running in a dream, her legs wouldn't do what she wanted and she stumbled down the driveway at half speed, moving by the slope's gravity and sheer force of will. A hand grabbed her shoulder and she lurched away, falling forward to hit the asphalt hip first and then with the side of her head. A blast of pain flashed across her skull.

Ana rolled over fighting the man who came down after her, jabbing fingers at his throat while her right foot kicked for his knee. It wasn't the driver of the car, but some goon with a dark hood over his face. His head dodged her jab, but the instep of her shoe connected and he yelped in pain. She'd crawl away if she had to. A second man, wearing a loose ski mask, grabbed her flailing arm and locked an icy metal cuff around her wrist.

She made a fist with her left hand and cracked it into the side of his head, and she started yelling. She yelled for help and yelled, "Fire!" and a string of obscenities. The first man recovered from her kick and his hands grabbed her free wrist while both men forced her onto her belly. She scissored her legs like a swimmer, trying to connect with anything. The driver's black leather shoes came into her field of vision.

"Enough," he said from above her head. His fingers touched the back of her skull and she blacked out again.

She woke on her side on pale canvas, with her head throbbing and her hands cuffed behind her back. Her body told her only minutes had passed: her mouth wasn't dry and her pulse was still elevated from her attempted escape. She heard a man's voice, but the words sounded foreign. Her eyes slowly adjusted to the dimmer light and she looked up at a wide, bare ceiling. The pain in her head was so fierce she didn't dare sit up yet, so she talked to herself silently, trying to calm down, take the measure of this place, find a way out. It didn't do any good to panic; that could come later when she was away from here.

You've got to survive, she told herself. *Don't think about what they might do. Don't add to the fear. Breathe slowly and use the brain God gave you. People have escaped worse situations. Damn it, girl, this is not how you die.*

Dominating the vast room was a large white cloth or tarp spread across the floor with designs drawn in black and a few unsteady brown lines. In the center of the tarp, near her, were two concentric circles with foreign letters in strings between them, and inside those circles stood a man in an unbelted black robe with a dark cowl cloaking his face. Around him were three other men each in a smaller circle and facing him was an empty circle inside a triangle. More men stood around the outside of the tarp on the bare floor. All of them were masked, some with plain knit masks, others with hoods that looked like silk or satin pulled over their heads with only the eyes showing.

She wished Ruben were here. He was strong enough to give these men the beating they deserved. But the image of Ruben hitting these men felt so alien to her, she found herself picturing her brother Gunnar instead, breaking the nose of this one and the arm of that one. She'd never seen Gunnar hit anyone, only seen him get hit, but she was certain he could do it. All the men in her family could.

Most of these men wore long black robes or tunics, only two had dark suits on, with bangles around their necks consisting of many pointed stars and symbols she didn't recognize. The driver was the only one in the room who didn't wear a hood. He was also the only one on the tarp not standing inside a circle.

One of the men glanced over at her. "She's awake," he announced to the room.

"Perfect timing," Driver said.

Ana pushed herself up to sitting and turned to get a view of the rest of the room. There were no windows and only one solid-looking wood door on the far side of the room. A layer of sweat increased the chill that rose from the hard floor into her muscles. Her handcuffs had been tied with a length of rope, about ten feet she guessed, to a metal ring that rose out of the floor under the tarp. A small hole had been cut in the fabric for it. Hysterical laughter threatened to burst out of her mouth and she ground her teeth together so hard her jaw burned. Setting a metal ring into a concrete floor meant a lot of planning had gone into this event. What the hell was it?

If she could untie herself, she would still have to find a way to run, in handcuffs, past all these men and up the stairs. Perhaps if she knew what they were doing, she could use it to her advantage, maybe talk them into untying her. Under the cloying, woody smell of the incense, she caught the frozen metal scent of fear, not just her own. They weren't unified; could she find the weak one and get him to help her?

A tremor ran up one of her arms. How long did she have until the insulation of shock wore off and the panic overwhelmed her?

She made herself count the men in the room: twelve. Some stood perfectly still while a few shifted from foot to foot. One had a censer like in a church that he dangled at the end of a chain. It smelled like hot sugar and pine trees. All the men had folded their street clothes neatly along one side of the room and she wondered if her purse was there with her cell phone in it— or had she dropped those outside of Helen's apartment when she tried to run? If her phone was in the room, was it better to run to her phone or the door?

The men's costumes weren't uniform; some of the hoods were ski masks, others like lopsided pillowcases in black satin. A few looked like they had been sewn together by a seamstress of uneven skill. She marked the three antsy men with sloppy outfits as the weak ones. Although they all wore black robes or suits and cowls, she thought of the one in the center-most position as Black Hood, because his head covering was the most well-made and elaborate, giving the impression of a neatly sewn hood over a close-fitting cloth mask. He faced the empty circle and began to recite a series of words that meant nothing to Ana. He paused and recited them again. Then Driver called them back to him and the two of them chanted together.

Ana despaired of identifying any of them if...no, *when*, she told herself, when she got out and went to the police. She could only make out the breadth of shoulders under their robes, from narrow and skinny to wide and well muscled, and only a few had enough gut to round the front of their robes. Black Hood looked like an iron pillar.

They reminded her, oddly, of a group of boys at her high school who played at being dark wizards, thinking they could talk to the dead and amass mysterious powers. Those boys came from nice houses and had new clothes to wear each year, yet they managed to be dissatisfied because they were not handsome or strong, because they thought they lacked power and were looking for any way that they could compensate. A few of them liked to brag to Ana, to try to spook her with stories of late night trips to the cemetery—when they spoke to her, which was a last resort considering her dirt-poor, outcast status back then. She didn't understand the kind of power they wanted; at that age, power to her was a fist or a sharp kick, and it was enough money and a car so that she could get away from there and never go back.

What did these men want? Was it the same kind of power as those boys back in school? Could she give it to them and survive?

Most of the men had taken places inside circles drawn around the outer edges of the tarp, and two suited guards took a handful of white powder from a dish by the door, carried it to a spot on the floor, then trickled the powder in a circle around them. Black Hood and Driver repeated the foreign sounding words until they all blurred together for Ana. Their voices rose in volume as they spoke, entreating at first and then threatening, dropping again to rumbling. The other men swayed at the sound of the chant. One slipped to his knees, but came up again still inside his circle. The air felt like the pause in a storm right before a twister forms.

As far as she could tell there was nothing inside one empty circle in the center of all of them. Everything else about this pageant was so real she almost expected to see something, a dark twisted figure or a cloud of smoke like a movie genie. How long would it take these men to admit their ritual hadn't worked? Her fingers struggled with the rope knotted tightly against the short metal chain of the handcuffs. She'd untied tough knots before; you just had to work at the rope persistently until it moved. It was only a matter of time, but how much time? Sweat covered her fingers, making them slip over the smooth rope.

The man who had fallen to his knees suddenly shook, once, violently and threw his head back with a shout. "The woman! She is calling for the woman!"

Oppressive silence filled the room. Ana bit her cheek so hard she tasted blood. She wouldn't scream for these men.

"Bring her!" Driver roared at the shaking man, his voice so loud it echoed.

The man staggered out of his circle toward her. "I hear her," the man was saying over his shoulder to the others who stood rooted to their positions around the room. "Drake, I hear her, like a wind roaring." He clapped his hands over his ears for a moment and then tore them away.

* * *

The mask hid the water pooling in Jacob's eyes, though he was certain the demon who called himself Nathan Drake could smell his grief and its accompanying rage. It should have been Helen here to take this possession, not this blond popsicle. Jacob still couldn't accept that she'd died; he had never meant for circumstances to play out the way they had. Why hadn't he forced them to wait? It had been so long already, what would another month or two matter? He'd been impatient himself, that was the sad truth of it and he'd been willing to believe Drake.

Drake said the stars were right, the omens—it wasn't worth it to wait. Earlier that night, when they'd first tried this, Helen had come down the stairs in her garnet red gown with the grace of an antelope, steady against her fear. He'd been so proud of her. Now Ana Khoury shrank away from them with all the poise of a whipped dog.

Jacob hadn't minded Ana in the office when they worked together. He'd even admired her shape, nicely put together though a bit on the sturdy side, and she was a fine publicist, did her job with enthusiasm and success. But she knew nothing about magic and demons. Drake said she was hot-blooded and that she had darkness in her. What did she know about darkness? His fingers strayed down to touch his right hip where the scars began, the decades-old pain forged into strength.

He'd caught his first demon when he was sixteen and back in the hospital for the fifth time. The creature came to feed on his pain, but he saw its smoky form and wrestled with it until it spoke in words he could understand and promised to bring something that could teach him. Twenty-five years he'd been studying, experimenting, and perfecting himself. He'd called Drake to him and now Drake presumed to tell him how they would perform this ritual and with this ignorant girl.

Helen had studied with him for two years and she'd been a surprisingly quick student. Tears closed his throat and he swallowed them down along with his rising anger. Only a fool let his emotions play freely in a summoning ritual. Jacob had learned the hard way; now nothing offered these creatures an entry into himself except his pure will. He reminded himself this ritual was only a stepping-stone, a formality for Drake, then they would get to the real work at hand. Let this one have his moment, Jacob thought; he could wait now that he'd seen the consequence of pushing forward too quickly.

Drake called again for Ana to be brought into the center circle and the young summoner they called DK left his own circle to walk drunkenly toward her. Jacob wanted to drag the man bodily back, but it was too late, he'd already broken his protection. If he picked up some creature drawn to this power tonight it was going to take weeks to get it out again.

"I hear her, Jacob, I hear her," DK kept repeating in a murmur. Poor idiot. They called him DK because the summoning name he chose, "Demonknight" was too embarrassing to use regularly. They all had summoning names that masked their identities. The group kept DK in the coven because of his extraordinary sensitivity to the ethereal world. He'd been the first to hear The Woman last time also. Jacob did not envy him.

"Please," DK begged Ana who flinched away from his grasping arm.

This is a disaster, Jacob thought and then banished the idea; *Focus or fail.* He couldn't speak aloud, Ana might recognize his voice from the office, but he bent his will toward her, lending strength to DK's efforts.

Drake had no such limits on his voice or appearance. He didn't care who knew he was involved here because he didn't expect Ana to survive, at least not as herself. "Come and get in the circle," he purred. "Or I will put you there."

If they were going to use trash as the vessel, they should not have chosen Ana. He understood Drake's logic: that if it went wrong and she died it would look like someone had targeted the publicists at Roth Software and they could frame the ephemeral "drug dealers" in shipping they'd set up months ago. Ana was too pretty, too young, too charismatic to use as a vessel, though those very characteristics were what Drake wanted. Some of the less disciplined men were hesitating now. DK seemed afraid to touch her and in his peripheral vision he could see two others fidgeting nervously.

"Come and get me," Ana spat back at Drake.

Drake crossed the room as fast as thought and hauled her to her feet so swiftly that Ana's gasp choked in the back of her throat. Drake's voice was pitched low, but it carried through the still room. "This will go more easily if you enter the circle willingly. It's less likely to kill you that way."

Ana's eyes flicked past him to the grand circle on the floor and up to Jacob's masked face, then past him. She was a bright girl, looking for the powerful and the weak in this group. Maybe this would work after all. If only it had been Helen.

"Fine," she told Drake. "If you uncuff me."

Drake shoved her forward to her knees and tugged at the handcuffs. They clicked open without benefit of a key and Ana had to throw her hands forward to avoid pitching on her face from the momentum of that sudden freedom. From where he stood on the far side of the grand circle, Jacob saw the expressions flick across her face as she crouched on hands and knees: the relief of having her hands free and the dismay of the distance still to cross to reach the exit, not to mention that most of the summoners were between her and the door.

What had killed Helen? If he knew he might tell Ana to prepare her to accept the demon that waited for her, even breaking his silence to do it, but he had no idea why Helen had failed. Jacob never had a problem letting demons into his body, only getting them out again. The bone cancer of his teens had given him a lot of practice with invasive procedures. He thought Helen had been open; had she only put on a brave face for him? If he could go back he would change so many aspects of tonight.

Ana's eyes were neither willing nor unwilling, they were furious. Jacob hoped that was enough. He did not want to have to prepare for this particular ritual again.

"Into the circle," Drake said. "No running."

Ana rolled over from hands and knees to sitting and unbuckled her sandals. Drake's eyebrows shot up and Jacob suppressed a chuckle. She really thought she was going to get a chance to run. But of course she did; she didn't believe in demons and thought this was all for show. She had no way of comprehending what was going to happen to her when she crossed that double line and probably thought it was just a silly design. She didn't understand it was the boundary into another world. He wouldn't have believed it either if so many years of experience hadn't shown him how the worlds really worked.

A pang of sympathy stabbed up from his hip with the memory of the times he'd let demons come into him, the mind-shattering pain of it and the violation of the last bastion of self. If they weren't going to take the time to train up another adept like Helen, they should have used someone older and less alive. It was a shame to destroy her.

CHAPTER THREE

The men waited for her to move, but Ana hadn't decided whether it would be better to run for it or bluff. She stood up and paused at the lip of the first line. She could see the door now and one of the men between her and that exit was shuffling nervously from foot to foot.

"What's going to happen?" she asked the driver, the one the shaking boy had called Drake.

"My demon lover is there to meet you," he said. "And ride you out."

Demon, he actually said the word "demon." And Drake had called the demon his lover. She wasn't going to ponder the implications of that too graphically, but if he was well disposed toward this demon lover then perhaps if they believed she was possessed they'd give her enough space to get out the door without being tackled by multiple men.

Ana wasn't the best actress under normal circumstances, but with her life on the line, she surely could pretend. It was telling that although they clearly thought they had called some demon, none of them were willing to get into the circle and face the fact that they had failed.

Ana pictured herself stomping around the room, ranting and shouting commands, and felt the first lift of hope in hours. If it didn't work, she couldn't possibly be any worse off. She intended to walk slowly to the center of the empty circle, stand for a few moments and then shake like the other man, maybe scream a little, and then fake a demonic voice.

Ana crossed the line of the circle and a cool breath raised the hair on her arms. *Don't psych yourself out*, she told herself firmly. Did some part of her want to believe this could work? Not that she would be possessed by a demon, but finally proof that this other, unseen world she'd suspected and pleaded to for so long was at last unfailingly real? A little dizziness rose up in her, making that next step toward the center of the circle a staggering affair. She went down on her knees. Was she losing consciousness again? Maybe when Drake knocked her out her head had hit the floor; this in and out wakefulness made it so hard to think of escape. She just wanted to lie down and sleep for days. Was that the sign of a concussion?

She was on hands and knees with only a small square of the off-white cloth visible to her, feeling dizzy and nauseous, when someone turned out the lights.

"Damn it!" she yelled and then clapped a hand over her mouth. She was supposed to pretend she was possessed, not swear at them. Or is that what demons did? She needed time. Could they still see her with the lights off? She let herself slump down, falling slowly onto her left side, going limp.

She hadn't actually seen *The Exorcist*, but Ruben had dragged her to see *The Exorcism of Emily Rose* and judging by that movie she should writhe for a while, speak in a deep voice, and maybe bang her head against a wall. That last part wasn't going to happen with this possible concussion. Which way had the door been, was it the corner in the direction of her out-flung right hand?

She threw her arms out to the sides and snaked on the floor and then started crawling on her belly in that direction. When someone tried to stop her, she decided, she'd let loose with the demonic voice. The room was so silent now it should have a good impact. But she couldn't even hear the men breathing; that wasn't right. She should hear someone shifting at least or a quiet cough, and now she'd crawled a good ten feet without running into a single person's legs. Either they'd all cleared out of the room after they shut off the lights or the much more likely answer was she was no longer conscious and had actually passed out when she dropped down to fake it.

Ana rolled over and sat up. It was still the kind of profound dark that only happens in interior rooms, where the sole movement came from flecks of color swimming in her own eyes. She filled her lungs and let out the deepest bellow she had in her. "I am here!" she roared.

The sound sank to the ground and no one answered.

"Oh great, I'm not even conscious," she said, relieved to be hearing her own voice, even if it was in a dream stage of injury.

The words felt so small after they fell away. This wasn't a room she was in, but a vast, empty place, or perhaps a non-place. Then came a sickening lurch in her gut and the cold fear that she hadn't passed out from her injuries. If possession were real, is this how it would feel? Could some entity be walking around in her body even now?

"Help me," she yelled upward into the dark. "I don't want to die! I don't want to die!" It became a sobbing chant and she rocked, arms holding knees. The words didn't even make sense to her—shouldn't she plead for freedom? But the animal part of her convulsed in terror that this could be its end.

Far above, a small light became visible, like a star in the void, growing larger. As she watched, it flared to the size of the sun, similarly blinding and yet still observable without pain, and her fear vanished because she knew for certain now she was only dreaming. The sun fell from the sky, down at her like a comet and dropped in a massive lump only feet from her, its blaze illuminating a vast space of nothingness where she sat. The fire separated into a thousand flaming serpents writhing over, under, around each other. She crawled away from it but then turned to look.

The serpents were joining together, twining in long strands to make the shape of a huge body. She put her hands over her face. The afterimage of the blazing, shifting body remained on her darkened sight: a slender man about twelve feet tall standing on a base of snakes.

"I want to wake up," she whispered, but it didn't work. The fear that she could never get back to her body edged into her lungs, crushing them tight.

A voice spoke, saying words that were hopelessly foreign in a tone so near the middle of the spectrum that she couldn't tell if it was a man or a woman, until she took her hands away from her eyes and saw a luminous man on his knees in front of her. He was smaller now, about her height, and only a few blazing snakes remained in place of his feet. He looked to be about her age with copper skin and a cleanly shaven skull. His honey-brown eyes squinted at her, puzzled.

He spoke again but she shook her head, "I have no idea what you're saying."

His expression was tight-lipped. He shook his head too, the mirror image of her gesture.

"Are you stuck here too?" she asked. "Are we someplace? Are you that snakey thing and you're just trying to look pretty for me?"

He shook his head again and held his hands open to her, palms up. His fingers had no knuckles. Yes, he was the snake thing; whether he meant her to understand that from his gesture or not, she didn't know. He was the only light here, glowing golden like the dawn. Ana reached out her right hand and touched his left, tracing the lines of his fingers with hers.

His right hand came forward slowly and paused a foot from her eyes, fingers forward. Pointing with his whole hand, perhaps?

She tapped her chest. "Ana," she said.

He bobbed his head and shoulders forward in a bow that was a nod and spoke a string of sounds that made so little sense to her that they were gone from her mind as soon as he finished.

"I can't call you that," she told him.

Puzzled look. He shook his head. Then he raised his hand pointing to her again and then tapped his chest as she had hers. Lastly, he brought his hands together, palms cupped as if he held something and flung them up and open like a man releasing a bird to fly. Escape!

Ana nodded. "Yes," she said.

"Yes," he repeated in his liquid voice with a smile. He reached for her very slowly, his eyes staying on hers, watching. She gave him no sign of refusal. Either it was a dream and she was in no danger or it wasn't a dream and this seemed the only way out. She really wanted it to be a dream. His hands closed on the sides of her face. He looked worried as he came toward her and that was the real reason she let him put his lips on hers. His face held no cruelty.

It must be a dream if this strange and beautiful man was going to kiss her here in the middle of a plane of nothingness under a fallen sun—and if she was going to let him. She relaxed. Everything was going to be all right when she woke up. His tongue touched her lips gently and she opened her mouth to him. First his tongue touched hers and then withdrew. Then he breathed into her, a warm sweet breath, and on the tail of that more heat burned her lips. It went on and on, searing pain and bright pleasure, and she knew that what passed through her lips was one of those flaming serpents.

She couldn't scream as it slid into her throat and then he rushed into her like a forest fire, tongues of heat and pain searing narrow channels under her skin. The air forced out of her lungs, the last breath sucked from her mouth. Pressure crushed her from all sides. She screamed in her mind for release as molten lava ran down her veins to her heart. Then she dropped into her body from a vast distance, like a stone statue toppling from a cliff, and her wakefulness shattered when it hit the ground.

* * *

Oh the joy of nonbelievers, that this woman would saunter so easily into his circle, Drake thought. She crossed the line like a girl going into a strange store, and once across it dropped to her knees and then fell motionless. That was all his human eyes saw, but with his greater power he knew she'd gone through the door. He hummed with anticipation, vibrating like a hummingbird's wing. How long would it take in this world for his consort to find her in that world and take her?

The men were restless, except for Jacob who stood unmoving as ever, blazing inside but cold as stone in appearance. Yes, Drake wanted to bring that one the money and influence he craved, even shore up his doomed control over his world. And maybe one day he would loosen up a bit and let Drake inside him to consume some of that bright fire of rage. He could almost feel it on his lips now, inside his mouth. But first, he needed his other half, the fuel to his blaze.

In the center circle, Ana's body jerked like a puppet. She rolled onto her back and her hands flopped independently like two fish. Then they settled and pulled in toward the body, feeling up and down the torso, touching her face. Drake hoped his consort was pleased with her new home. He wanted to rush forward and crush her in his arms, but he had to let her break the circle to know she had full power to come into this world. Ana's body sat, eyes still closed, and rocked forward into a crouch. She stood unsteadily and walked to the edge of the circle as if it were a wall.

She bent down, legs wide and ungainly in her dress, and touched her fingers to the inside of the line like a blind man feeling gently forward. Then her hand pushed through, swept right and broke the binding. She was free! He crossed the room to her. She stood and opened her eyes to him.

Fire bright gold, burning like the sun! Her whole body was lit with it. This was wrong. Where was his consort? Some other creature had displaced her, taken her vessel as its own. Drake would take this burning power and consume it to add to his own.

"Grab her!" he shouted. Half the men would not move from their circles but the others did. He began the words of a binding against the creature in the woman's body.

The first man reached her at a run and she turned without having first looked and struck him in the chest with both palms. He was thrown back off his feet and knocked down a second pursuer. The other men hesitated and the creature in Ana's body sprinted for the stairs.

Drake finished the binding and threw it as an invisible net. It fell where he intended but as it hit the body it evaporated. The creature was not possessing her. She'd let him in willingly. He owned her body now. Dammit! What power she'd given away in her ignorance.

She was on the stairs and the man who reached her and grabbed her arm received a quick blow from her elbow that stunned him. He tumbled down the few stairs he'd climbed while she continued up to the door. Drake dodged him and pelted up the stairs after her.

On the landing, she threw the bolt back and pulled the door open, but the action bought him time. He caught up to her in the doorway and closed one hand around her upper arm, the other raised to ward off any blow. She didn't strike him. He turned her, closing his hand over her other arm so that he held her immobile.

Her eyes were golden. "Shaidan," she whispered and then a series of words so old he couldn't at first remember their meaning.

A flash of light came from her, bright and stinging. Then her hands struck the inside of his wrists and broke his grip while he was blinded. When he could see again, she was across the yard and sprinting faster than a human body should. He might catch her on foot, but the humans would not. In cars, they could get ahead of her. He bounded down the stairs.

"We have to catch her," Drake said. "Put on your street clothes and pair up. Two pairs on foot as spotters, four in cars. Go."

"You didn't tell me she was going to run," Jacob said.

"*She* wasn't," Drake said. "That is not my consort."

"Who—?"

"Power, Jacob, great power if we can bind it. Come, you and I will take my car."

* * *

This time when she came back into the world, Ana's body wasn't tied up or immobilized. She was already running. That sensation felt familiar enough. She knew how to run and get away from men. It was possible for her body to do that on autopilot. She didn't remember how she'd made it out of the cellar, but she could worry about that later. The night air was cold on her skin and the pavement abrasive against her bare feet.

At first she thought her vision was blurred but the edges of the houses and trees weren't fuzzy—they glowed. In the night the trees should have been gray but they were bright green as if the sun shone through each leaf. The houses had colors that didn't match their exteriors, some of them different from room to room. They looked like stained glass windows of themselves.

She'd have to ask for an MRI or CT scan at the hospital, or whatever they used to check for brain damage. For now she had to hide herself better. She was running down the middle of the street and any moment they'd be coming in cars to find her. She tried to turn but her body wasn't responding to her. In her periphery she watched the houses flying by. How fast was she running? She had to turn off the street and get behind those houses.

Her feet turned and sprinted between two houses and then took a sharp left so she ran behind them. They came to a privacy fence and her hands grabbed and catapulted herself over it. She could never have done that before. Adrenaline? Or was there something else inside her now pushing her on? The thought should have caused her fear, but she didn't get cold or feel tingly. She really wasn't in charge of her body.

Later, she told herself, *I can panic all I want.*

She ran across more yards, setting off some automatic security lights. That couldn't be good.

Her sight wasn't the only sense that had changed. She smelled each plant in the neighborhood separately, like notes in a symphony. And she had an extra sense that told her where everything was around her. She didn't need to see the houses to know where they were or to see a fence that was coming three yards away to know how high it was. She felt the men who were chasing her before she heard or smelled them. There were two falling further and further behind, but they must have called others because she heard a car come up the road and slow when she triggered another security light.

We need to hide, she thought loudly, hoping whatever controlled her body could hear and obey. She accompanied the words with mental images of crouching under shrubs or in a small building if they could find one, like a shed.

The senses of her surroundings expanded, rolling out on all sides like a hologram. There was the bay and the docks on one side and the park on the other. Neither of those were good directions. She needed to shake her pursuers and then find someone who could call the police, not get pinned down in an underpopulated area where the summoners would have time to look for her. She wished herself to go northwest, deeper into the residential streets and her feet obliged, turning them that way.

She wanted to run up to one of the houses and pound on the door, ask the inhabitants to call the police, but she couldn't be sure the house she chose would be occupied and during the time she was standing on the porch making a racket, the black hood gang could find her. Even if she got into the house, she couldn't be sure that the lights and commotion wouldn't draw enough of them that they'd just push in and grab her again. The yards here were large and beautifully kept with enough trees to look lush but not enough to hide her. She spotted a gazebo.

As soon as she thought how good it would be to hide there, her body wheeled and sprinted newly with no hint of fatigue. The door slipped open with a metallic whisper. Inside was a large hot tub and on the far side a wooden bench with a few towels set out on it. Ana crawled under the bench as a car drove slowly down the street in front of the house.

CHAPTER FOUR

The luminescent sight and extra sense were gone. Wind rushed by her ears and the inside of her skin itched as if filaments were being drawn across it. It wasn't a painful feeling, just intensely discomforting. She shivered uncontrollably and her legs burned. A hundred small hurts made themselves known: her lungs and throat ached, the bottoms of her feet had been scraped by the asphalt, and her eyes burned. She blinked and brought her fingers up where she could watch while she wiggled them.

She was alive, she reminded herself, and there were a dozen crazy men out there looking to catch and kill her. She had to assume they were still combing the neighborhood on foot and in cars; she'd seen Drake's face, so clearly she could identify him and he hadn't planned for her to survive the night. From her occasional morning jogs, she could estimate that she'd run about two miles but not all in a straight line because she had to avoid the men, so she was at most just over a mile from where they'd had her.

When Ana could bear to move again, she rolled to her right and used her arms to push herself up to sitting. The muscles in her legs felt like oil set on fire, liquid and burning. Sitting and leaning back against the wall she saw that the soles of her feet were bleeding, not as badly as she'd have thought from the pain, but oozing blood and plasma onto the wooden floor. Her pantyhose were trashed and the sight of the frayed ends around her ankles made her chuckle. That turned into a laugh and then she couldn't stop crying.

She let her arms stay at her sides, lowered her head and wept in hacking but nearly silent, dry sobs. A few tears made it to the lower lids of her eyes but there wasn't enough moisture in her to let them fall. It hurt to cry, it all hurt, and she wanted to use that hurt to fuel her anger. She pulled the emotions in, breathed deep and held that breath until it ached, then rubbed one dirty hand across her face to scatter the half-shed tears.

If she waited until morning, would she be safer? She tried to think it through but she couldn't. The fear and pain took over and insisted she get help now. She inched herself to the door of the gazebo and pushed it open far enough to see out. A large backyard stretched up to a broad two-story house with the gazebo off to one side, thankfully at the bottom of the lawn. She was about twenty feet from the house and the enclosure was edged with gravel. Ana didn't think she could hit the house from where she was, but the strength in her arms surprised her. The first few fell short, but then she hit the back windows squarely.

The clatter of the stones sounded impossibly loud in the night. What would it take to wake the homeowner? After a few minutes when no lights went on, she decided she needed to move in case the summoners heard her. She crawled out of the gazebo and moved from one clump of shrubs to another. Where was she?

Another car crunched slowly down the road and turned a corner. In the distance, she heard it turn again. It was circling the block. She had to keep moving before all the men closed in on this area. She ran from cover and crossed an expanse of lawn heading for the street where the car was most recently—

wanting to cross behind its path and get back under cover before it returned.

Her feet stung on the cool street surface and she was across and looking for a new hiding place.

"There," a man called softly.

Two of them stood down along the street, one pointing in her direction. She bolted, but one was already closing the gap between them. He tackled her but his grip was loose. She rolled as she went down. He was trying to move up her body and get a better grip on her.

His face looked pale and soft in the yellow streetlight glow. This wasn't a man used to fighting. Ana drove her elbow into the side of his head and he dropped—onto her legs. She struggled to pull free, but the other man was standing over her now, pointing a boxy, black stun gun at her.

He fired it.

A million points of pain exploded under her skin. Her body jerked hard as every muscle spasmed. A fog covered her vision. Under the pain and the dizziness, under the thick refusal of her muscles to move, she felt that other presence moving in her body. It whispered along the paths of her nerves and set them right again.

The man with the stun gun was standing a few feet away. He had his cell phone out and lifted it to his ear. Ana knew she had to get the unconscious body off her legs and incapacitate this guy, but her muscles wouldn't do anything she wanted. The presence had cleared her mind, but it was still working to right her body. She looked around desperately for anything she could use but even if she found a weapon, she wouldn't be able to lift it.

* * *

The hair bound around Sabel's fingers tugged and she turned right and then quickly left into an alley. After being dormant for hours, it was active again and directing her toward Ana. She'd entered this neighborhood and driven in fits and starts, trying to figure out where Ana was going. Ana had paused for a few minutes and that nearly allowed Sabel to find her, but then she started moving again.

She had a window cracked so she could scent the air as she drove. Power lay heavy around these houses and once she caught a flash of something acrid and hateful. When the witches asked her to watch Helen, they gave her everything they had on the woman. Helen had studied with the Hecatine witches but left after just a year. She didn't fit their slow, measured discipline. She'd wanted more power at a faster rate of speed.

The Hecatines usually checked in on former pupils, and in the last year they'd seen Helen's fate entwined with dangerous powers.

"Let's hope it's just hedge magicians," her mentor, Josefene, told her.

"What if it's demons?"

"Your role is to report to us," Josefene said. "You may not become involved if there are demons in this. You're too valuable."

Well what was "involved" exactly? Sabel was going to be in trouble when she reported in about tonight's activities, but she couldn't leave Ana to whatever these people had planned—not after seeing Helen dead. The other Hecatines were cautious, sometimes to a fault, but Sabel agreed with their philosophy that the greater one's power, the greater care one must take with it. She had been studying with them for just over a decade and what they'd taught her was beyond anything she imagined when she began her training. Whatever Helen sought, Sabel doubted it compared to the full power of the Hecatines.

Sitting in the alley, she let the car idle for a moment so she could give the neighborhood her full attention. The tug on her finger moved right and right again. Ana was running perpendicular to her. The night air smelled of eucalyptus, a banked barbecue fire, and fog, but it tasted like bitter power and the burning metal of raw need. And there, a half-block toward the direction Ana's hair pulled, she heard two men speaking in short bursts and the slap of their shoes on the pavement.

She kept the lights off and drove silently down the alley. When she saw caught sight of people again, two bodies struggled against each other on the ground. Ana's hair flashed golden in the porch lights. Sabel slid silently out of her car and ran crouched in her stocking feet along the inner edge of the lawns where the hedges gave her some measure of cover. She saw the standing man point at Ana's prone body and heard the zap of a stun gun and an agonized half-sound from Ana's spasming mouth.

The standing man had his back to the houses and was intent on the cell phone that he dialed with shaking fingers. This wasn't a man accustomed to chasing women along dark streets at night. He was in a black robe over jeans. No luck on the hedge wizards, this looked like an amateur, but successful, demon summoner. That put at least one demon out here on the streets with them and probably more.

Focus. Sabel straightened up and drew in a long breath of air. The air went all the way to the bottom of her lungs and its power continued through her abdomen to connect everything from the bottom of her pelvic floor to her throat. She opened herself to the power and drew it up. She didn't have to speak loudly to use the Voice, she only had to have breath pass her lips and have the listener hear what she said.

She stepped up to the man quickly and silently, stopping with her mouth about a foot from his ear, the one that didn't have a cell phone to it. It was important that Ana not hear this word. The last thing she needed right now was to have to drag an unconscious Ana to safety.

"*Sleep*," Sabel commanded him.

He dropped to the pavement. Her word had enough force in it that the fall didn't wake him. He'd be out for at least an hour or two. She bent and grabbed the phone from his lax hand, hitting the red button to end the call and then throwing it as far into the street as she could.

Ana stared at her wide-eyed. At least she was awake; she hadn't heard the command. One of her hands was jerking toward the other of the two men. This one lay across her legs. Sabel wanted to curse the stupid stun gun, but at least it hadn't been a bullet that hit her. She braced herself next to the unconscious man.

In a nearly inaudible whisper, she commanded herself, "*Strengthen.*" If Ana heard that one, so much the better, though she hated to use the Voice on allies.

Her muscles seemed to firm and thicken, though she knew there was no visible change. She heaved the man and he moved easily off Ana. That revealed the ruin of Ana's stockings and the bloody soles of her feet. How far had she run already tonight?

"Can you walk?" she asked Ana.

"Don't know." The words came out with minimal slurring and even Ana looked surprised.

Sabel had another minute of increased strength at best before her body burned off the magic's augmentation. She grabbed Ana's closest arm, her right, and put it around her shoulders. Then she slid her left arm behind Ana's back and pulled her up to sitting. Ana's right hand closed on her shoulder. She was getting muscle control back very quickly. From the length of the stun gun zap, an average person would have been immobile for twenty minutes. Sabel was prepared to drag her if she had to, but walking would be faster.

"Up we go," she said softly and pushed up hard with the strength in her legs. Ana teetered but Sabel gave her a moment and then she nodded. She half-dragged Ana into the shadows of the nearest house. With each step, Ana seemed to gain significant control and soon she was moving at a fast walking pace.

Sabel's car waited around the corner where she'd parked in a pool of darkness. Behind her, men shouted as they found the two unconscious bodies. As she pulled Ana around to the passenger side and helped her fold herself down into the seat, she tried to pick out the voices. Four men? Five? How big was this group?

Two men reached the end of the street and spotted them in the mouth of the alley. They yelled to their companions and started running toward the car. Sabel darted around the front of the car and jerked open the driver's side door. She slid into the seat and slammed the door shut as her fingers hit the ignition button and the engine purred. A dark magic grasped toward them but the general protection magic she had on the car prevented it from sinking into the hoses or the tires and causing a catastrophic failure. The next attempt would be more specific and get through.

She gunned the car into the street. For the first few blocks she kept accelerating and turned as soon as she could, hoping that none of them had the presence of mind and ability to see her license plate and that the stronger magic couldn't reach them. When she saw the signs for the highway, she started to relax.

"How many are there?" she asked Ana.

"Twelve," Ana said in a flat voice. She stared out the windshield but her eyes didn't seem to focus on anything. Sabel understood that feeling—she was having a version of it herself at the moment. *Twelve*! A full complement of summoners. How did Ana escape?

Sabel took in Ana's condition in a series of quick glances as she drove. There was a bruise forming on her left shoulder under the thin silk strap of her dress where she'd hit something hard enough to make the skin purple up quickly. Her wrists had angry red lines on them where she'd strained against restraints. In addition to the bloody soles of her feet, a thick trail of blood was drying on the right side of her dress from some kind of head wound. She looked like she'd battered her way out of whatever captivity these men planned for her.

"I think you need a hospital," Sabel told her, keeping her voice as gentle as possible. "Do you have a preference?"

Ana shook her head so Sabel turned off at the next exit where she knew they'd find a good hospital. They drove in silence for another minute and then when they'd stopped at a light, Ana turned to her.

"How did you find me?" she asked.

Sabel almost told her the truth, but at the last second she turned the first syllable of "magic" into, "Masterful detective work."

Ana's broad mouth quirked up, but her dark eyes swam with pain. "Why?" she started but choked on the word.

The silence in the car was absolute as Sabel released the brake and moved through the intersection. She couldn't think of any right words to say. Had this bright-haired, clever woman really just fought her way free of a dozen men and then tried to ask why Sabel would bother to come after her?

As they were pulling up at the hospital, Ana tried again in a lighter tone. "I thought you were just a professor," she said.

Sabel made herself laugh a little. "I'm not *just* a professor. Let's get you looked at."

The hospital staff let her go into the exam room with Ana and she didn't ask if Ana preferred for her to wait outside. She told herself that she needed to stay close to Ana to find out what kind of magical damage had been done to her—but the truth was that she felt a shockingly strong need to protect her. Ana was bigger than Sabel and her body displayed years of casual athleticism, but tonight that easy physicality was covered in dirt and blood. Ana's wheat and gold hair was matted with blood on the right side and decorated with bits of twig and leaf. The lovely silk dress hung in tatters under her knees and the bottoms of her stockings were completely gone, worn away from her running, and along with them a lot of the skin on the bottom of her feet. She'd limped into the hospital leaving bloody footprints that made Sabel wince.

From the way Ana gingerly sat herself on the exam table and levered herself back on it by inches, Sabel understood that her whole body must be burning with pain and fatigue. She wanted to take Ana's hand and tell her it would all be okay, but she didn't dare. She remembered the words of her mentor: "*Maarevas*, when you become emotionally involved, you put everyone in danger."

It was a little late for that. She'd become curious about Ana when the HR director at Roth volunteered her to help set up the diversity training sessions, but she'd assumed Ana was just another corporate pretty face. Now that she was soundly proven wrong, she didn't know what to do with all the emotions colliding together inside her.

Sitting in the cold, plastic hospital room chair, she bowed her head for a moment to compose her thoughts. When she looked up, Ana was watching her with dark, curious eyes. Sabel straightened up in the chair by reflex and Ana's look turned to one of dismay.

"Oh no, your suit."

Sabel glanced down. A long stain of blood ran from her shoulder to the curve of her breast. She touched it with a curious fingertip. It was Ana's, from whatever head wound she'd sustained. She liked the suit a little better now, but she could hardly say that out loud.

"It's all right. I'll get another," Sabel said.

"But Ruben made it sound ridiculously expensive..."

"Not if you get it from eBay."

Ana smiled.

"Should you call him? See if he can come pick you up?" Sabel opened her purse and pulled out Ana's phone.

"Where did you find that?" Ana asked.

"On the street down from Helen's apartment."

"And that's how you knew I was in trouble...but what were you doing there?"

"I thought you were right to be worried about Helen," Sabel told her.

"Did you see her? Is she okay?"

Sabel stood up in alarm. "You didn't go in?" she asked, hoping she was wrong.

"No. I just saw them carrying in what looked like a body. Oh no, no, no. It wasn't Helen. Tell me it wasn't Helen!"

Sabel couldn't deny the truth, even if she didn't say it aloud. Realization broke in Ana's eyes and she rolled on her side away from Sabel and started crying. Sabel wanted to put her hands on Ana's back and comfort her. She wanted to pull Ana into her arms and let her cry herself out but she was afraid that would embarrass her more than comfort. She put the cell phone on the table and slipped out of the room.

In the hallway, she leaned back against the wall and slowed her breathing down so her thoughts would settle. She lifted the left side of her jacket and put her mouth close to the dried blood. Cupping her tongue just under her palate, she drew air in slowly—there was a woody, balsamic scent like myrrh and then a lance of pain across the roof of her mouth. She gasped and jerked her head back.

Whatever happened to Ana, it was tremendously powerful—but she hadn't felt any of that energy rolling off her in the room. Had it passed through her and gone or was it lying dormant in her body? What kind of demon magic left that signature? She hadn't been around a lot of demons in her life, okay none, because the witches didn't let their precious *maarevas* do that work, and the few times she smelled the magic of little, bothersome demons, it was nothing like this.

A small, blond woman in scrubs came down the hall and went into Ana's room, and Sabel followed her back in. Ana was half sitting against the raised top half of the hospital bed and staring at the phone in her hands.

"Do you need a ride home?" Sabel asked.

"I don't want to trouble you."

"I'm taking you home."

Ana's mouth quirked up in the ghost of a smile.

"What?" Sabel asked.

She shook her head. "Just a joke with Ruben earlier about the security system."

The doctor interrupted before Sabel could ask what the joke was and gave instructions for the care of Ana's injuries. Most of them were straightforward, but the doctor did think she had a concussion and recommended someone be with her for the next twenty-four hours. If Ruben didn't show up, Sabel resolved that she was staying over whether Ana asked her to or not.

While the doctor was talking about how to change the bandages on her feet, a police detective came in to get a statement. He assured Ana they would do everything they could to find the men who abducted her. She gave a very full description of the space she was in, but she changed something in the middle. Sabel noted a pause in her story and a distant look in her eyes. She said she'd pretended to be possessed and used the distraction to escape, but Sabel could tell more than that happened. Had she seen other magic at work?

Ana invited Sabel to chime in for the account of the rescue. The Hecatines didn't approve of average humans finding out about the magic operating in the world and it was surprisingly easy to keep it from them. A fundamental aspect of this material world was its resistance to persistent magic. When Sabel had asked the Hecatines why they didn't tell more people, they'd only said that it wasn't time.

Sabel explained that it was pure dumb luck that she found Ana and said she'd taken down the man on the phone with a solid double-handed club strike to the side of his head.

"That self-defense class finally came in handy," she added with a wide-eyed smile.

* * *

"You can't find him?" Jacob asked again, the annoyance clear in the tight clipping of his words.

"He is riding in her body. She let him in. No, I cannot. There is no way to distinguish her from any of the other millions of people in this city. But we know who she is, we will wait and then go take him," Drake said.

They were standing in front of Jacob's house, having sent the men home after the woman got into the unexpected rescuer's car and escaped. Drake stroked his fingers along the back of the stray orange tabby that wandered by and let it rub its soft head against his knee. He'd take this one home too except he already had three women living at his house and they wouldn't tolerate more than the couple of cats he had. It was always easier to pass up a new friend than to make trouble with women. In another day that wouldn't be an issue. Maybe he should have Jacob hold onto the cat for him. No, Jacob was too focused and Drake didn't want to use up his favors.

"She saw you," Jacob said. "And she heard you named 'Drake.' She'll know you and the whole deal at Roth is in jeopardy."

Drake sighed. "We'll just have to kill me."

"I assumed you had another body handy," Jacob said. Drake didn't appreciate the hint of a smile he saw on Jacob's face.

"We'll plant evidence that I killed Helen and then we'll get me killed. Case closed. I'll be back in a few days as my brother who, in case of my death, inherits my business."

"Perhaps then we can get on with the real plan," Jacob said.

CHAPTER FIVE

Ana felt four kinds of grimy—layers of fearful sweat and exertion, dirt, and emotional smudge. Five layers, if embarrassment counted. She directed Sabel toward the garage under the house because there was no available street parking and Ana didn't know how far she could walk. Tomorrow she'd have to send Ruben to get her car, if he ever showed back up from his wild night. She gave Sabel the code to open the garage door and watched her glide out of the car to the number pad and back again. There could not be a worse way to spend time with this self-possessed, beautiful, cryptic woman.

The soles of Ana's feet were thickly bandaged and she wasn't sure if she could walk across the basement floor on them. The process of cleaning them at the hospital hurt at least as much as running on them, and now they both stung and ached despite the prescription dose of painkillers they'd given her. If Sabel wasn't here, she'd seriously consider crawling out of the car and up the stairs.

"How can I help?" Sabel asked.

"Could you just go up and open the door for me? I need a sec."

The other problem with crawling was how many muscles she'd have to use. Her shoulder was sore from hitting the ground and she didn't want to have to put weight on her arms. She clenched her teeth and stood up. She'd sprinted on the balls of her feet and they'd taken the brunt of the damage, so she put her weight on her heels and hobbled to the stairs. She hated Ruben for a moment for forgetting to reinstall the railing after he'd painted months ago, but she put her good shoulder to the wall for balance and went up one slow step at a time.

If only Ruben were there, he could have picked her up and carried her. She'd texted him a few times from the car, but there was no answer. Clearly his night at the clubs had turned out the way he planned. She'd also sent a quick email from her phone to Detlefsen to let him know that she wouldn't be in the office that morning. She assumed the police would be contacting him about Helen and he'd have his hands full without worrying about Ana's absence.

Sabel waited in the hall. She didn't say anything as Ana continued her painful progress up to the second floor. Ana made it to the bathroom and then paused in the doorway, swaying slightly, because she couldn't figure out how to turn on the tub and get her clothes off.

"Oh by everything holy, let me help you," Sabel said.

"But you already—"

"Let you get kidnapped? Took forever to find you? Yes, I'm batting a thousand tonight. Go. Sit."

The bitterness in her voice surprised Ana. She limped to the closed toilet lid and sat on it. At least she'd used a bathroom at the hospital so she was spared trying to figure out how to navigate peeing, bathing, and Sabel.

"You knew I was going to be kidnapped?" Ana asked.

Sabel turned on the bath water and rinsed out the tub, letting the cold water swirl down the drain.

"You're going to have to get in first or you'll soak the bandages," she said. After a pause she added, "I thought Helen might be in danger. I had no idea it would spread to you. If I'd known more, I'd have warned you. But I should have come with you to Helen's. If I'd just come with you…Hindsight. It's hard to know what I should have known."

Sabel's gray-blue eyes were stormcloud dark. She held her fingers under the running water for another moment and then turned off the faucet. Ana had too many questions trying to get out of her mouth at the same time. Why hadn't Sabel come with her? Was it just because they were strangers to each other? Why did Sabel seem to think she could have prevented both of them from being taken? What did Sabel know about Helen? And, when Ana was running at random through an unknown neighborhood, how could Sabel pinpoint her?

She asked the most radical question that came to mind: "How did you drop the man with the stun gun?"

"Why don't we take care of you first, okay?"

The four feet between the toilet and the bathtub looked like a chasm, but Ana nodded resolutely. "I can do this," she said. She wanted some answers, but she wasn't sure she wanted them now.

"Yell if you need me," Sabel said. She paused in the doorway and gave Ana a stern look. Her face, framed by the open collar of her black shirt and her loose, windblown hair, looked like an ivory carving of some fey queen with fierce sapphire eyes. "Promise?"

Ana nodded. When the door shut, she slumped against the back of the toilet and tipped her head back. At least Sabel hadn't offered to undress her. The shock and fear were still dampening every other sensation in her body, but some part of her mind warned her that tomorrow she was going to feel unbelievably horrified.

She hitched the dress up and struggled out of it, then threw it into the far corner of the room. Her bra followed and then the underpants. This part of a crisis was familiar to her: get clean, shake and cry from the shock, remember to eat something as soon as she felt hungry, and get to sleep if she could manage that; otherwise maybe she could stand some mind-numbing television.

She took the opportunity to put a tad of weight on her feet. They didn't hurt as much as she expected from the trip up the stairs—the painkillers must be doing their thing. She was able to get to the edge of the tub with minimal ache. She braced on her hands and slid back into the cold porcelain basin, propping her heels up on the sides to keep the bandages out of the way. Then she leaned forward enough to close the drain and turn on the water. Sabel had run it until it warmed and made sure that it wouldn't freeze her.

As the warm water embraced her, the shivery adrenaline of the last hours began to ebb, uncovering her deeper fears. She wasn't supposed to get hit ever again in her life, or have to fight and run. San Francisco had been safe for her the last nine years, nothing like where she'd grown up. She hated the way that part of the evening felt familiar: feeling afraid and threatened, being trapped, the anticipation of pain that was as bad as the real pain when it came. But this was different, she insisted to herself. This time she could fight back effectively. She wasn't a kid anymore.

Hell, even as a kid, she fought. In the trickle-down economics of their family, their father's frustration and rage was passed on to her oldest brother Mack, who doled it out to her and Gunnar with all the brutal simplicity of a child. He hit them when he felt like it, choked them and laughed at their panic, and most often simply threatened and then mocked them. It was such a natural part of their lives, Ana used to think all families were like that and then she hit puberty. Mack stopped hitting and wrestling her and his attentions took a crueler turn, until the day she went after him with a knife. He never touched her again, but much about that day and all the days before it left her feeling like a monster.

The familiar heat of rage simmered under her breastbone and she wanted to strike out. She put her hands under the water and forced them open. She'd given all the details she could to the police. She had Drake's name and she'd seen the faces of two of the men and had listened carefully to all of them. Although she couldn't identify most of them, or where they'd taken her, she would use every resource at her disposal from the police to the media to the Internet, and she wouldn't stop until these men were found and arrested. This time the right people would get hurt.

When the warm water had eased some of the soreness in her muscles, Ana picked up the soap and washed as well as she could without hurting herself more. Then there came the problem of getting out of the tub. She opened the drain and let the gray water out. That made it easier to turn sideways and put both feet over the side of the tub. She levered herself up until she was sitting on the edge of the tub and then snagged a towel.

She wanted pajamas but she was so tired she didn't care enough to get them. She stood up and grabbed Ruben's huge, white fluffy bathrobe and pulled it on. Then she limped into the hall and paused at the top of the stairs.

"I'm going to bed," she yelled down.

"Good." Sabel's voice rose from the direction of the living room.

"Thanks for bringing me home."

Sabel came into view at the foot of the stairs. "You shouldn't be standing," she said. "I'm going to stay for a bit."

"You don't have to."

"Doctor's orders. I'll just stay until Ruben gets back. You're not supposed to be alone."

Sabel walked back toward the living room. Ana didn't have the strength to argue. She took the few steps into her bedroom and collapsed across the bed.

In the darkness behind her eyelids images flashed like a slideshow: Drake's cruelly beautiful face, the hooded men, the circle, her dream in the darkness of the falling sun, blazing serpents, running, and the feeling that something outside of her conscious mind moved her arms and legs.

She rolled onto her back and sat upright because she smelled hot sunlight. Was she dreaming now? Could she dream just a smell? Her fingers edged their way around the band of her skull as if she could pry it open and feel inside. The right side was too tender to put any pressure on.

What had really happened to her? Whenever she'd been hit in the past, she hadn't seen visions or blacked out for long periods of time during which, apparently, she'd acted without the benefit of being conscious. And she'd been hit enough that if this was going to happen, it should have happened before. Was there some kind of lasting damage from the abuse that just now showed itself? She put her hands over her ears, wishing her freaked-out brain would just shut up for a while. She felt hands covering hers, larger and warmer, but when her eyes snapped open no one was in the room.

"Who's there?" she whispered.

No one should be able to answer that, but the liquid voice from the man in her dream rolled through her mind. The words came with perfect clarity from the back of her skull into the gray space between her ears like any other thought she'd ever had, except for the pure alien quality, a tone utterly unlike any she'd used with herself, and a language she never knew.

She screamed with surprise and then she couldn't stop. Deep screams came up from her gut, rough and tearing in her throat. "You fuck! You son of a bitch! No!"

She made a fist and hit the side of her head by the temple. Pain wracked her already sore skull. It triggered her body's alarm that she'd damage herself even worse and that cut through her panic. She hit herself again, harder, and meant to again, but someone had her wrist and was forcing her hands down from her face.

Sabel knelt on the bed, her knees on either side of Ana's legs, her hands on Ana's wrists. Ana didn't want to fight her, but her body reacted to being trapped with rage and renewed panic. Her right hand got loose and grabbed a fistful of Sabel's jacket, trying to drag her off while her legs kicked.

"No, don't...don't!" Ana heard herself panting. She was trying to convey that Sabel needed to get off her and not try to hold her down. Constraint always made her fight, and in her already overloaded body it was so much worse, but she couldn't make the words.

"It's okay," Sabel said as a counterpoint. "It's okay. You're safe."

How could she be safe if the threat was inside her own head? Her body fought reflexively, spurred by the panic of being restrained. She wrenched at Sabel's jacket again making her lose her balance and slide to the right. The pressure of Sabel's weight came off her legs and she kicked up with her shin and knee. The force of Ana's kick shoved Sabel to the edge of the bed and momentum carried her over the side. Ana heard the breath rush out of her as she hit the floor between bed and wall.

Ana crawled to the edge of the bed, her right hand in a fist, not sure what to hit next. Sabel stared up at her from the floor and her blue-gray eyes shimmered with a golden fire around the pupils. Her lips parted as she took a long breath in through her open mouth. The voice that came out of her held a deep resonance, as if each sound was a struck bell.

"*Sit down. You will not hit.*"

Ana's body obeyed and sat her back on the bed. Her fist fell open and she stared at it. The rage was still there and it swelled in her arm, trying to close her fist again. She watched her hand slowly curl inward. How the hell did Sabel do that? Why couldn't she just ball up her fist like normal?

Sabel pushed up from the floor. Her slender fingers touched Ana's closing fist and gently opened it. For a moment she held Ana's right hand in both of hers and pressed the muscles with her thumbs until they relaxed. Then she pulled back the corner of the blanket.

"*Get into bed,*" she said in the resonant voice.

Ana did.

"*This is a dream,*" Sabel told her. "*You will remember feeling safe. You will not wake fully until you are rested. Sleep.*"

* * *

Sabel stood over the bed watching Ana slip from light sleep into deep sleep almost instantly; she needed the rest badly. Sabel hated having to use the Voice on an ally—and especially with the power and intention she just put into it so that her command would last for hours. Usually she gave short, light commands that held for a few minutes.

One of the first lessons she learned when the Hecatines began training her as one with the gift, or curse, of the *maarevas*, "the dangerous voice," was that if you commanded a person too often, you began to destroy their mind. Command a friend and you started to destroy their trust in you as well. It could become impossible to relax around someone whom you knew could make you do whatever she wanted.

She rubbed her hip where she'd hit the floor. So far so good, she'd managed to terrify Ana at least once and get herself bodily thrown out of the woman's bed—could she count this as the worst first date ever?

She shook her head, trying not to think that way. She wanted to touch Ana but she stepped back from the bed to put more distance between herself and that temptation. This was not the time. Very few people could fight against the Voice, and she replayed the moment in her mind when Ana struggled against her command to make a fist. Did she have that much anger in her or was there another power alongside the anger?

What had set her off in the first place? Was it a memory of something in the past or had the summoners magicked her? Just because Sabel couldn't smell it on her now didn't mean there was no magic working in her. It had to extend a little outside of her body to become something others could perceive, because the human body itself was one of the most effective tools to hide magic. Sabel really needed help on this one, but she dreaded the restrictions that came with that help.

She paced out of the room and down the stairs. It was possible to contact Josefene from here if she could manage enough focus to concentrate. It was what she should do. The problem was that she wasn't just remembering Ana trying to close her hand into a fist or Ana fighting off two men in an A-line dress and torn stockings; she had a very clear image of Ana leaning over the side of the bed to see where she'd thrown Sabel, heedless of the fact that her robe was open. She'd seen just enough to have a very clear idea of how divine Ana's breasts would feel in her palms. She shook her head. There were ill-intentioned men and demons afoot and all she could think about was sex—some witch she was.

Sabel went to the kitchen and hunted through the cupboards until she found mugs and tea. They only had two kinds of tea, but one was a calming blend so she filled a mug with water, nuked it and dropped in a tea bag. She started sipping it as soon as it was cool enough to drink.

She liked this kitchen with its cutout window to the dining room where people could sit and talk to the cook. It was a galley kitchen, the same as most of these narrow houses, but well-organized and pretty. Did Ana cook? She took her mug of tea into the living room and set it on an end table. In the mirror over the fireplace she caught a glimpse of herself in the bloodstained Armani suit.

Was it some combination of blood and magic that made her react so strongly to Ana right now? The jacket's button was gone, a consequence of being thrown out of bed, so she shrugged out of it easily, folded it and set it across the couch's arm. There was blood on the shell under the jacket too. She sighed and headed back up the stairs. Was it worse to borrow clothes from Ana or Ruben? He was almost a half foot taller than Sabel, so Ana it was.

With Ana sleeping soundly, she took time to look around the simple bedroom. The bed sat on a plain wooden frame and the worn, broad bedside table looked like it had been passed from person to person for the last twenty years. The dresser was another mismatched hand-me-down. Did Ana not care what her bedroom décor looked like or were these pieces from past relationships or past homes that she did care about? Sabel ran a finger along the edge of the dresser. The wood was thick and heavy, warm in color and scuffed with use. Next to the dresser the open closet showed all of Ana's work clothes hanging in no particular order above a half-full laundry basket.

Sabel opened the middle drawer of the dresser to find two neat stacks of T-shirts with a couple of extras tossed to one side. She picked up one of the extras. It was charcoal gray and so well worn that the collar had frayed all the way around.

She knelt and opened the bottom drawer. Sweatpants and pajama bottoms. She pulled out the top pair of sweatpants but they had elastic at the ankles so she folded them and put them back. Again there was a clothing item crumpled to one side of the folded stacks—soft black pants by the look of them. Sabel lifted them out and held them up. Perfect.

When she looked down again to shut the drawer, something else caught her eye and brought a rush of blood high into her cheeks and a ripple of heat down her body.

"Oh," the word breathed out without conscious intent.

She touched the worn leather with a cautious fingertip. This was not the time to imagine Ana wearing *that*...but the picture formed in her mind anyway. It would fit her well and the other part of the ensemble, yes that would be perfect. It made her ache from the base of her spine to the roots of her teeth. There was no magic at play here, blood-based or otherwise: she just wanted Ana.

She shoved the drawer closed and hurried out of the bedroom. On the first floor there was a tiny bathroom behind the kitchen and she changed there. She scrubbed off her makeup and put her jewelry in the small side pocket of her purse. In the living room she knelt on the hard stones of the hearth as a concentration aid to pull her mind back to the problems of the night rather than its secret revelations. Despite the painful pressure of the stones on her knees, she kept thinking back to that moment when Ana began making a fist again—defying the power of Sabel's Voice—and she wanted to curl herself inside those fingers and be the one who felt protected for once.

CHAPTER SIX

Ana dreamed she was walking in a desert, surrounded in every direction by gigantic sand dunes. She knew she was dreaming but that knowledge didn't cause her to wake up. It was a relief to be in a true dream, to be able to set down her expectations about reality and her concerns and just look around at this golden setting. Maybe if she stayed lucid she could fly. She was walking barefoot, but the sand didn't burn her, and she had on some kind of white dress or tunic that blew around her knees in the hot, slow wind.

A man walked beside her, but she couldn't turn her head to look at him. The best she could do was to look down at an angle and then she recognized his feet, if you could call them that: the flaming serpents of the vision.

"I know what you are," she said. "Don't think I don't know that you're using this dream to lull me into some sense of safety so you can lay your sympathetic story on me. As soon as I figure out how to do it, I'm getting rid of you."

They crested a rise and overlooked a valley. The moving air held the kind of heat Ana only felt on vacations, and it slid in through her pores and relaxed her muscles. She only half cared about his response to her words, more interested in the fact that she didn't hurt, or fear, or want to scream.

A vision appeared in the valley. It was historical. She didn't know how old, that wasn't her thing, but old enough that everyone looked dirty. They were pulling stone blocks with oxen to build something enormous. It wasn't a pyramid. From the finished side it looked to be a rectangularly shaped building. Alongside some of the people were creatures of smoke and fire who were helping them, by showing where to lay the stones to make them strong, and talking about foundations and arches. In the strange manner of dreams, she understood the meaning of what they discussed without knowing the words.

Beside her, the creature was speaking. He didn't use English, but if she didn't focus on his exact words she found she could understand the sense of them as well.

"We came into being before you," he said. "Long ago we helped your people. Sometimes with knowledge and other times with a strong fist to protect you from yourselves. When your people called out for adversaries, some of my kind agreed to be what you wanted and to fight against you. That is the kind of being the one who calls himself Drake is. I am not that kind."

"Are you saying that people wanted to be attacked by demons? That's crazy. You're totally blaming the victim."

"If some of humanity want the experience of being beset by adversarial forces, where do you think those come from? Someone must agree to play the antagonist," he said.

Ana understood the basic meaning of what he was saying, but that didn't mean that it made sense to her. "I thought all demons were evil," she said.

She hadn't meant to voice that question and wasn't sure she'd even said it out loud, but in this in-between space of being awake inside her dream, her thoughts had a voice of their own.

"We are harsh," he said. "Divisive, pain-bringing, wrathful. But that does not prevent us from using those capacities to protect humans. I am one of the protector demons, not the adversaries."

"Then why call yourself a demon at all?" she asked. "Where I come from, demons are evil and tricky and just out to take your soul."

"We call ourselves many things, humans came up with the name 'demon.' Is there no one among you who understand this?"

"Why don't you go looking for someone who knows what you're talking about? I want you out of my dreams and out of my life."

"I can't do that."

"Why not?" she asked.

"I traveled a long way. I'm too weak to stay in your world outside of your physical body." He paused and they stood watching the ancient construction taking place for a while before he spoke again. "The men who captured you sought to put an adversarial demon in you, a creature of great malice. I helped you escape with your life and gave you back control of your body."

She shuddered. He had a point, but the idea that having control over her own body was now optional horrified her.

He went on talking. "I can make you stronger and faster, as I did when we ran together. I can make your body mend itself more quickly. And I can teach you."

"I don't make deals with the devil," she said.

"I am not anyone's devil."

She turned away from him. In the valley below, the scene faded and the wind blew sand in great mounds to obscure it all. She was alone and the air turned cold.

Her eyes opened on a white ceiling and sunlit window. According to the clock, she'd slept a good six hours and she felt surprisingly well-rested. It was late morning now and she had an agenda. Before evening, she wanted to be closer to seeing the summoners in jail and this thing out of her head.

After that dream she couldn't go on toying with the notion that she was just losing it from the trauma. She wasn't sure if the thing was actually talking to her or if her own mind was interpreting the experience for her, but either way it was time to assume she had some kind of spirit creature in her. In her life she'd seen a few incidents she considered miraculous and felt the presence of something supernatural and awe-inspiring, so it was possible there were other forces she didn't know about, but this wasn't how she planned to explore that part of the world. She had two goals now: get rid of the thing in her head and bring the guys who'd put it in her to their personal experience of hell.

The smell of frying bacon drifted up from the kitchen and her stomach growled. She pushed herself up. The dream remained so clear she expected to see sand on her toes, but they were clean and taped at the base where the gauze bandage stuck to her foot. Scrunching forward, she peeled the tape away and looked at the sole of her foot. Many small scabs dotted the pink landscape, but it didn't look nearly as raw as it had at the hospital. The man in her dream of the desert said he could make her heal faster and that seemed to be true. She pressed the tape back into place and swung her legs over the side of the bed.

Although her bedroom was sparse, it was one of Ana's favorite rooms in the house. As the only girl in her family, she'd gotten her own bedroom at an age when her two brothers still bunked down together. If not for the mystery of girlhood, it would have been a point of great contention. Of course her bed was an old, strange-smelling mattress in a walk-in closet, but late at night when her family was asleep that bed was all the comfort in the world to her. Alone in the dark she could think anything she wanted and imagine a life in which kids didn't stare at her and her raggedy brothers, and talk about them in undisguised whispers. She could dream of a time when her oldest brother Mack didn't take out his rage on her and Gunnar. Through college and after, in her apartment, she always loved having her own room and being in her bed.

Ruben had the bigger room on the other side of the hall with a grand bed and two huge armoires, plus a makeup table, dresser, and matching bedside tables. He was always the refinement to her carelessness. They'd met three years ago when she was dating his former roommate. He seemed to like living with lesbians, though he was a lot better with home repair than she was, so it wasn't from any mistaken notion about her butch skills. If she had to guess, she'd say he liked living with someone who never competed for his attention and had a completely different set of values about what was attractive. Her relationship with his former roommate hadn't worked out because of the restlessness that killed most of her intimate relationships, but she'd come out of the deal with Ruben and that seemed like a more than fair trade.

They'd lived together for just over two years now and she only regretted it on the nights when she heard loud sex from his bedroom or when she had to limp up basement stairs without a railing. He'd bought this house as a foreclosure and restored most of it himself, but he had a bad habit of leaving the fix-up jobs ninety-five percent finished. Ana was about ready to teach herself to tile just to complete the downstairs bathroom sink backsplash.

She stood up slowly but her feet didn't hurt beyond a light ache that was easy to ignore. Her muscles were another matter. She felt like she'd seriously overtrained. Her head ached and her left shoulder was badly jammed into its socket. As soon as she had some food in her stomach, she was taking another dose of the painkillers.

One of her favorite T-shirts for sleeping in and a pair of loose sweatpants sat on the chair next to her dresser, where she'd thrown them a day ago when she got ready for work. She shrugged out of Ruben's robe and got herself into the pants and shirt.

Once she made it into the downstairs hall, she caught the scents of savory onions and dark coffee. She picked up speed heading toward the kitchen. Ruben was an average cook, but he had a few dishes he knew well and bacon and eggs was top of the list. He said he practiced it so he could impress lovers with his morning-after breakfast skills.

When he saw her, he wiped his hands on the dishtowel tucked behind the string of his favorite dark gray apron and pulled her in for a hug. She winced as his arm brushed her shoulder but hid the gesture by turning her face into his body. They'd been mistaken for a couple fairly often and they did make a handsome pair. Ruben had the classic good looks of a Calvin Klein underwear model and Ana knew her smile made up for the Midwestern rest of her face.

Ruben let her go and she settled on a stool by the cutout window between the dining room and kitchen. He put a cup of black coffee in front of her and she wrapped her hands around it gratefully.

He waited for her to take a few sips and then asked, "Honey, what the hell happened last night?"

She really had no idea where to start. He needed to know, particularly if she was going to keep talking to the police until this was resolved, but how could she tell him she'd been taken to a demon summoning ritual and...

"That must have been some date," he added under his breath as he poured a mixture of eggs, sour cream and scallions into the skillet.

"Date?"

"Sabel lit out of here like a cat with her tail on fire as soon as I got in—and I'm pretty sure she was wearing your yoga pants."

"She was?"

"Mmhm, the stretchy ones that make your ass look cute and that gray rowing shirt that has to be yours. I'm sure girlfriend hasn't rowed a day in her pretty little life."

"Oh. God." Ana dropped her forehead to rest on the windowsill.

If she hadn't been so sore, she'd have run up the stairs to confirm her suspicion about what that particular pair of yoga pants was supposed to keep covered up. Fate had to be allied against her if, after everything, Sabel chose to lift *that* particular pair.

While her head was down, Ruben let out a long whistle and one dry fingertip touched the side of her collar and pushed it out so he could look further underneath it. "Sweetheart, how big is that bruise?"

"Big," Ana mumbled without lifting her head.

"She is *not* worth that."

She snapped upright. "Ru, this isn't from Sabel. We didn't do anything." *Other than me bodily throwing her out of my bed.*

He raised an eyebrow and shifted the eggs off the burner.

"I went to check on Helen and some guys grabbed me—really fucked-up, crazy-ass guys. I got away but I was pretty banged up and Sabel...she was worried about Helen too and she helped get me to the hospital. Then she stayed."

"I need to hear the long version of that story," he said, staring at her. "One minute."

He finished the scrambled eggs and put them on two plates with toast and bacon, carried the plates into the dining room, and set them at two adjacent places. Ana sat at her plate and took a few bites before launching into a longer version of the events of the night before.

"At Helen's building there were these men carrying in what looked like a body, so I called 911—"

"Was it?" he asked.

The eggs caught in Ana's throat and she washed them down with a long drink of her cooling coffee. "Helen, yes," she managed. "I think they killed her. Then they saw me so they grabbed me and took me somewhere. They wanted to do this ritual."

"Seriously? Like Satanic cult stuff?"

"Pretty much. So they uncuffed me to offer me to their demon or whatever and I ran for it." She touched her shoulder. "I think I got this busting through a door, or maybe when I fell in the driveway. It's all muddled. I just ran like hell and then they were chasing me and Sabel...she went to Helen's after I did and saw my phone in the street and realized I was in trouble. So she was driving around—"

"Wait, she found your phone and just started driving around looking for you? How long were you kidnapped for?"

Ana tried to add it up in her head and it came to a much longer amount of time than made sense in the story—three or four hours including the time she was unconscious. Had Sabel really driven around for that long looking for her? How did she know which way to go and was that ability connected in some way to whatever she did that dropped the man with the phone? It had to be.

"A few hours," Ana told him.

"And you two have met what, three or four times? And she drove around for hours looking for you?"

"Um."

"And then somehow, miraculously, she finds you running from the bad guys?"

Ruben set his fork down and sat back in his chair with his eyebrows drawn in and his stare completely focused on her.

"They weren't exactly quiet about chasing me," Ana said. "She probably just followed the yelling."

"Where were the cops?" He spread his hands wide.

"At Helen's, I'd guess."

"So Sabel just pulls up in her badassmobile and you jumped in to safety?"

"Something like that."

"Ana." His arms folded tightly across his chest. She wasn't going to get away with being that vague.

"Two guys caught me and I knocked out one of them and the other one tased me with a stun gun. Then Sabel knocked him out and kind of half-carried me to her car. I tried to call you from the hospital."

"Oh shit, I turned my phone off."

"Jerk."

"I'm sorry. If I'd known you were going to get yourself kidnapped and tased…" His joking expression turned serious and he unfolded his arms to reach across the table with one hand and touch her wrist. "Are you okay?"

Ana shrugged. "I'm shook up a lot and I hurt, but nothing serious. Oh, I could have really used a basement railing or a big strong guy to carry me up the stairs. And I'm pretty sure I demolished any chance of getting a date with Sabel."

"You're kidding."

"I kind of kicked her off my bed, literally, and I almost hit her while I was panicking."

"Sweet thing, this woman drove around for hours trying to find you, pulled you out of a serious scrape and then brought you home and stayed all night to make sure you were okay. That's the most fucking romantic story I've ever heard."

"When you put it that way..."

She couldn't suppress her grin. The way he said it made it sound like she still had a pretty good chance to salvage things. He opened his mouth to go on, but the phone rang. The number was the general exchange for Roth Software.

When she picked up, Detlefsen bellowed into her ear, "Ana! How the fuck are you?" When under stress or agitation, he had the foulest mouth of any executive she'd ever met. He only got away with it because he so clearly cared about the people who worked for him that no one could take offense.

"I'm all right," she said. "I really didn't get hurt much, just scared."

"After they told me about Helen..." He trailed off.

She swallowed hard but couldn't think of anything to say.

He continued, "Hell of a thing! That goddamned motherless fuck killed her."

"What? Who?"

"Nathan Drake, that asshole playboy investor. He and Helen were an item, apparently, did she tell you?"

"No, never a word." Ana tried to remember if she'd missed something, but she felt certain that Helen had never mentioned Drake. She was under the impression that Helen didn't know him.

"Police got a tip. Went to his house early this morning. I've got a good friend on the force keeping me updated. He was all fucked up on coke and started shouting at the cops about how Helen betrayed him. He was waving a gun around. He shot at the cops and they killed him."

Ana pulled the phone away from her ear for a moment and stared at it. That didn't make sense at all. "What?"

"They think Helen dropped him and he killed her, then saw you and...I don't know what. Maybe he was going to punish you for what Helen did. He was pretty heavily into drugs, they say. Thank God you got away. Such a tragedy. I want you to take as much time off as you need."

To buy herself more time to think, Ana switched into professional mode. "You're going to have to come up with some statement for the papers."

"Don't you worry about that!"

"I think I can come in on Monday. If I stay home I'll just worry."

"I've upped the security in the building," he said. "But with Drake gone I think it's over. Ana, I'm very sorry and if there's anything at all that I can do, tell me."

"I will," she said.

Ruben was watching her and sitting very straight in his chair, all traces of his casual, playful attitude gone.

"It doesn't make sense," she told him. "My boss says Helen was seeing this guy Drake and he shot at the cops and got himself killed, but she never said a thing about him to me. I need to look at something up in my office."

"Lead on, Nancy Drew. You want me to carry you up?"

She shook her head at him but the image of him carrying her up the stairs like a pair of awkward newlyweds made her smile. He followed her into her tiny home office and watched as she woke up her computer and searched recent news for Nathan Drake. The story was on every local paper's website.

Police had gone to Helen's apartment minutes after Ana's call and found her deceased in her bed with no signs of a cause of death. They'd initially suspected a heart attack until they received an anonymous tip from a man who said he was one of the group that had kidnapped a woman the night before— that woman was Ana, but her name was mercifully absent from the story. He said he was afraid of what his group had become: Nathan Drake had killed Helen when she said she was leaving him and wouldn't go along with their ritual.

When the police showed up at Drake's house that morning they'd found him intoxicated and with cocaine in plain sight. He'd appeared cooperative at first but then pulled a gun and started shooting, at which point the officers shot and killed him. The medical examiner's report wasn't complete, but they expected to find that an overdose was responsible for Helen's death, presumably administered against her will by a vengeful Drake whose ranting to police before his death included a confession that he'd killed her.

Reading over her shoulder, Ruben made a couple of "Hmh" sounds and said, "Well, I don't mind how that ended."

The words foremost in Ana's mind were: *I don't think it's ended at all.* She had the oddest feeling that Drake wasn't done. His death felt staged, though she couldn't imagine how. And there were still twelve other men out there who'd been involved. Maybe they'd let Drake take the fall for them. He was one of the few Ana could identify.

The police would try to find them but with the ringleader gone, Ana imagined this wasn't going to be high on their list of priorities. That left a dozen men loose and dangerous in the world.

"I want to look into this more," Ana said.

"Holler if you need anything, I'll be downstairs hounding my agent—after I put that railing up, of course."

She pulled her folio out of her work satchel. She'd dropped it there Thursday before she changed for the anniversary party. In addition to using the folio for note-taking in meetings, she kept her most critical information in the back zippered pocket. Along with her own passwords, she had a small note card on which Helen months ago wrote the password to her work email. They shared their work passwords in case either was sick or unreachable on a day when they had a big product release or announcement.

Now Ana used the web interface to log into the work email system as Helen. At first she thought she wasn't logging in properly and then she realized that Helen's email was empty. Everything had been deleted.

Puzzled, she clicked into Helen's Sent Mail folder. This was full. Someone—Helen or someone else?—had deleted all of Helen's mail but forgot to look in here. Many of the outgoing emails were to Ana, many more were routine and work-related.

Two months back, Ana found a glimmer of hope. Helen's new upstairs neighbor sent her an invitation to a housewarming event. She must have written her personal email address on her business card because he'd sent the invitation to both addresses. Helen's reply said she'd try to stop by and asked that future invitations only go to her personal email.

Ana opened another window in her browser and tried logging in to Gmail with Helen's personal email account name and the same password she used for her work account. It worked!

Her sense of victory was short-lived because there were almost no emails in Helen's personal account. She'd been deleting them as she went and the oldest was from Wednesday. It was the same in the Sent Mail folder. Helen didn't want information sitting around in this account, apparently. There was some junk mail and then a very short note in Helen's Sent Mail dated Wednesday morning, "Jacob, I don't need anything else for tomorrow night, thank you. But I'd still like to see you tonight. Call me after work."

Ana's memory flashed on the dark men in the underground room and the young-voiced one saying, "I hear her, Jacob, I hear her." He hadn't been talking to Drake but to Black Hood, the other leader of the group. Maybe that was the man who turned Drake in to the police. It sounded like he, and not Drake, had been Helen's lover. Why would Drake confess?

She picked up the phone and called Andi, a reporter for one of the local dailies. Andi answered her phone as always, even on a Saturday. She could have been downhill skiing and she would answer her phone, a habit that had cut short the second of their two dates and insured no third date.

"It's Ana," she said. "I saw your story on the murder and abduction."

"Yeah, what the hell happened? They grabbed some other woman you work with? The police are being tight-lipped."

Ana took a deep breath. Last week, she'd talked Andi into running a short piece on the Roth Software anniversary party, even though it was barely news. That put her in Andi's debt. She intended to repay that debt in a moment, but she couldn't say so much that she got herself in trouble.

"This can't get out," she said and paused to make sure Andi muttered assent. "I need your help, so you've got to promise me that we're so far off the record I don't even exist."

"I promise," Andi said.

"It was me."

She laughed and then stopped so abruptly Ana thought she'd hung up.

"Andi?"

"You're joking."

"I'm not," she said.

Her voice changed from light and joking to hard-edged, "Do you need me to come over? Are you all right? I can be there in ten minutes."

"I'm fine. Ruben's here and I'm okay."

"What happened?"

Ana told her, obscuring some of the details about the possession and outrunning a dozen men barefoot.

"Demon-summoning ritual?" she asked in a dubious tone when Ana finished.

"I'm serious, Andi. Plus, if I were going to start lying to you, I wouldn't begin with something so ridiculous."

"Ruben didn't put you up to this? He was an extra in that possession movie, right? It's kind of down his alley."

"I need you to help me figure out who these guys are," she said, ignoring the question. "And I need to know exactly where Drake lived."

"All right, let me see what I can do with what you've told me so far. I've been getting some strange reports from Roth, including people up all hours at that building. My contacts say drugs, which I think is a lot more likely than black magic."

There was a pause while she fanned through her notes. Ana heard the paper rustling. With Andi nothing from her notes made it to a computer until she started writing the story itself.

"Nob Hill," Andi said. "Drake was renting a condo there."

"Okay, keep me updated."

"You too," she said.

Ana found herself staring at the wall a foot to the left of the computer screen. Drake had driven her to Marin, so either he had another house there or it belonged to one of the hooded men, probably Jacob. Helen had emailed Jacob, so he was her primary connection to the summoners.

Whether she'd been involved willingly or not, maybe the ritual had killed Helen. But that wasn't what the summoners expected to happen. They drove her body back to her apartment to make it look like a natural death. They clearly didn't want to be discovered.

When Drake saw Ana watching them, he probably thought he could kill two birds with one stone—taking her so she couldn't identify him to the police and using her as Helen's replacement. He didn't expect her to survive, at least not as herself. He hadn't worried about her seeing his face. After she escaped, he'd framed himself. She believed he'd made the police shoot him on purpose, but why? And how?

CHAPTER SEVEN

Friday was one long blur to Sabel, from running out of Ana's house in the morning to staggering through her afternoon classes on very little sleep and then failing to make contact with Josefene. That night, she fell into bed and lay awake for hours in the darkness thinking about Ana struggling against her in bed. That wasn't the sort of memory of Ana she wanted to have right now, but her brain kept dredging it up.

She woke feeling gritty and trying to muster up some kind of steely resolve, but it felt more like soggy paper resolve. With tea and a bowl of fruit and oatmeal, she sat at the dining room table she used as a desk in her compact three-room duplex. She had a copy of the police reports about Helen Reed and Nathan Drake that she'd talked a friendly forensic expert in Anthro into getting for her, plus she had the news stories about Drake's death.

She'd scanned them the night before, but now she read them carefully. She already knew that Helen had wanted power over life and death—that was the reason she began training with the witches and the reason she stopped her training. The Hecatines didn't deal in immortality. The idea of it was offensive to them; they were on the side of time, change, and transformation. To their way of thought, death was necessary and important. At the same time, Sabel could empathize with Helen because when she contemplated her own mortality, she wasn't nearly as level-headed about it as she was in the abstract.

Helen must have thought she could get some serious power from the summoners in exchange for her cooperation. Because the Hecatines had selected Helen as a initiate, Sabel could assume she had a good amount of raw talent or power to offer. The Hecatine witches weren't a big group and they were highly selective. Whatever Helen had planned with the summoners, she must have reasonably expected she could pull it off. What went wrong?

Her phone rang and she glanced at the faceplate. "Ruben Cooper." The only Ruben she knew was Ana's roommate. She snatched up the phone, realizing it was Ana.

"How do you feel?" she asked Ana in what she hoped was an even tone.

"Pretty good really," Ana said. "I hope it was okay to call, I just…I need to know more about what those guys were trying to do and I thought maybe I'd go to some of the occult bookstores tomorrow and ask around."

"What time?" Sabel asked.

"I didn't know if you'd want to come along."

"I'm looking for answers too," Sabel told her. She didn't add that her answers were of a different order than Ana's. Maybe there would be a time to talk about that later.

There was a prolonged pause on the other side, then Ana said, "I'm sorry about kicking you. I hope I didn't hurt you."

"Not even my pride. When do you want to hit the bookstores?"

"Let's start around elevenish tomorrow and we can get lunch while we're out?"

"Why don't I drive?" Sabel offered. "I'll come pick you up."

"Thank you."

She hung up and stared at her phone. Bad idea? Probably. How bad? Medium bad. On the one hand, this gave her a chance to see how Ana was doing and follow up on the line of investigation about what the summoners had done to her. On the other hand...the other hand wanted to brush along the soft side of Ana's jaw, cup her chin and find out if her lips felt as agile as they looked.

* * *

"I thought we'd start at the Dark Knife, unless you know a better one," Ana said when she got into Sabel's car late Saturday morning.

Her gaze ranged from the floor mat to the inside door panel but she couldn't see any traces of her blood from Thursday night's escape. It looked like she'd never been in the car and Sabel was similarly impassive, as if none of the events had even occurred. The arch of her dark eyebrows was just visible over the top of her narrow, oval sunglasses. It was hard to tell if she was smiling or not because the corners of her small mouth turned up naturally. They rode to the bookstore in silence.

The Dark Knife sat at the bottom floor of a decaying old house on the less prosperous side of San Francisco State University. It was not a stately old house, just an old wreck of a place with parts of its plank siding coming loose and a cracked window that had never been replaced. Ana eyed it dubiously as they walked up the crumbling concrete steps.

A narrow hallway ran the length of the house. The door to the bookstore was on her immediate left and she pushed it open to an alarming jangle of deep-toned bells. The décor was early gothic revival, complete with wrought iron candleholders that looked like miniature lanterns spaced along the one wall that held art rather than books—though it was a stretch to call some of it art.

As Ana and Sabel walked in, a group of five kids clustered around the cash register all straightened up and stared at them as if controlled by a single mind. Between facial piercings and necklaces, they wore enough jewelry to accessorize a small tribe. Ana's eyes flicked back and forth, working to take it all in at once. One of the kids was behind the register, presumably the sales clerk, and the other four leaned against the long, rough-hewn wooden counter that was crowded with iron candlesticks and goblets. A display case held pentagram necklaces and small, ornate knives. Three walls of the room held thick-planked bookshelves crammed with dark-spined tomes.

Two of the boys looked them up and down and elbowed each other. Ana ignored them and fixed her eyes on the one behind the register, a skinny boy with long, greasy black hair and a goatee that came to an uneven point under his chin.

"I'm looking for books on demons," she said.

"No shit," he said. "What school are you guys in? Crowley? Chaos magic?"

"I'm not in any school. I just want some details about demon possession, or inhabitation."

"You should study with us," he said abruptly. "We're the best in the city. We've summoned spirits."

"Really?" Sabel asked, her tone thick with disbelief.

"We did the Abramelin ritual," the kid said. "The whole thing."

"For six months—?" Sabel started, but Ana missed the rest of it because a strange sensation hijacked her attention. She became completely certain that these kids had nothing to do with spirits or demons or whatever they were called, but that they were only interacting with lingering patterns of the dead that hadn't dissipated yet. That thought was foreign to her and bordered on the ridiculous since she'd never spent any time before thinking about the dead, demons, or the difference between the two.

You shut up, she thought fiercely. *I don't want you taking over my thoughts. I will knock myself out first, do you hear me?*

The odd sense of certainty withdrew. Ana rubbed her temples. She wanted to get out of this cramped and busy room. Sabel was listening to two of the kids detail how they'd set up an oratory for this ritual. Ana touched her elbow.

"They don't have what we need," she said. "They're not talking to demons. Let's go."

"Sorry, guys," Sabel said cheerily and followed Ana out the door.

In the closed silence of the car, she asked, "Do you mind telling me how you knew that?"

"I don't know," Ana said. "I just did. The other store is out in Oakland. Do you want to get something to eat afterward?"

"Sounds good."

Part of her reason for asking Sabel on this errand was to get her talking too. She'd seemed reticent on Thursday night to say what she'd done to the man with the phone to drop him with a single word, but the longer she thought about it, the more Ana knew she needed the knowledge Sabel had.

This wasn't the way she imagined they'd spend their first outing together. She'd only just started thinking about asking Sabel to get together when all this happened and hadn't figured out where to suggest going or even how to ask.

She'd noticed Sabel the first time she walked through Roth Software on a tour ten months ago, but it was more like "she's hot" than an actual thought about connecting with the woman. Even for San Francisco, Ana's office was mostly a desert of straight men and a few straight women, predominately in marketing and sales. She remembered Sabel pausing in the doorway to Helen's cubicle accompanied by the director of HR. Helen's cubicle was across from hers so when Ana turned around to the sound of unfamiliar voices, she saw a slender woman in a milk chocolate brown sundress and those fashionable Greek-style sandals with straps around the ankle. Her eyes followed the flow of straight black hair down the woman's back to her shoulder blades and from there she had to appreciate the way the soft material of the dress clung to her body.

When they all turned around to face Ana's cubicle, she was left blushing and trying to pretend she'd been waiting to ask Helen a question. She should have known then that Sabel liked women because somehow, mysteriously, Ana was the one requisitioned to help set up the two-session diversity training with her—but it really didn't dawn on her at the time. She just figured that the HR director was swamped with hiring and that he assumed since Ana was the one out lesbian in the office, she'd be the logical choice.

She didn't know that Sabel wasn't just a pretty straight girl until after the second training was completed. Ana had been helping to gather up the materials around the room when Sabel said, "I was glad the clouds cleared off for the festival last weekend."

Ana stopped with a handful of dry erase markers and tried to remember what bag they went into. How many festivals were there in the city of San Francisco on a given weekend? Dozens? Did she mean the Pride festival?

"You were there?" Ana asked, keeping her question neutral.

"I spent two hours at the SFSU booth and then wandered. You?"

How many festivals could SFSU have at booth in? She had to be talking about Pride. She hoped Sabel would volunteer whether she'd gone by herself or with someone.

"I went with Ruben, my roommate," Ana said. "He had a schedule of all the stage acts he wanted to catch."

"I meant to see some of those, but I got caught up in shopping." Sabel held up her delicate right wrist to show off a thin leather bracelet with a pearl clasp.

"Pretty," Ana managed through dry lips. Did the right side mean top or bottom? She tried to remember the complicated handkerchief code that gay men used and Ruben seemed to know intuitively. Did a leather bracelet count or did Sabel just prefer it on her right wrist even though she was right-handed? Did it even matter? Maybe Sabel was just showing off a pretty bangle.

"Well that's it for me here." Sabel snapped shut her soft-sided, burgundy leather briefcase. "You have my contact info. Call me if there are any questions."

Ana unstuck her tongue from the roof of her mouth. "Thank you."

"Anytime," Sabel said with a small smile and a bright flash of her eyes. She had turned and walked out the door and Ana watched the way her loose pants swayed as she moved.

She and Ruben had dissected that conversation every which way and decided that yes, in some subtle way, Sabel was coming on to her in a completely appropriate corporate diversity trainer fashion and she'd be insane not to fabricate an excuse to call her. Ruben also felt that the bracelet should be significant and reminded Ana more than once that the right side meant the receptive partner. Ana had trouble picturing Sabel as all that receptive, but it didn't stop her from trying.

She had forwarded Sabel the information about the company party and was working on a question that would warrant a phone call—but she still hadn't figured out how to turn that into an actual date. And then everything happened with Helen and the men in black masks and the hospital. Now it was all backward. Sabel had already spent a night at her house, and been in her bed, however briefly, and it was all wrong.

Sabel pulled into a parking spot near a small storefront in a strip mall sandwiched between a drugstore and a children's clothing outlet. The door opened with a tingle of chimes and Ana smelled sweet sandalwood and floral musk. A lean, older man stood behind the counter with his graying hair pulled into a ponytail hung with two feathers that trailed down his back. As dark as the other store had been, this one was light. White bookshelves sparsely populated with bright titles lined the walls and display tables held little bowls with unburned sage bundles, small drums, carved totem animals and other friendly knickknacks.

"May I help you?" he asked.

"I'm looking for books on demons," Ana said. "Specifically, possession."

"Well, I've got Dion Fortune's *Psychic Self-Defense* here, but that's about it."

Sabel wandered toward the back of the store. Ana watched her pick up one box of incense and smell it, wrinkle her nose, and move to another.

"When you say 'demon,'" the man asked quietly enough to reach her ears only, "Are you speaking literally?"

"I think so," she said.

"What did you do?" he asked.

"It was an accident."

He raised an eyebrow and shook his head. "I hope it turns out well for you."

He walked back to the counter and beckoned her to follow. From a drawer under the register he pulled out a business card in a subtle, designer eggplant color with gold script. *Ingenious Books*, the card read in a florid but very readable font, with the tagline, "Put Our Power to Work for You," and below that the name Lily Cordoba, a phone number and an email.

"Go see Lily," the man said. He was still speaking quietly and watching Sabel as she moved along the bookshelves, making sure that she didn't see him give Ana the card. His secrecy and discretion told Ana that this referral was serious. This man believed in demons and knew she needed help, and he was going to be careful about how he gave it to her.

"Who is Lily?" Ana asked him.

"She's the one you need. She's not cheap, but she's the only one in the city who really knows what she's doing."

She slipped the card into her pocket with a grateful, "Thank you."

Sabel walked back toward the front of the store and raised her eyebrows in an unspoken question. Ana considered showing her the card but suppressed the urge to share. If Lily could get the creature in her head to leave, maybe Sabel didn't need to know that part of the ritual. On top of her other transgressions, Ana didn't want to add hosting some otherworldly demon.

"He suggested another bookstore," Ana told her. "But let's go eat."

They picked a little Asian place where Sabel could get sushi and Ana ordered noodles. Their tiny table was crammed into a corner by the window with an excellent view of the parking lot. The whole place held maybe twelve tables and appeared to do most of its business as carryout.

"What's 'Ana' short for?" Sabel asked when they were settled with tiny cups of hot, woody-scented green tea.

"Nothing. Really, it's on my birth certificate like that. I used to make up names it could be short for. I even had an Anabelle phase for like three weeks. What about you?"

"Sabeline."

"Nice."

"Pretentious," Sabel said. "I've been going by Sabel since I started college."

Ana smiled into her tea. She didn't want to threaten the light mood, but she had questions. She remembered very clearly how Sabel seemed to step out of the darkness when Ana was running from the summoners and how she spoke what looked like a single word to the man holding the cell phone and he dropped like a sack of potatoes.

"Thursday night," she started, paused, and then pushed on. "What did you do to that man?"

"I made him sleep," Sabel told her. She stopped and Ana feared she wouldn't continue, but then she went on while her slender fingers played with her half-filled cup of tea. "There is magic in the world; it's just not the kind you see in movies with fireballs and all that. It's invisible and hard to do and not many people know how to use it, but I do. Lots of people do magic and don't realize that's what they're doing, but I've only met a few people who really train in it. I think it's a vicious cycle— people don't believe it exists so they see magic events as chance or explain them away, and then they never learn how to do real magic. You've been trying to explain away parts of what you saw the other night, haven't you? When the summoners took you, did they do anything to you that seemed…uncanny?"

"They said they wanted to put a demon in me," Ana admitted, though there was a lot more uncanny to the event than just that. She thought of the flaming serpents falling from the sky and how she assumed it was the result of a concussion.

"Did they?" Sabel asked.

"I think it's my turn," Ana said in order to deflect the question. She wasn't ready to answer that question fully for herself yet, let alone share the answer with anyone. "Did you make me sleep also?"

"Yes," Sabel said quickly and then looked away out the window though there wasn't anything of note to be looking at. "I'm sorry. I hate doing that to friends."

"How do you do it?" Ana asked.

The corners of Sabel's mouth quirked up. "It's my turn. Did the summoners' ritual work?"

The server showed up with their orders and Ana turned gratefully to her bowl of noodles. They were hot and savory. She took a mouthful but it was hard to swallow around the nervous tension in her throat. She made herself eat a few more bites and then answered the question.

"I'm not sure. I don't think it went the way they planned or I wouldn't have gotten out but—I don't know how I got out."

"Shock and adrenaline?" Sabel suggested. "Or did you do something you can't explain?"

Ana shrugged. "How does your…ability to do magic work?" she asked.

"What I can do is usually a lot more subtle and takes planning," Sabel said. "And with the Voice, it's an innate ability that my training has honed. I can use it to give commands, basically to override the information in your brain for a moment. I never use it to harm anyone. I'm not like the summoners."

"I know."

The muscles around Sabel's mouth relaxed and her shoulders settled back against the chair.

"Where are you from?" she asked.

Ana laughed. "That's your next question? South Dakota."

"A long way from here."

"Thank God. It's not the best place to be a lesbian, or a smart woman of any kind. At least not the part of town I was from. When did you come out?"

What passed for a grin on Sabel's delicate mouth would have been a wry smirk on anyone else—she had a way of packing a lot of mirth into a very small gesture.

"Well, I started having sex with women when I was sixteen. Coming out took a lot longer, maybe ten more years. My family wasn't particularly open to the idea. They wanted me to get married and come into the family business. Your family wasn't supportive either?"

Ana stared down into the tangle of noodles. "I didn't come out until college. All the shit with my family was just…shit." She didn't know how to describe it to Sabel and she wasn't sure she wanted this woman to see her as the girl she'd been in South Dakota. Finally she settled on, "You know: alcohol, no money, no education, no hope. But we got out, my brother Gunnar and me. He lives here too. My other brother…he's not worth thinking about."

"College?" Sabel asked. "Girls?"

"Yes to both. You *were* coming on to me after that last training, right? Ruben and I talked about that for days."

"Of course. You were one of the few people asking the smart questions. And anyway, Helen outed you to me when we first talked about setting up a series of trainings, probably to demonstrate how cool she was with diversity."

"Helen," Ana said with a long sigh. "Why did they kill her?"

"My guess is it was an accident. Whatever magic they were doing, with that many people and the setup you describe, it would have been tremendously powerful and it probably just went wrong."

"Your magic…?" Ana started but then wasn't sure what she meant to ask.

"Can kill," Sabel said. "But I take a lot of care with it and I have mentors who train me so it doesn't go wrong like that."

"What do you call yourself?"

The little smile arrived on Sabel's lips again. "A witch. It's not a perfect name because it gets me confused with the Wiccans. But I like its etymologies and it's what the Hecatines call themselves."

"I like it," Ana said and meant it. Something about the way Sabel said the word "witch," combined with her black hair and fair skin and those blue-gray eyes, elevated it to a place of wisdom and power. "Do witches…" she began and paused because she didn't know how to ask what she wanted. She started over, "The guy who grabbed me, they really thought they could summon a demon. Is that real? Can you do that?"

"No," Sabel said. "I don't work with demons."

The flat, almost angry way she said it chilled Ana. By all accounts this thing in her head was a demon and Sabel made it sound like she wanted nothing to do with that, so where did that leave her? She'd been hoping that Sabel would say she could banish demons. Then Ana might be willing to admit to her about the voice in her head and the strange dreams, but not if it was an issue that would drive them further apart. She was suddenly glad she'd instinctively not shared the name of the last bookstore with Sabel.

"They exist," Sabel said. "I've only ever met a few half-breeds. You did see something, didn't you?"

Ana nodded. "I don't know how to talk about it yet," she said.

"When you're ready, you can talk to me," Sabel told her.

Ana managed to smile back at her, but if Sabel couldn't get this creature out of her head, then it probably wasn't worth having a conversation about it.

The bill came and Sabel picked it up. "I'll get this one. You can get the next one."

"Thanks," Ana said, lighthearted that Sabel believed there would be a next meal together.

They walked out into the cloudy afternoon light and Ana paused a few steps from the door. Sabel turned and looked at her.

"Thank you," Ana said and opened her arms. Sabel hesitated and then stepped forward and hugged her. Ana could tell from the quick tightening of Sabel's arms that she meant it to be a brief gesture, but instead her body relaxed against Ana for a moment and Ana held her tightly. She rested her cheek against the side of Sabel's head and inhaled apricot musk and wildflowers.

Sabel pulled away and went to the driver's side of her car. Ana ducked her head to hide her smile.

"I forgot to bring your T-shirt and pants back," Sabel said.

Ana was glad Sabel wasn't looking at her just then because the reminder of that specific pair of pants made her blush.

"Whenever, it's fine," she said.

"I'm running errands tomorrow early afternoon."

"Perfect. Why don't we hit the other store then too. I'm feeling like I should nap. Everything's not all mended up yet."

She'd been developing a headache for the last hour or so, probably from too much moving around, and had put off going home so she could sit and eat with Sabel. But now that there was going to be a next time, she thought she'd better go lie down for a bit. Her body felt stronger than usual but at the same time more exhausted. Whatever the creature in her did to make them run so quickly seemed to have burned through all her reserves.

She went home and slept for most of the afternoon, then woke long enough to eat dinner and watch a movie with Ruben before she was ready to sleep through the night.

* * *

Sunday morning, Ana planted herself on the couch to watch a crime show marathon. She was eager to go see the Lily woman on the card from the bookstore, but she still felt a lingering exhaustion and a deep drive to keep her life seeming normal.

Ruben took himself off to the gym and he'd been gone about an hour when the doorbell rang. She considered ignoring it completely but after the second knock, she heard a woman's voice say, "I guess she's not home, do you think we could leave it?" Ana peered out the side of the living room window and saw a man and woman in casual clothing. Salespeople most likely, but she grabbed her phone on the way to the door in case she needed to call for help.

When she cracked the door, the woman and man were facing away. She opened the door another inch, leaving the chain on to stop further motion, and keeping the phone ready in her left hand where they couldn't see it.

"Yes?" she said. They came back up the two steps they'd descended. She didn't recognize either one.

"Ms. Khoury?" the woman asked. "I found your purse, I wanted to bring it back to you."

This could be the bright spot of her day, still Ana didn't move. The most likely people to have her purse were the people involved in the ritual, although they didn't have any women participating as far as she could see at the time.

"Where did you find it?"

"Outside our apartment building, in the street. If you had any cash, I'm afraid it's gone."

Twenty-five percent chance, she figured, that these two were telling the truth, and seventy-five they were trying to lure her out to grab her. She should tell them to leave it at the base of the door and back away, but she was tired of feeling that paranoid. She undid the chain but braced her foot at the base of the door so that anything short of a battering ram wouldn't move it.

She reached out a few inches through the narrow opening, forcing the other woman to come forward to hand her the purse. Her fingers closed around the soft leather and she was starting to feel optimistic about the whole transaction when she saw the man's hand come up quickly with something in it.

Ana pulled her hand and purse in the door, but before she could slam it, the man popped the lid off the small, gray glass bottle he was holding. A cloud exploded out of the top and slammed through the narrowing crack in the door to flood Ana's face even as she shut the door and threw the lock.

Fire raced over her nerves and she would have screamed but her mouth wouldn't move. It felt like hot liquid was being forced under her skin, as if her body were being inflated. She wanted to fall to the floor and curl into a ball but her muscles weren't responding to her mind anymore. She could still feel her body breathing, but the man on the other side of the door said a few words and her sight went dark. It wasn't like the time in the vast, open place when the man came down from the sky and kissed her. That pain had come on softly and given her time to adjust. This burning took her over immediately.

She still felt every detail of her body, the air shifting the tiny hairs on her arms, her blind eyes blinking, heart beating, but she could not do anything. Wherever she reached out with her mind to move a muscle, there was a searing wall of pain.

What's happening? She cried out desperately into the darkness of her own mind.

The original creature in her didn't answer in words, but she understood suddenly that they'd put another demon inside her and this one was made to overtake and control its host.

There's another demon in me? she asked and the answer came at the same time as her question, allowing her to feel this new demon distinctly. Its borders created that puffy, hot feeling under her skin. Its impulses overran her own neural commands and laced pain along the pathways to keep her out of her own body. *How many damned demons can I hold? Get it out!*

Anger or frustration, not her own, flashed inside of her. He was trying to push the other demon back out of her. His will inside the landscape of her body was like a wall of white fire. She felt a flash of unwelcome pity for him, to have traveled all this way and now be as much a prisoner in her body as she was. He had been very powerful once, she understood, he could have taken care of this easily, but it had been so long and the journey here made him weak like a child.

The pain created a fog across her mind, she wanted to crawl far away from it, but the first demon, the protector spirit, whatever he was, pointed her toward it as if he'd taken her head in his hands to direct her gaze. He wanted her to look into it. At first it was like reaching into a fire, but as she pushed into the pain it cleared the haziness in her mind and she became more aware of the boundaries of the two creatures fighting for control of her limbs.

The guy on her side was hot and bright, like the sun on sand. The other demon felt and smelled like smoke and mold. She pushed against it but it kept shifting and moving around in her.

A new pain lanced through her, radiating out from the top center of her chest, blazing out from her spine. It pulled her attention into her core and away from her right hand that had begun to slowly unlock the door. The demon fought her for her muscles. Underneath the pain, the alien presence ran its information through the nerves of her body telling it what to do. Her lungs started to fill again with air on the inhale, but then the creature stopped them.

Her chest was being crushed; she couldn't breathe. Ice-water fear flooded through her, pounding her heart and turning her bones to liquid. Her field of attention narrowed as she began to lose consciousness, her senses pulling themselves in from her fingers and toes, from the surface of her skin. Her mind was closing itself down to conserve power.

As the sensation from her body grew more distant, she watched the man on the porch turn the knob and swing the door wide. Burning consumed her left arm as the protective demon used it to lash out and slam palm-first into the chin of the man. He flew backward, missing the first three steps completely and then tumbling down the last seven. The woman glared at Ana and commanded, "Stay!" and then ran down to him.

Her left foot stepped back and dragged her body behind it. The good demon—that was a funny thought—had taken control of most of the left side of her. She realized she could help him.

I'll move, she said. *You hold him back.*

A rush of affirmative feeling passed through her and then her guy forced himself into the middle of her body, making a barrier. The foreign demon had shut down her right side on the command to stay. She could barely feel anything and the sensation of half a body terrified her, but not quite so much as the possibility of having no body at all.

With her left hand she slammed the door shut and locked it. That wouldn't hold for long; they could make it through a window given a few minutes and she couldn't speak to call for help. She held onto the wall for balance while she shuffled backward with her left foot, unable to feel her right leg at all.

Step after step she dragged her way down the hall to the door above the garage steps. She opened it, snared her keys off the hook by the door, and looked down the steps. There was no quick and easy way to get down there.

She bent her left knee and tried to swing her right foot down to the step, watching to make sure it had solid footing. Holding the railing tightly, and silently thanking Ruben, she shifted her weight to it. The knee buckled. Her body hung for a moment sideways, supported entirely by her left hand. Then she let go.

On her left side where she could feel, the stairs hit her shoulder and hip. She landed at the bottom and lay still for a moment. In a little while, when all sensation returned to her right side, she was really going to be in pain. Now she crawled on her good side around to the driver's door. The demon on the right side, who'd been told to hold her still, seemed confused about what to do and his efforts to get her standing again made the crawling easier.

She pulled herself up into the car and thumbed the garage door opener. She had to reach across and use her left foot on the gas pedal, but she made it out without hitting either wall of the garage. Then she floored it down the street. They'd seen her leave, she'd caught a glimpse of the woman's face at the side of the house, where she was probably trying to jimmy a window, and they might try to follow in their car.

First she focused on getting distance, but as soon as she had to stop at a light, she fished along her body into her right pocket and pulled out the business card she'd put there that morning like a talisman. The further she got from her house, the more pain she had in her right side. Bones felt bruised, then her skin scoured with glass, then it all became so cold. She clenched her good hand around the wheel, ground her teeth against each other, and drove.

* * *

Lily Cordoba had no appointments, no client meetings, nothing at all that she had to do that morning, so she took her chai down into the store to sit with the books.

The long, narrow space included glass cases for the rare books, two display desks, and a meeting area for the marketing work she did. Books had been her passion for the last fifty years, but she didn't mind this new addition of a profession that also relied on words and cleverness. Along the left wall of the meeting space was a couch with throw pillows and she sat against an arm with one of the newer acquisitions: a book she'd bought from a friend about the building of the Temple. It wasn't a classic, just aligned with a hobby of hers.

Outside a car horn blared. It sounded again and again, irregular, not an automated alarm. She lifted her face toward the front door and opened her senses. Other demons, two of them. Yes, that was a call for her. Who would bring her two demons on a Sunday morning, she wondered as she set the book down and slipped her feet into her boots. On the way out of the store she grabbed the kit of useful tools she kept on the sill and clipped it to the waistband of her pants.

There was a silver Mini Cooper pulled sloppily into one-and-a-half of the two visitor parking spaces in front of her store. The woman in the driver's seat looked on the surface like a contestant for a Midwestern beauty pageant turned surfer girl. Very blond spiky hair and that amber-honey color white women got when they tanned naturally. Lily couldn't see the demons or tell what kind they were, her powers weren't that strong, she could only feel them like a density of space.

"What did you bring me?" she asked as she approached the driver's side. The woman had the door open and her left leg out, but she seemed otherwise frozen. Fashionable sweatpants but no shoes and there were patches on her hips and shoulders smeared with dust and dirt. She'd left somewhere in a hurry.

"Can you walk?" Lily asked.

With her left hand, the woman pointed at her right arm and leg, then shook her head.

"I'm going to loosen your tongue, is that all right?"

The woman nodded with her eyes wide and hopeful. Lily took the bitumen salt out of the kit and pinched a few grains between thumb and forefinger. With her other hand, she forced the woman's jaw open. It wasn't hard to do; whichever demon was in charge of shutting down this woman's ability to move and communicate had his non-corporeal hands full. She dropped the salt onto the woman's tongue and was rewarded with a series of obscenities.

"Jesus, Mary Mother of God that's nasty," the oaths concluded, and then the woman said, "Oh, I can talk. Thank you." After another pause she added, "I'm Ana and you're Lily, right? Can you help me?"

Lily got the impression that this woman didn't know the half of the trouble she was in. But the local powers-that-be paid Lily to take care of situations like this, and besides, she enjoyed it. She laughed with the light, upbeat sound that made demons of control cringe. Then she blew into her right hand, shook the bracelets down from her wrist so they rested at the base of her thumb and tapped Ana's right knee. The creature that had been holding it immobile jumped back reflexively, curling itself into Ana's arm and freeing the leg.

"Thank you," Ana said and pulled herself out of the car. She winced when she put that foot on the ground but tested her weight on it and nodded.

Lily took her into the entryway and then slowly up the stairs to the apartment above the store. The creature that now huddled inside her arm and upper right chest had more power than it should for its size and yet it seemed frightened. There was a second being in Ana's body, something so strange Lily wasn't sure it could be classified as a demon, though she didn't know what else she'd call it.

Her apartment had the basics: living room, kitchen, personal library, plus a sunroom converted into a summoning or banishing circle. She kept her bedroom and any truly private items on the third floor because of the number of people she had to bring up to this circle in the course of a year. She was among the best, if not the best, banisher in the city. That didn't mean she got a flood of work. There weren't that many demons running around in the physical world, but when they did get through in San Francisco, they tended to end up here.

Ana balked at the edge of the circle, or rather the young demon in her did, grabbing control of her right leg again. Lily was going to shove her over the line but Ana threw her left leg forward and dragged the unmoving side of her body after her. Not bad for Ms. Midwest. Lily spoke the words of consolation, the shortened version she'd created for herself, and watched the demon trickle out of Ana like smoke. She traced her left hand in the air, defining the boundaries he was permitted to inhabit. She gave him a square foot of space and he chose a crow shape, gray and indistinct.

"You're a young one," she said. "What were you offered? No, ignore that question. Who brought you over?"

"Drake," it hissed. "Calls himself Drake."

"He'd dead," Ana said.

"What kind of dead?" Lily asked. "Human dead, banished or destroyed?"

"The police shot him," Ana told her.

"Little crow," Lily addressed the trapped demon, "could you remain here if the one who called you was destroyed?"

"I can if you let me serve you, dark woman."

"No." She made a gesture to avert connection. "You will not serve me. You will answer me thrice more and that in payment for the binding you put on this woman. How could I bring myself to the demon who called you into this world?"

He pointed with one wing, "You could walk in that direction for about eight-hundred breaths."

"What did he command you to do?" she asked.

"Take the woman and hold her still for the humans."

"What is his name?"

"I don't know it! Woman, I answered true, let me serve you and stay!"

"No, this is not your world. Go home." She spoke three words of banishing and struck her palms together with a crack. The smoke crow was gone, back to whichever spirit world it had been pulled from.

"Now, let's see about this other one?"

"Can you get him out too?" Ana asked.

"I don't see why not."

She said the words of consolidation as she had with the first and something began to take shape but it didn't conform to the size she'd given. In the faintest mist she saw the form of a man as if he were standing beside Ana with his arm around her protectively. He looked young and clean-shaven. Even his head was smooth except for the hint of brows. His lips moved but she couldn't hear him. He couldn't draw enough substance to himself to make sound.

She took a handful of ash from an incense burner set inside the circle and blew it into the air where he was. It fell to the ground. He pointed to the candle next to it. Lily shrugged. She wanted to talk to him before she sent him on his way, what could a candle hurt? She lit it and pushed it across the floor to the base of where his form was.

The tiny flame of the candle turned into a lattice of fire, each line a tiny filament of flame so thin it was almost invisible. He made a body of fire out of lines so small they gave off virtually no heat. Ana stepped sideways and he disappeared.

"Could you stand by the candle? I know it seems strange, but he can't be any distance away from you and I'd like to talk to him."

Ana rolled her eyes but Lily saw the white of fear in them alongside the dramatic exasperation. She stepped back to the candle. He appeared out of her without Lily having to call the consolidation again. Had he learned her words of power already? How could he use them on himself?

"What are you?" she asked.

He answered in another language.

Lily shook her head. "I don't understand you."

He tried another and it sounded slightly familiar.

Lily tried Spanish but he shook his head.

Then his eyes lit and he spoke again. "I am a traveler," he said in Hebrew.

Lily translated that into English for Ana. "From where?" she asked him. His dialect was strange, but she could make out the words and apparently he could understand her well enough because he answered.

"Years ago I left this world. I do not know when I am now."

She gave him the date by the calendar of the Sangkesh demons, which was almost a thousand years older than the 2013 date of the Roman calendar. If he spoke Hebrew, he might be a distant relative, which meant he would calculate the current date from the building of the Temple. "It's 2974," she said.

He hissed in surprise, "I remember the year 1997. I have been gone nearly a thousand years. No wonder this world is so strange to me."

"What were you before you left?" Lily asked.

"I have been many things but I was known most often by the name Abraxas."

"Oh." The gasp escaped her before she could close her lips on it and Ana stared at her in alarm.

"What did he say?" she asked.

"He's very old." That was the best short explanation she could give. Ana looked exhausted and on the edge of panic. The last thing Lily wanted was for her to bolt and take this fascinating creature with her. In Hebrew to Abraxas she said, "You're one of the Protectors, like I am, yes?"

"I am Sangkesh, a demon of Solomon."

That was enough for her to understand she wasn't going to toss him out of Ana as she had the little crow, and she didn't want to. He would do this woman no harm and she could learn so much from him. Lily called down her circle.

"Ana, come sit on the couch. We should talk about this and you're swaying on your feet."

"You can't get him out?" Ana's voice held a protest, but when Lily took her arm she let herself be led easily to the couch in the living room.

"Not quickly, no. I'm sure there is a way. There's always a way. But…you might want to keep him for a while."

CHAPTER EIGHT

When the small, dark-haired woman said "You might want to keep him," Ana almost bolted for the door, but it felt so good to sit after having fallen down the stairs and dragged herself here that she stayed. Plus Lily was the first person she'd met who seemed to know something about demons. She had banished one, and compared to everyone else's track record, that was a great start.

"Tea?" Lily asked.

"Please."

The apartment was decorated in oranges, reds and golds with accents of mahogany and black lacquered wood. This couch and the love seat were thickly cushioned with plenty of extra pillows. The side tables and narrow table along the wall looked antique. There were a few pieces of art on the walls, two of them paintings Ana didn't recognize and the third a photograph of a person in a white robe standing in a beam of sunlight that filtered down from a round hole in the roof of a building that looked like a mosque or temple. Three large glass cabinets held a variety of items, vases, books, statues and stones.

Lily came back carrying two thick ceramic mugs filled with a creamy, dark liquid. It smelled like chai and when Ana sipped it, she found it very sweet and spicy. She could drinks cups of it. Lily settled into the other side of the couch, a pillow propped between her back and the armrest. She tucked one booted leg up under the opposite knee with the grace of a habitually unconscious gesture. Ana wondered why she didn't just take the heavy boots off. Maybe they were magic anti-demon boots. The thought made her smile.

"Why won't this one just come out like the other one?" she asked.

"If you told me what happened, I'd be better able to answer that."

Ana told the story, this time with as much detail as she could remember about the ritual and the men performing it. Lily's brown eyes seemed to darken to near black as she talked.

"A group of men are summoning in the city?" she asked when Ana finished, but didn't wait for an answer. "From your account, they have a powerful demon guiding them and they wanted to bring over his consort, to make him more powerful. But something went wrong, perhaps connected to your friend Helen's death, that prevented the consort from coming through into this world and instead you found...someone else."

"I think he found me," Ana said. "But that other thing the little demon said, that you could find Drake by walking in that direction." She pointed. "What does that mean? The police shot him."

Lily shook her head. "They shot the body he was using. He's not gone. He'll find another body."

"How?"

"Accident, illness, addiction, there are quite a few ways."

"Does that mean some of the people out there just walking around on the streets are really demons?"

"Yes," Lily said. "Now, the situation you're in, sharing your body willingly, that's very rare."

"I wouldn't say willingly."

Lily smiled sympathetically but her eyes were still bright with curiosity. She asked, "May I speak to him more?"

Ana shrugged and stared down into her tea mug. This whole experience was so...beyond. But now that she felt a measure of safety with this woman and her circles and spells, or whatever they were, she had to admit in the far corner of her mind that she was starting to feel curious too.

Lily brought over a few short candles and set them on the narrow table that ran along the back of the couch. Filaments of light streamed from the flames and built a lattice of glowing threads in the shape of a man sitting cross-legged between them.

Lily said something to him in the staccato language she'd been using when they were in the circle and repeated her full name. As he replied, Lily translated for Ana and added her own commentary.

"He says he has had many names, but that Abraxas is one of the more recent and most pronounceable by humans," Lily told her. "He also says Nathan Drake is a demon strong enough to cause bodies to be shaped for him."

"What does that mean?"

Lily looked up and her mouth drew into a pensive line. "Bodies are key for powerful demons who want to operate in this physical world. If a demon doesn't have a body, it can be banished or controlled. A body is freedom and power."

"For demons?"

"For anyone. Abraxas is saying that Drake has the resources to get human bodies to inhabit that have been vacated by their original owners. He probably uses lesser demons to keep the body alive until he needs it."

"He really isn't dead," Ana said suddenly. "That's why they shot him. If he can have more than one body, he just set it up so the police would stop looking into Helen's death and my kidnapping, but he's still here."

"Yes," Lily told her.

Abraxas went on talking. Ana thought she had his name right, but then if memory served that was also the name of a

Santana album, which contributed to the feeling that she wasn't really in her own life anymore but in some strange television montage of history and pop culture. Feeling so profoundly outside herself was a form of shock, she assumed. It was useful; it kept her from running screaming from the room.

After a few minutes, Ana held up her hand. "Can you explain some things to me?"

Abraxas and Lily stopped their conversation to stare at her.

"I thought all demons were evil," she said. "Well, I mean...I thought they didn't exist but if they did they would be evil. And Abraxas says they aren't, but couldn't he just be lying to me?"

"Anyone can lie," Lily said. "But his answers are on track for what he says he is. The Sangkesh demons are protectors of humanity."

"A protector demon? That's a real thing? Wouldn't that be an angel?" Ana asked.

"Angels are messengers, they don't usually choose to live in this physical world like demons do."

"But they fight the demons?"

Lily shook her head. "That's in movies and books. Demons fight demons. The Shaidans, the adversaries, harass humanity, and so the Sangkesh came into being as the protectors, who keep humanity safe from other unseen beings as best they can."

"I still don't get why they call themselves demons."

"That's because you think there's something wrong with having a dark power rather than a light one. Just because your powers are based in darkness, divisiveness, anger and hurt doesn't mean you can't use those just as effectively for good. Think of the human soldiers who want to fight and found a place where they can fight to protect others—or the surgeon whose ability to cut into a person and cause a wound is what saves that person's life."

Ana rolled the mug between her palms, watching the remaining inch of froth rock from one side to the other. An unwelcome image of her brother, Mack, came to mind and she wondered if people like him could ever learn to turn their rage to good. And yet, it made a kind of sense to her. In the fight against the men who'd kidnapped her, she wanted the biggest, baddest, meanest creatures on her side. Maybe that was demons and not angels.

"Can the protector demons take care of these summoners?" she asked Lily.

"We can't allow them to continue to operate in this city, but the local demons have limits to what they can do and how much they can interfere in human matters."

"I'd like to see them all go to jail. Can you help me do that?"

"I can try."

"And can you get Abraxas out of me?"

Lily watched the man's shimmering form. "Not right away. He needs a body or a vessel to contain him while he gains strength. It's best if it's a living human body, but I could theoretically put him into a vessel of power."

She asked him a question and he answered with a few words. Lily choked back a laugh. "He's asking if his current vessel would like to become more worthy."

"I am not your damned vessel," Ana snarled at him. "I have a life of my own that your nonsense is screwing up right now. What's Sabel going to think if I tell her I've got a demon sharing my body? Or Ruben? Oh my God, Ruben! Lily, can I use your phone, he's going to be frantic if Sabel shows up to meet me and I'm not there."

Lily brought her the phone. In a coincidence of great luck, she got him five minutes after he'd come in the door with groceries, while he was still trying to figure out if she'd left him a note somewhere.

"I'm so sorry, I forgot to leave a note," she said. "I just had to get out and I went to that third bookstore. The woman here is really great. But Sabel was supposed to come with me and she's going to show up soon."

"Oh honey, I can keep her entertained," he said. "I'll see you soon."

His eager tone worried her. She didn't like the idea of the two of them talking about her. She looked at the time on the phone and resolved to be out the door in twenty minutes or less.

"What's so good about a living human body?" Ana asked.

"Well the dead ones start to smell," Lily said and then shook her head at herself. "I shouldn't joke. Demons were originally created without bodies and as a result they were easy to bind and control. Solomon found a way for younger demons to be born with bodies and that paved the way for humans and demons to interbreed. Through those crossbreeds, the nonphysical demons learned how powerful they can be when they have access to everything that's in a human body. While Abraxas has his home in you, no one can compel him and it's much harder to work magic on him, though I suspect he can still be banished, yes?"

She asked that again in the other language and Abraxas made an affirmative sound.

"What's banished?"

"Sent back to one of the nonphysical realms that they come from in the Unseen World. Most demons hate to be compelled or bound, and aren't too happy about banishing either. Being in your body gives Abraxas a place to recover and learn about the world he's in now. If you were willing, you could help him accommodate to this world more quickly."

"And that would get him out sooner rather than later?"

"It improves your chances."

"What do I need to do?" Ana asked.

"Give him access to your senses and some of your surface thoughts so he can learn English."

"Can I reverse that later or push him out if I don't want him to hear what I'm thinking?"

"Yes." Lily got a pad of paper and wrote down a simple phrase to let him have access to her senses and surface mind and another to cancel it. They were in English and seemed silly and unceremonious to Ana.

"Shouldn't it be in Latin or something?"

"The words are the focus, it's your will that works the change."

Lily watched as Ana read the first set of words off the page and the shimmering form of Abraxas slid back into her body.

Then Lily got off the couch saying, "I have an idea," and disappeared up the stairs.

She returned with a worn leather book the size of a family Bible in her hands, holding it with reverence. If there had been words on the cover, they'd long ago worn away, but when Ana opened it a title was written three times in neat script, twice in English and once in an Arabic script.

Demonologie of the Moderne Aeon and below that a signature she could not decipher. Next was a date: 1604. Below that, another, even neater hand, had penned a second title: *Modern Demonology*.

"This is a four-hundred-year-old book written by hand?" she asked in wonder.

"It's been copied by hand from the original. There are only a few copies of that in the world."

Ana turned a few pages and saw that each right-hand page was in an older dialect of English, one that reminded her of Shakespeare, and the left-hand pages were the Arabic text. It wasn't too hard to read in the English and as her eye scanned the page her mind easily translated it into the modern English she was used to.

"If you let him move your hand, he can find pages in the Arabic and you'll see the English translation. It will help you communicate and also let him learn English faster." She reached into her pocket and pulled out a small tan envelope. "I think you'll need this too. It's the banishing salt I use, in case you get more little adversaries at your door."

Ana tucked it into her purse gratefully and, while she was in there, pulled out one of her cards. "My cell phone number's on that."

Lily was scrutinizing her again as she handed the card over. "You seem to be holding up pretty well," she said.

Ana laughed. "That's just because you didn't see me screaming and hitting myself early Friday morning. I'm eager to get this over with."

"You may not want to be so eager. Few people on the planet ever get an opportunity like the one you have there."

"It doesn't feel like an opportunity. It feels like my whole life getting completely screwed up."

"Sometimes," Lily said, "that's what opportunity feels like." She helped Ana up from the couch, and Ana found that she could put a modest amount of weight on her right foot. They made it down to the car easily.

Her mood lifted as she started the engine. Now she had someone on her side who could get this demon out of her head and call in the cavalry to help deal with the dozen crazy men who might kill her in order to keep their mischief a secret. Ana wanted to see them pay. Could she help to discover their identities and turn them over to the police? *Put that down as the next item on the to-do list*, she thought.

* * *

When Ana pulled into the garage and tried to get out of the car, she was surprised by how strong her legs felt. Despite the fall down the stairs, she stood up without trouble. She had the impression that Abraxas was helping her body heal itself—at least he came with benefits.

With her right hand, she held the heavy tome to her chest. Its leather felt like rough skin against her palm, as if it held her as much as she held it. She braced her hand against the wall and took two slow steps up the stairs. There was no pain at all. Grinning, she went up the rest at a normal pace.

When she turned to peer into the kitchen and dining room she saw two people sitting on the back porch chatting and drinking what looked like mojitos. Ruben's tousled brown mop and broad back sat next to now familiar straight black hair and slender shoulders. Sabel turned as if she heard a sound and saw Ana through the window.

She was on her feet in an instant and Ruben got up with her. He pushed open the glass door and strode through the dining room.

"What happened?" he asked with a tone that suggested Ana had a fresh bruise somewhere obvious. She should have looked in a mirror before driving home.

"I'm okay," she told him. "Are those mojitos? Where's mine?"

Ruben rolled his eyes at her and huffed into the kitchen, but that was just his way of showing he was worried. Ana put the thick leather book on the coffee table and settled back into the support of the couch.

Sabel walked into the room and looked down at Ana and then the book. She reached down to touch the book and hissed through her teeth like she'd hit a thorn. Her hand pulled back quickly. She took the armchair in the far corner of the living room and waited while Ruben handed Ana the cold, skinny glass. Then there was nothing for it but to tell the story—or at least most of it.

"The other night with the ritual and the summoners, the demon thing, well, they think I ran off with their demon and they want it back." She talked quickly so they couldn't interrupt with questions she didn't want to answer. "And the bad news is that demons really do exist and these two people showed up at the front door with my purse. No, I didn't let them in, I'm not stupid. But the guy had a demon in a bottle and it came through the crack in the door and possessed me."

"Slow down," Ruben said. "I didn't see this movie. What are you talking about?"

At least Sabel was watching her with eyes full of steady comprehension. Ana didn't know if she should even tell Ruben this, but he needed to understand a little of it in case the summoners returned to the house when he was there.

"Just...listen as if I'm talking about something that could maybe be real," she told him. "These two people looked like an average couple, but the guy had a bottle and when he opened it this smoky thing came out and then I couldn't move. The guy tried to push into the house, but I managed to get my left arm and leg free and slammed the door. I fell down the stairs on the way to my car, but I got away and drove to another bookstore where I met Lily. She did something that pulled this demon out of me and questioned it and then sent it back to...wherever they go. And she gave me the book."

Ana slipped a hand into her purse and came out with the small envelope Lily had given her. "She also gave me this," she said. "As defense against future possession. I'm not making this up."

Sabel pushed out of her chair and took the envelope from Ana's fingers. She opened it and sniffed, then lifted a pinch to her tongue. "Tastes like salt and bitumen and something else. Crude but it should work."

"That black sand drove a demon out of you?" Ruben asked. "And that's, like, a real thing?"

When he said it that way it sounded ridiculous and stupid. A wave of fear and nausea passed over her.

"I'm not crazy," Ana insisted.

Sabel held up a hand. "Give him some space. He still doesn't know what we're talking about."

Ruben looked back and forth between them and his sculpted, expressive eyebrows conveyed his deep doubt and confusion. His chest rose with an extended inhale and then fell with a whoosh. "First things first, I'll bring the phone and you call the police and describe the people who showed up here."

He was walking back into the room with the phone in his hand when his cell phone rang. He gave the house phone a puzzled look and then figured it out and pulled the cell from his pocket.

"My agent," he said apologetically and put the house phone on the coffee table by Ana. Then he answered his cell phone and disappeared toward the kitchen.

Ana took a long sip of the mojito and the minty alcohol warmed the back of her throat.

"You should think about how much you tell him. You're putting him in danger too." Sabel's voice sounded low and accusing. She was sitting in the armchair but balanced forward with her hands on her knees, her lips thinned, a frown creasing the sides of her mouth. The expression didn't make her any less attractive.

"Don't lecture me," Ana shot back. Her good mood was shifting into anger. She thought about the way Sabel had touched the book and recoiled and felt blamed for things she didn't understand. "Ruben needs to know to be careful if people are going to show up here."

"I read the police report. You'd have to have a lot of money and dedication to outfit a basement like that. These guys must have been in operation for a long time. You have no idea how dangerous they are. Ruben needs to be more than careful."

"You read the police report?" Ana asked. "*My* police report?"

"I read everything I could, not just yours."

"And somehow you think this is fair, that you can look up whatever you want and tell me what to say, but you won't tell me the least bit about what you're into?" Ana asked. The words carried more emphasis than she intended, but hearing them come out of her mouth made her realize how truly frustrated she was.

Sabel's voice didn't rise. She looked surprised. "I was in the room when you gave the police statement," she said.

That was true, and it wasn't the contents of the report that upset her, it was the idea that Sabel could go around finding out information without her. Or maybe that Sabel had years of information more than she did about magic and demons and all of this.

"What aren't you telling me in the name of protecting me?" she asked. "Because I'm pretty sure you just told me the barest fraction about yourself and this witch business yesterday."

The heat of anger rose in her chest and she got off the couch and walked toward the fireplace where she could pace a few steps back and forth. Looking down at the hearth tiles, she recalled a half memory of Sabel here the night she stayed. Ana had gotten up to use the bathroom and come part way down the stairs, just to look and see if Sabel was really asleep on the couch. She'd seen Sabel kneeling on this hearth, her hands on her thighs with the fingers turned in. Her head was bowed and her hair falling straight and dark on either side of her face, hiding her expression.

Then and now that image evoked a powerful longing in Ana for something she couldn't name. She tried to shove that wanting feeling away, but it only made her general frustration worse. Her life felt upside down and too jumbled for her to be able to name what she wanted and find a way to it.

"My secrets are worse than yours," Sabel said in a quiet voice. Ana doubted that, but Sabel went on talking. "Just be careful with Ruben. And I don't think you should go to your office tomorrow. If these people were brazen enough to come to the front door of your house in the middle of the day, what's to stop them from trying to take you from your office? They have to be connected to Helen somehow and maybe to your company."

"I am not staying home." She spat the words out. She hated feeling trapped in any building and she hated being told what to do by anyone.

That brought Sabel to her feet. "You're so...heedless. You're just going to rush in wherever you want?"

"They came here today and they could come back any time. I'm not willing to wait for that, and I'm not going to sit as a prisoner in my own house. I'm going after them."

"You are not prepared to fight them," Sabel said. Her voice softened toward a plea, but the words stung.

Ana let out a sharp laugh. "When have I ever been prepared for a fight?" She took a step toward Sabel and met her eyes. "And don't tell me what to do."

She expected a challenge from the other woman; the frustrated boil of emotion in her wanted a fight. Instead, Sabel dropped her gaze. Her whole body shifted subtly: her head tilted down, her shoulders lowered a fraction, and her hands turned out in acquiescence. It was a precise and eloquent set of gestures. Every angle of Sabel's body seemed to defer to her.

In an instant all her anger transformed itself into a noble and protective instinct. A second ago she was ready to hit something and now she wanted to wrap her arms around Sabel and hold her.

In awe, Ana reached out and touched her fingertips to Sabel's downturned cheek, intending to tip her face up. Instead Sabel turned a fraction of an inch and pressed her skin and the corner of her mouth into Ana's hand. The brush of lips on her palm was almost a kiss, but not quite. A bolt of electricity traveled down Ana's hand and arm to her belly and then along the inner edge of her legs to her toes. She sucked in a sharp breath. Sabel held perfectly still with her head still turned down and her cheek against Ana's hand.

Ana thought she should step away, but Sabel's stillness itself was an invitation. She'd never seen anyone be unmoving, her breathing slow and measured, and yet look supple and hum with a thick sensual energy. There was no doubt that if she didn't want to be near Ana, Sabel would have been well across the room by now, but she simply waited.

Ana brought her free hand to Sabel's other cheek and tipped her face up. In this interior light, Sabel's eyes looked like a stormy ocean as they met Ana's and turned down again. The barest brushstroke of a smile changed the angle of her lips.

Ana kissed her. It would be quick, just the idea of a kiss, the hint of something they could have when this was all over. Her lips touched Sabel's, drew back for a half breath, and returned to find Sabel's mouth meeting hers with a hungry strength. Sabel's fingers touched the sides of her waist. Ana kissed her hard and felt Sabel's hands pull at her until their bodies pressed together.

Sabel's lips opened and Ana touched her tongue lightly and then harder, tasting the mint, rum and sugar flavors in Sabel's mouth. Sabel's moan was a low vibration against her body. She felt Sabel's knees start to bend and moved her left arm to circle her back and help hold her up.

Both of Sabel's arms were around Ana's back now and she felt the heaviness of Sabel's breasts against hers. She pulled her mouth back enough to take a quick, gasping breath, and then kissed her harder. Against her back, Sabel's hand convulsed into a fist around a handful of Ana's shirt.

Ana needed to feel more of her. She tucked her hand under the back of Sabel's shirt and spread her fingers across her cool skin, feeling the muscles shift under her touch. How far was it to her bedroom? Could she even suggest it? Ruben could be back any moment and she felt a real danger of them just sinking down to the floor together. She wanted Sabel underneath her, caught between Ana's body and the unyielding floor.

A hot, dry wind shifted under the skin of her arms and she flinched back with a gasp.

"What?" Sabel asked, her voice low and soft.

Abraxas, dammit! She'd forgotten all about him, but how could she possibly do anything more with Sabel, knowing that he was in her body and could feel it too? She'd just given him access to her senses at Lily's. Of all the rotten timing.

"I can't," Ana said. She took two steps back from Sabel and tried to get her breathing to slow down.

Sabel's expression closed in on itself: her open lips compressed to a hard line, the flashing blue-gold of her eyes flattened to gray as her eyes narrowed, a muscle clenched in her jaw. It made Ana burn with the need to touch her again and feel her soften.

"I'll go," Sabel said.

Ana nodded. What could she come up with to have her stay? There was no excuse, no reason that could combat: *I'm sorry I can't kiss you, there's a demon in me.*

"I'm sorry..." she started to say, but the rest of the words crumbled to dust in the back of her throat.

Sabel picked up her bag and let herself out while Ana stood in the living room by the fireplace. She stared at the closed door until Ruben came around the corner and put his hands on his hips.

"What did you do?"

"I kissed her."

"I saw that part, what did you do to drive her out again? I thought for sure you two were going to hook up."

Ana just shook her head at him and slumped down on the couch. "It's complicated."

"Demons, huh?"

"It sounds sexier than saying I was abducted and may be having some PTSD stuff come up," Ana said. Sabel was right that she didn't need to bring Ruben any further into this than necessary.

"I can't figure you out," he said.

"That makes two of us." Or three, she thought, if she included Sabel. No, counting Abraxas—and she had to count Abraxas now—she was pretty sure the total came to four.

* * *

The darkest hour of night this time of year fell between one and two a.m. Lily set up her tools in the room at the top of the house facing cold north. She wasn't good at this. Years of study and she still felt a pit of dread every time she had to make contact with the noncorporeal entities in the city. Alone and secure in her house, she'd taken off the heavy boots that hid her clawed feet, removed her contact lenses, and the caps on her teeth. She imagined to an average person, or someone like Ana, she looked more alien than the noncorporeal demons were to her. Still, at a fundamental level she just didn't get how creatures could survive so long with nothing physical to cling to or steer by. Maybe this was just her own fear of death come to stare her in the face again.

Enough woolgathering. The powers that protected the city needed to know they had an enemy in their territory and if she got this done quickly enough she might even get some sleep. Lily splayed out on her back, arms and legs relaxed and outflung. She concentrated on her own fear for Ana and for the city she loved and threw it out from her body like a flare attached to the name of the one she wanted. After decades of practice she didn't need ritual implements or to draw any more sigils than already existed in her house; she just needed to send out this intention with enough emotion to draw attention and then hold in that state for much longer than a person should have to.

She was starting to get cold when Asilal saw her from across the city. They'd known each other for decades but this part always made her panic a little. With her eyes closed and inside her room, she still saw a face the size of a mountain turn from the spires of downtown and search across the houses until he saw her. Then he came forward like a tidal wave.

The moment he passed through the wall into her room he appeared only a little larger than a man. He dropped into a cross-legged position on the floor—or rather he seemed to. He gave off enough image for her to pretend he looked like the ghostly figure of a man, though he was so much larger.

"Lily." His silent voice shook her to her teeth. "Sit."

She rose to sit and inclined her head to him. "Asilal, please turn down the awe. You're making my head hurt."

His laughter was short of terrible, merely chilling. In his gray-black face with its leonine nose he shut his storm-gray eyes for a moment and then squinted at her. "Is this better?"

It was doable. Little bones in inner ear still protested, but she knew he was toning himself down seriously in deference to her delicate half-humanity. She nodded and got on with it.

"There's a shaidan of some power in the city. He's drawn a group of humans to him, at least a dozen, and is trying to bring his consort into a body here. He's already killed one woman in the attempt and nearly another."

And then she had to pause because in all the preparations she hadn't thought through whether or not she'd tell him about Abraxas. Stupid mistake. If she did tell him, he'd want to bring this long-gone traveler into his world and question him. Who knew how long that might take. Lily found she was strangely protective of Abraxas. Maybe it was his vulnerability. At his age he should be near growing into a creature like Asilal if he willed it and knowing all that power was in such a small and humble state had an oddly intoxicating quality. She wanted to get to know him now while he could be easily known, before he became something she could barely listen to.

Into her silence, Asilal placed questions. "How do you know this? Have you had contact?"

"A woman came to me with a small creature placed in her so the shaidan could capture her. She'd seen his face and heard his name: Nathan Drake. I banished it after I questioned it. It confirmed that he is in the city still. I believe he is finding another body."

"I will watch this."

She knew he couldn't just swoop down and nail Drake. Not only would that be far too convenient for her own life, but the Sangkesh were cautious not to make overly aggressive moves against other demons for fear they would spark a conflict that could catch humans in its crossfire.

"I will also," he went on, "improve the wards on the city so no creature within my boundaries can summon anything larger than a gnat."

"It would be beneficial to have protection for the woman," Lily pointed out. "He will try to take her again, not only because she saw him but I believe he is a creature of anger who cannot stand to be defied."

"You have a specific protection in mind," Asilal said.

She had to be careful here not to ask for anything that would also affect Abraxas. "Ward her house. Elsewhere she is surrounded by humans and I can deal with any small demon he sends to her, but if she knows she is safe in her house, that no creature who has not already been there can come in without her clear, spoken assent, that would help greatly."

"Give me her location and it is done."

She told him and felt the sharp snap of his power. He did not control the whole city, but he was one of a few of the older ones who watched over it and so he knew every brick, stone, board and pane as if it were part of him. He'd been here for over a hundred years.

"What else are you hiding from me, Lily?" he asked, as gently as he could.

"This worries me. No, it scares me. Usually I deal with accidents, people who are fooling around with powers they don't understand and often don't even believe. Whoever Drake is, he's easily hundreds of years old. And this woman...I like her. She has spirit. I'm afraid for her." It was enough truth to cover the other fact she meant to keep hidden.

"Would you have me reach down and smite this Drake?"

"What if you try and you can't?"

He looked at her, unblinking, eyes as cold as the moon. It was almost a foolish question. On the rare chance that Drake was as old and powerful as Asilal, the protective demon had enough allies in this city and in the hierarchy of the Sangkesh that it wouldn't matter. The problem was, he couldn't call on that help unless Drake did something much worse than what he'd done so far.

"You will tell me what you find out, yes?" he said. "I will do the same."

She gestured around the room and at him and the direction he'd come from. "Is there a better way for me to send you information?"

"Write it in black fire on white fire and I will see it," he said. Then he was gone, striding away over the city again and warmth rushed back into the room. Lily was shivering.

She went out of the small room she used for these personal magics and into her private library, turning on all the lights. She'd heard the phrase before, "black fire on white fire" she just couldn't remember where, so she woke up her computer and searched for it.

It was a reference to the creation of the Torah, the first five books of the Hebrew Bible, and some speculated it referred to black ink on white parchment. She scrolled through a few various interpretations. Was she supposed to get some parchment? Sitting back, she stared at the screen and suddenly got it. The screen behind the words glowed white, the words themselves black.

She opened a fresh document and wrote at the top: "Asilal, you could have just asked me to email you."

Below her sentence, words appeared all at once on the screen: "Email is so human. Forgive me my drama but you are one of few I can genuinely play with."

Lily shook her head. Demons on the Internet now, well that would make her life easier.

She wrote: "Good night."

The reply: "Guard yourself, little one, I cannot watch everything."

CHAPTER NINE

When Sabel walked into her apartment, she realized that the shirt and pants she'd gone to Ana's to return were still in her bag. She took them out and then found it hard to let go of them. She sank down onto her couch and held them against her chest while she replayed the memory of Ana's hands pulling her close.

In the moment when Ana broke the kiss, Sabel had been too upset to think. One moment she was safe and alight with desire and the next cold and alone again. Her reason turned itself off and she only wanted to get out of the house before she did something stupid like cry.

For the first time, she'd found a woman whose will was at least as strong as hers—and Ana had pushed her away. She'd said, "I can't." But why? At the noodle place when they were talking and flirting, Ana didn't seem to have any reservations. The only element that changed between that lunch and the kiss was the appearance of the summoners on her doorstep with a demon to possess her. That was a significant change for anyone. The logical conclusion was that Ana felt overwhelmed and was afraid for herself and the people around her.

Now that she'd replayed the scene a hundred times in her head and her higher brain functions were coming back online, Sabel had to admit to herself that Ana's reaction probably had more to do with circumstances than with Sabel herself.

So it was time to change the circumstances.

Sabel went up the stairs to her two-room second level. She put the shirt and pants on the foot of her bed and changed into loose clothes. Then she stepped into the smaller room and approached the altar along the far wall. It was a simple wooden table with framed photos, candles, incense and symbols of the four directions. She had a traditional dagger for the east and a wand, given by a friend, for the south. But the west was represented by the action figure of Death from the Sandman series and the north was a necklace of semiprecious stones made by an old friend.

She lit the candle and from it a stick of incense and invoked the space of this room. Technically it was more of a re-invocation because she never completely dissolved the circle of magic that protected her space. Then she knelt on the meditation cushion and began to quiet her mind.

Every witch had to create her own interface for working with the layers of reality and the powers available in the many worlds. Sabel had begun building hers as a teen, before she knew what she was doing. In the silence of night, apart from the pressures of the day, she imagined a place for herself—a pristine white house by a serene blue sea. It was a place she had been during the summers as a child and it always reminded her of calm and freedom. The Atlantic was the first ocean she ever met, so when she discovered the Mediterranean, it's warm, inviting, beautiful water came as a joyful shock. By the time she was a teen, her family no longer spent summers in Greece, but she returned to that place in her mind until it was as real a part of her daily life as her bedroom.

The Hecatine witches taught her how to simultaneously protect that place and to open it to select guests. And they showed her how to create a workroom within it that she could use to perceive the greater forces of the world.

To get to her home in the Unseen World she relaxed her body and then turned her awareness inside of herself and stepped backward out of her body and onto a short flight of white stairs. Six steps up and she opened the door to her home. While her body remained motionless in her room in the material world, she could use this space to direct her magic and to meet with Josefene.

Over the years this small house had grown into a sprawling whitewashed complex of rooms, some open only to her. She went into the long front room with its expansive windows open to the dark blue sea and bright blue sky. Josefene waited for her there.

The image of herself that Josefene chose to project in this space looked like a movie producer's ideal of the goddess Athena, but aged over fifty. Josefene was tall and elegant in a white draped chiton: sleeveless, gathered at the shoulders in myriad little pleats, V-necked, belted at the waist with a golden cord. She had copper-gold hair piled high on her head. Her eyes were hawk-bright and well-lined with wisdom.

Sabel had never met Josefene outside of this imagined place. She had no idea what the woman actually looked like, nor did she know how much of this image she now saw was created by Josefene's mind or by her own.

"There's trouble," Sabel said and told her about the summoners taking Ana and then showing up again on her doorstep.

"Why do they return to her?" Josefene asked. Her voice was throaty and lightly accented in a way that Sabel had never been able to place.

"She said they thought she had their demon."

"Does she?"

Sabel paused. "It's possible she does have a demon in her and doesn't know it. I didn't sense it the night of the ritual, but it could be dormant inside of her. Otherwise the summoners may simply be using that excuse as a reason to silence her."

"Or she's one of them and seeks to escape her commitment to them," Josefene pointed out.

"Unlikely," Sabel said. "Unless she's really good at hiding what she knows…but she doesn't strike me as a person with that level of guile."

"You will continue to watch her?" The words were part question, part statement.

"I want your blessing to do more than that. I want to find the summoners and I need your help."

"Go on," Josefene said. They'd worked together long enough that Josefene would already know Sabel had a plan before she proposed a course of action.

"There are thirteen summoners plus Helen and their demon. Do you have anyone who can find the identity of any one of them? If I have a name, I can pretend I want to join the group and see if I can get an interview with them. I can find out how much they really know and if they're working with the local demons or if it's a rogue."

"Why involve yourself in demon business?"

"It's human business. They killed Helen. If Ana isn't one of them and they think she has something of theirs or that she can identify them, what's to stop them from killing her? Do you want a group of killers attracting and then disposing of the magic-gifted people in this city? I don't."

She didn't say that the real reason she wanted to pursue this was entirely for Ana, so she could be free of the threat of the summoners, and by extension for herself. That argument wasn't good enough to earn her permission for what she wanted. Her family had taught her that the easiest way to mask her feelings was to channel them in a similar but different direction—to turn her concern for Ana into a general worry, to turn her desire into indignant anger.

"Do you know what a demon could do with your Voice?" Josefene said. "One of those profane creatures with the power already to entice a circle of humans to do his bidding, given access to the power to directly control the minds of others— have you considered the consequences of that?"

Sabel bowed her head. She had not looked at the consequences because she didn't want to. After a long silence she asked, "How would you deal with it?"

"Wear a leash," she said.

Sabel's head jerked up. "No," she breathed.

The energy leashes woven by the Hecatine witches gave them a profound level of control over the person who wore one. Sabel thought they were only for the mentally unstable. She'd only seen a leash in action once and it brought a powerful witch to her knees faster than thought. Sabel worked on her own self-discipline arduously just so that no one would ever have to control her from the outside and the thought terrified her.

"As you will," Josefene said.

"Wait. Tell me what it would do. Please."

The lightest brush of air went across the back of her neck and Josefene circled her. "It would sit under your skin around your throat, heart, and center. If demon magic touches your energy body, it would begin to tighten—slowly if the magic is slow and fast otherwise. If you're just close to the magic, you'll have time to get away, but if a demon tries to possess you, it will render you unconscious immediately."

"How close can I be?" Sabel asked. If she was going to try to infiltrate the demon summoners, she couldn't do it while wearing a magical device that would knock her out as soon as she got physically close to them.

Josefene seemed to understand the nature of her question. "If there is a person with some demon blood or a half-breed, or a skilled fully human summoner, as long as they don't use magic, you can be next to them and not trigger the leash. The same goes for a demon in a host body. You would be able to shake their hand without loss of consciousness, but if anyone is actively using demon magic you'll not want to sit next to them for very long. You would feel the leash start to close on you; there is a warning time period. It's only instant if the magic moves quickly into your body."

"So if someone is using demon magic but not using it on me?"

"You'll need to keep some space between you—about five or six feet. It's not a perfect system and the leash can't discern between them using magic near you with the intent to influence you and using it near you with no intent."

That seemed doable. It wasn't like she wanted to cozy up to the summoners, she just didn't want to sit down next to one in a restaurant and suddenly pass out. Still, it wasn't her first choice to wear the leash.

"May I think about it?" she asked.

"Of course," Josefene said and then abruptly she was gone.

Sabel walked to the windows and looked out on the calm ocean. Gray clouds were coming from the far horizon as the weather here often mirrored her internal state.

It felt strange to her to be so afraid, considering how she preferred to give up control in the right situations. But it was one thing to willingly surrender for the pleasure of it and another entirely to give the other witches the ability to knock her out instantaneously.

She had been studying with them for over a decade now, but still they were human like her and she never trusted other people completely. Everyone had their vulnerabilities. Once they put a leash on her, what else could they do with it? How could she know it would stop where Josefene said?

* * *

Ana woke in the early morning darkness still thinking about the kiss with Sabel. She pressed her fingers to her lips and tried to remember exactly the feel of Sabel's mouth under hers and the slender body in her arms. How long would she have to wait until she could do that again and not stop? What could she do to speed up the process?

She slid out from under the blankets and went down the hall to her office. The modern demonology book was on her desk. She opened it to one of the first pages and looked at the English, letting her mind translate from the early modern to the modern:

The demons pressed me to write this chronicle of their realms and principalities that they be known to humanity. I have been able to live among them because of the form given to me by my friend and I have become like one of them.

Under the skin of her right hand, a tickling breath moved. It was a question.

"Yes," she told him. Lily said they could use this book to communicate. Now that she had an ally who could get this creature out of her, Ana felt safer talking to him. She wanted to be able to ask questions and get answers. And if more demons showed up in her body, being able to talk to Abraxas might save her another fall down the basement stairs.

The tickling filled up her hand, like a hot balloon under the skin. He turned the pages with her fingers, then came to rest on one.

The reader should not think that I speak of a world other than this one that we currently inhabit, for the realms of the demon princes, and indeed the angels and the divine, all that make up the Unseen World, overlay the worlds of human—which I am told are themselves numerous: worlds upon worlds, each perceptible to those who have eyes to see them. These demon spirits have lived alongside humanity since before creation and will be with us forever.

"Are you a prince who lives alongside humanity?" she asked him. Was that the point he wanted her to glean from this passage? Or was it the worlds overlaying worlds, which she didn't understand?

The sound in her mind was faint but came from inside. It reminded her of wearing headphones, the way the music seemed to originate between her ears, only now the headphones were turned too low. She couldn't hear words but only a sound, low and burbling like water.

No, not water, laughter. Was he laughing at her?

"What's so funny?"

Now the sound was still soft and breathy, but she heard words. *Amir*, he said and then, *Prince*. Laughter again.

"All right so you're not a prince, whatever, what are you?"

He leafed through and showed her another page.

The word demon comes from the root meaning "to divide" and they are known for their ability as divisive spirits. However, the beings known to us today as demons had their origins in civilizations far older than this etymology. They are half-ether and half-substance, being made primarily from fire, where humans are made primarily of earth. While the essential mode for angels is that of a messenger, a conduit, and the essential mode for humans is as creator, the essential mode of demons is that of will and passion. This will is what leads to their divisive natures and has caused them from time to time to be considered evil.

It was still dark outside the windows and now she'd begun to feel tired again. She thought about going back to bed but instead moved to the overstuffed armchair. There was a question in her mind from Abraxas, a wordless wondering if he might read while she slept. That sounded harmless.

No sooner had she thought that than she fell into a deep sleep and through that darkness into the dream of the desert she'd had once before. It looked brighter here today, the sand more white than gold. Again he walked beside her and she couldn't turn to look at him.

"I thought you wanted to read," she said.

"I am reading." His voice sounded exactly as she expected it would, a thickly accented male tenor. Then she realized that wasn't his voice at all, it was her own mind turning his intentions into words. What would he sound like when she could hear him? Was his voice more like the laughing, distant wind and water sound she heard in her mind earlier?

"You can read and dream at the same time?"

"As easily as you can travel and talk. Now, you asked what I am and I do not know how to answer you save to say that I will never seek the destruction of your spirit and I will work to protect you from forces that would."

"But if I try to put my hand on a hot stove you're going to scare the living daylights out of me?"

"Precisely that."

"The Black Hood Gang, they weren't trying to get you, though, they wanted someone else, one of the bad ones. Why would humans summon one of those? It seems like a really bad idea."

A warm wind spiced with an acerbic plant smell brushed against her cheeks.

"Shaidans are not opposed to being used against other humans," he said. "Many of them relish the opportunity. They believe part of their challenge to humanity is to make power available to them. Naturally they are also likely to betray the ones who summon them when they get the chance, so it is, as you say, a really bad idea."

Ana wondered what would be worth that risk.

"Power over an enemy is a common request," he said. "Also wealth, which is its own power."

That made sense, but what caught her attention was the fact that he had answered a question she hadn't voiced. She'd been hoping he could only hear her when she put distinct words to her thoughts and projected them across her own mind, but apparently not. Did he know everything that went through her head? Every annoyance she had with Ruben, every time she looked at a woman on the street, every desire-laden thought about Sabel, every petty judgment she had about a person's weight or looks or way of speaking—did he hear all of that?

"Yes. All of it," he told her.

"Oh fuck." She put her head in her hands, swearing into her palms. "Fuck this. It's bad enough…everything else. I don't want you to…" she struggled for the words, "… to know me like that."

"You are afraid," he said. "That is all. You can handle it and you will."

Her fingers scrubbed away the tears that had started down her cheeks. She wouldn't cry like a frightened kid, even though she very badly wanted to. Any time in her life that she had felt lonely and longed for someone who could know her intimately now seemed pathetically short-sighted. Being known completely from the inside terrified her in a way she could hardly explain to herself—but Abraxas probably could explain it to her and she hated that even more than her fear.

"Do you believe you are your thoughts?" he asked. "Do you think you are made up solely of these uncontrollable, fleeting notions?"

She wished she could go somewhere and puzzle his question through without him in her brain eavesdropping. This was probably the kind of thing that Sabel was good at. She would have the answers. What did Ana know about thinking? Thoughts just happened, didn't they?

"I'm not just my thoughts," she said. "I mean, they're part of me. It's like asking if I'm my hand."

"Try this: don't make a fist."

She opened her hand, palm up to the bright sun of her dream.

"Now, don't think about a horse."

Of course she immediately pictured a large bay gelding she'd known from the farm down the street as a kid, and then Black Beauty from the movie, and a cartoon horse that had recently plastered the city on movie posters.

"That's not fair. How can I not think about something? As soon as you say it, it's already in mind."

"So your thoughts are not like your hand that you can open and close. Maybe they are more like your ears. Perhaps the mind is a sense organ like sight or smell. Are you afraid of me being able to hear what you are hearing? If not, then why be afraid that I hear what you are thinking?"

"Because thoughts are personal. They're inside me and some of my thoughts aren't nice at all."

"Then be grateful I'm not an angel."

"Would that be bad?" Ana asked.

"That was a joke," he replied and his rich voice held a wry turn to it.

"Was it funny?" she asked.

He paused beside her and then after a moment he started laughing and so did she, though hers held more of an edge.

At last he said, "Just consider that you are not the sum of your thinking. Perhaps you are not your thinking at all."

"Then what am I?"

"Good question." He was silent for a while and then said. "Ruben is awake and moving in the house. I must give you back to your body so we don't startle him by letting him see me sitting up reading in your body."

"Do I look different when it's you running my body?"

"Your eyes do."

And then she woke up in the chair with the book open in her lap. Why hadn't she told Sabel yet about Abraxas? She should call her and apologize for being so abrupt after the kiss. Was it better to meet in person rather than just apologize in a phone call, or was she looking for an excuse to see Sabel again?

She also wanted to ask Sabel these questions that Abraxas raised, but how could she bring them up out of the blue? Sabel wasn't afraid of magic, but did that extend to demons? Did it extend to a demon being in the same body with the woman she'd kissed? Could Abraxas hear her thinking that? Double creepy.

* * *

The circumstances hadn't given Drake enough time to properly prepare his death. That was usually how it went, but still it annoyed him to have to drag himself along the lines of old power he'd laid down rather than being able to hop from vessel to vessel. There was that awful moment when he had to wonder if any of his minions would try to turn against him and bind him while he was disembodied. He could destroy them, of course, but it would be a waste of time and power.

The creature he'd put in Simon Drake's body had been instructed to make it strong and vacate it when he needed it. Now it whined and begged and he had to draw smoke and fire around himself and threaten it. Once inside the body, Drake thought he might actually like the set of these shoulders better. This body was narrower than the Nathan body, but rich with lean muscle. He'd have to arrange for the next to be like this one. Reliable bodies were easier to come by these days now that the world population was so immense. He preferred a living but soulless body to any other conveyance, but he'd also had golems made over the years and on occasion impregnated a woman to birth his next body for him. That last was a terrible way to go because of the long childhood. Granted, it let him create with more detail and finesse than picking up a lost body and rehabilitating it from the addiction, abuse or trauma that drove out its original soul. Those lost bodies also held unfortunate energy patterns from their creators. He was looking forward to advances in cloning that someday soon might allow him to make endless copies of his favorite vehicles.

Nathan and Simon had come to him through a combination of great luck and significant preparation. They'd been brothers in life until a boating accident put both into a vegetative state. He'd watched over them for two years to make sure the boys had truly moved on and wouldn't be coming back, and then staged their final death and a subtle accident in the hospital that allowed his human minions to get out with the still-living bodies. He'd renamed them, of course.

He put lesser demons into them for a few years to strengthen the bodies until he needed them. Nathan was the older of the two, a high school athlete at the time of his accident, and he bulked up more over the years because he had one of those frames that put on muscle easily.

Now that he was in Simon, he could feel the lightness of this body and it suited him. The only disappointment was that the man still looked young. Chronologically he should have been about twenty-seven, but the lesser demons had been instructed to make the body lean and to age it faster than normal. Despite those efforts, he still looked to be about thirty, even with the fat gone from his cheeks and strands of gray in his short brown hair. Well then, Simon would play the prodigy.

He levered himself off the bed where the body had lain and stood in front of the mirror admiring the lines. Then he thumbed open a channel on his speakerphone to his best legal assistant.

"This is Simon," he said. "I've just arrived in town to take over Nathan's business and I need some documents drawn up. I believe Nathan had an illegitimate son, find out what I need to do to recognize him as my heir." That would be his next body, of course. He'd have to start watching for a suitable accident to furnish him with the actual physical part of this plan. "My schedule is open, tell the attorneys involved in my inheritance that I'm at their complete disposal for the next few days. I'd like this to be seamless so I can continue the deals my brother was involved in."

He opened the closet and looked at the outfits hanging there, the lush carpet feeling sweet on the soles of his feet. They'd had to fly the Simon body out here on Saturday and put him up in this hotel while he worked his way back from Nathan's corpse through the paths he'd created to get him to Simon. It was hard to do with Simon's body in transit for some of that time, but his other option would have been to put himself into a thing and be carried here, and he just didn't trust these people well enough to risk it. They could decide to try to bind him instead of release him. So it took him three days instead of a few hours and he'd have to make up for lost time now. Along with Simon came a wardrobe of six different styles. He never knew what he wanted before he took a new body, and so in the hours before Nathan's death as he settled the details that he could, he'd asked the professional shopper to choose a variety for him.

Not the expensive suits this time. That became cloying after a while and they made him look like he was trying too hard. But this time not too casual either. He considered a British style but it would make him appear too effete. Well then, upscale surfer meets Kenneth Cole: loose khakis and a zip-front, long-sleeve cardigan in classic navy over a white silk T-shirt. For the finishing touch he selected a pair of small, rimless eyeglasses that he had no real need for other than making this young face look uncannily smart.

He stepped into his boxer briefs and the khakis and then hit another number on the phone. This call went to his on-staff hacker who knew a few things about his nonhuman abilities.

"I'm Simon now," he said without preamble. "Can you doctor my school records? Give me a PhD in consumer psychology or something like that. Send me an outline of what I should know. Make me look brilliant but with a history of trouble in my early twenties that held me back from early success."

"Consider it done," his hacker said. "Welcome back."

Welcome indeed. He pulled the silk shirt over his head. He wanted to call Jacob next but couldn't. The man was at work and

Simon didn't have an untraceable cell phone yet. He decided to pull out a little invisible minion to go whisper in Jacob's ear, both to deliver the message and as a reminder of his power. He always had many small creatures waiting just outside the physical world to be pulled in for his tasks. They loved being able to come to this place and run around fueled by his power.

He spoke a few words, to hear his own voice say them, and reached with both his physical hand and his power into the realm of demons closest to him. His fingers touched nothing and his power slammed into a barrier. He swore and shook his hand as if he'd stubbed it against a wall, then tried again. A smash against his reaching power, like a concrete wall in the middle of an open room.

He howled and swore. The locals knew! He'd been so careful to hide himself and now they'd shut the gates on him and he could only work with what he already had in this physical realm. Who could have done this? Was he betrayed? No, that woman, Ana, she could not have known what to do, who to contact. He should have given better instructions for dealing with her while he was out of circulation. If it turned out to be her, he was going to destroy her. Killing wasn't enough, he would ruin her completely from the inside out.

His phone rang and he punched the line open, "What?"

"Jacob here to see you," his admin said.

There was a reason he enjoyed working with this man. He was intelligent and anticipated. Simon crossed the room in a few steps and slammed the door open. Standing by the broad windows, Jacob didn't flinch, but only barely. Simon saw the hard set of his shoulders against the reflex.

"The woman, where is she?"

"She hasn't come into the office yet," Jacob told him. "But they say she's coming in this afternoon."

"Where has she been? Has she been watched this whole time?"

"Not all of it, why?"

"Someone tipped off the locals. They know I'm here. They'll be watching now, we can't play fast and loose with power as we have been. We must be smarter."

"Why not leave off Ana and go back to summoning your consort? Ana will be hard to get to now."

Simon snarled, "We can't do any more summoning. The local powers have blocked it. We need that creature in Ana. He is much older than my consort. You can't imagine what his power would allow us to do. I need you to begin to prepare the others for a ritual to remove him from her when we do snatch her up."

"We're short one," Jacob said. "DK took off. Left the city, actually."

"So find someone."

"He'll need to be disciplined and have some training already."

"Then you know what to look for. I'll send an apology gift and work on getting back in with your company. Maybe we can two-birds-one-stone this whole situation. We have to move more slowly. It will give you time to find another member for us. Does Ana know what she has inside of her?"

Jacob gave a half-smile. "You're the demon, you tell me."

"I need to get closer to her. Get me an appointment in your office."

"One step at a time," Jacob said. "I've have a couple of the senior execs under my thumb, they'll push the others to see you."

Simon stared at the man for a moment and then smiled. It was fun to have a person around who didn't simper in awe and fear all the time. He might actually give this one everything he wanted…for a while.

CHAPTER TEN

By Tuesday afternoon, Sabel felt like she'd been dragged over rough ground. After her office hours on Monday she'd hurried home and started working on finding the names of any of the summoners. She made calls to her few magical contacts in the city and when that didn't pan out she tried to use her own magic. The trouble was that her abilities in the field of magic governing information were very limited. Her only gift in that arena was the ability to send herself information over short periods of time. She could stutter time and she could reorganize the information in a person's brain with her Voice for a short duration, but she had no way to look across the city and find what she wanted. There were witches who could do it, but they would all know the bargain Josefene insisted on and wouldn't work with her unless she took the leash.

She was running on three hours of sleep when she left for the university that morning and after her classes she wanted to fall into bed and crash. It wasn't only the sleep deprivation, she could shoulder that for days running and still function, but trying to do magic outside her expertise drained her. Leaving her class she was starving and nauseous, light-headed and heavy-limbed.

She pushed open the doors of the building and stepped into the open air. It was another heavy, foggy day when the temperature didn't crack sixty-five and she felt clammy under her light jacket. A familiar figure with short white-gold hair sat on a bench along the main walk. She felt a surge of happiness and a counterbalancing wave of caution. As glad as she was to see Ana, she wasn't eager to repeat Sunday night's closeness followed by sudden distance.

"Hey," Ana said and stood up. "They said you'd be out of class soon."

"Are you stalking me?" Sabel asked with a smile.

Ana held up a bunch of flowers wrapped in green paper, a mix of alstroemeria, carnations and some baby's breath—the kind bought on impulse from a stand on the street—and it was beautiful. Exhausted and aching from the inside out, she wrapped her fingers around the bouquet and blinked hard.

"I'm sorry about Sunday night," Ana said. "I really didn't want you to go. There was just so much going on."

Sabel didn't know what to say and what ended up coming out of her mouth was, "I still have your pants."

Ana grinned. "Good. Do you have other work stuff you need to do?"

"I need to eat," Sabel said. "And I'm falling-down tired. There's a decent sandwich place next to the parking garage."

"Lead on," Ana said.

Sabel walked across the quad to the little shop where she often got lunch. They settled into a booth near the back with sandwiches, hot tea for Sabel, and a bottled juice for Ana.

"I haven't been to my office yet," Ana said and her tone still held a hint of apology. "But I think tomorrow I will."

"No one else came to your door or tried to contact you?"

"All clear. I've just been poking around online and talking to Andi at the paper, but she doesn't have any good leads yet." She paused and reached across the table to touch the back of Sabel's hand. "Trouble sleeping?"

Sabel shook her head and finished the bite of sandwich before answering. "Trying to find the summoners."

Ana looked confused.

"With magic," Sabel added.

"And it wipes you out like that?"

"I look that bad?"

Ana laughed. "You look stunning," she said. "You always do. But your eyes are dark and you were swaying on your feet a little back there."

Sabel took Ana's hand in both of hers. She turned it palm up and brushed her thumbs across the broad, calloused surface. She was so relieved to have Ana there with her that she couldn't put it into words. It made everything feel easier. Now she knew that she would go home and take a nap and then tell Josefene she would take the leash and the information she needed. It seemed so simple in the plain light of Ana's smile. They would find the summoners and figure out how to turn them over to the police and then they could have as many lunches and dinners and kisses as they wanted.

"It's not a kind of magic that I'm any good at," Sabel said. "There are witches who can look across distances, through walls, even through time to find information, but I seem to only be able to do it in very limited circumstances and this isn't one."

"Are there different kinds of magic or is every person different?" Ana asked.

Sabel remembered Ana's accusation from Sunday, that she was only telling her the barest information about magic, and she tried to be forthcoming. She wasn't used to having a regular person in her life that she could talk to seriously about magic. Most of her former girlfriends saw it as more of a religious practice, like Wicca, without real-world impact. That wasn't exactly being fair since many of the practices of Wicca did have real-world impact, it was just too slow and subtle for most people to see. But the fact remained that most people she knew, if they knew she practiced magic at all, saw it as something unreal and fanciful.

"Magic is like most kinds of human endeavor," Sabel told Ana. "You can be gifted in music or dance or sports and then if you practice you get really great at it. And two people can be great soccer players or dancers and still have different strengths inside their field."

"So information just isn't your thing?"

"Specific kinds of information aren't my thing," Sabel said. "The Hecatine witches deal mainly in information, and time, and to some degree in transformations, but those are really big fields." She paused and looked at the confusion in Ana's face. "Let's just say my time magic is a lot better."

They finished eating and left the small shop. Outside, the sky was lighter, it might even clear completely in time for the sunset. Sabel had enough time to get home and sleep for a few hours and then try to contact Josefene.

"Are you in this garage?" she asked Ana.

Ana nodded and they started walking in that direction.

"Do you want to...do something else?" Ana asked. She paused outside the door to the parking garage and Sabel stopped with her.

"I do," Sabel said with a smile. "But I need to go home and try another avenue on this search."

"More magic?"

"Yes."

Ana paused and a look of caution flickered across her face. Sabel hoped she was wondering if it was okay to kiss her on campus and not something more bothersome. She wanted to kiss Ana fiercely, but not now—not when she felt half-dead on her feet still and muzzy-headed from all the failed magic.

She held up the bunch of flowers. "Do these mean that next time you kiss me you won't stop?"

Ana grinned. "Yes," she said.

"Then let's get this summoner situation handled so we can do that."

She turned away and headed for her car before she could override her own better sense. Let them put the damned leash on her. Maybe her reward for getting a list of the summoners' names could be a return to Ana's living room and to that kiss that should never have ended so abruptly.

* * *

Seeing Sabel on Tuesday put her in a good mood for the rest of the day, but the next morning as she drove to the office, anger came over her again and she steered her car through traffic like a missile. She parked in one of the two-hour visitor spaces right in front of the building entrance. Let someone try to ticket her car, Detlefsen would take care of it. Standing in front of the ten-story building, she squinted up at the glass windows that sparkled like shiny diamonds in the bright light of early morning. She set her shoulders and pushed into the lobby.

When the elevator reached her floor, she used her keycard in the side door and ducked around to the back hallway between the outside wall of the building and the last row of cubicles. No one had spotted her. The women of the MarComm department could be terrible gossips and she felt sure they'd already discussed Helen's death and her abduction for hours over the past few days. They would discover her soon enough, but she wanted to settle in before that happened.

Her cubicle was one row in from the outside wall and just off a hallway between the MarComm cubicles and the analysts. A man stood at her desk with his back to her. He had short brown hair, cut neatly, and an expensive, chestnut-colored suit jacket with a stylish, casual cut to it. She walked closer. The office sounds of the big room covered the tread of her steps, but he turned anyway and looked right at her.

Square glasses almost balanced out the roundness of his face, but they did nothing to cover the malice in his eyes. In his hand he was holding a photograph from her desk—the one of her and Gunnar and his wife standing at the wharf in front of a sunset. He smiled, like a vulture, and set the photo very carefully back in its place.

"Ana," he said. "I came to apologize."

"What?" Her disbelief came through in her voice.

"Yes, let me introduce myself to you. I am Simon Drake. I've come to remedy my brother's mistakes." He held out his hand. She looked at it. What was the relationship between him and Nathan?

From the look in his eye, she thought that they must have been in close communication, that Nathan had told his brother all about his plans. Maybe Simon was in town now to clean up after his brother and take out the people who'd set up his death, unless he'd set up his own death. Lily said that as a demon he could survive the death of his body and would find a new one. Was Simon here to make sure that happened or was Simon the new body?

Ana shook his hand. His skin was dry and feverishly hot. She held her palm against his and asked Abraxas, *Is he the demon?* He didn't answer in words, but a soft sense of agreement rose inside of her.

"You seem *very* familiar," she said.

"There is a strong family resemblance," he said.

He had Nathan's strong cheekbones, though they were muted by his rounder face. Both men had the same shape to their eyes and the same long lashes.

"Yes, it's uncanny."

"You have a brother too, I see. Are you close?"

He was threatening the part of her family she actually cared about. She brushed her fingers over the tops of the pens that sat in a mug to one side of her cubicle and pulled out a heavy fountain pen she rarely used. Slowly she unscrewed the top and looked at the delicate point of the pen. She wondered how much force it would take to ram it through his eye and into his brain.

But then she'd be arrested for murder and he'd just find another body. She had to ask Lily how they got rid of him for good.

"Not particularly," she said.

"Family relations can be so complicated, can't they? I am truly sorry for my brother's actions."

Ana had no idea how to respond to that. She stared at him for much longer than was socially acceptable and he didn't seem to mind. He held her gaze, blinking calmly, as if they were having the most natural conversation in the world.

"Ah there you are," a voice called from one row over. Charles Johnson, the VP of Sales, was coming toward them with Detlefsen on his heels.

"Ana, welcome back!" Detlefsen bellowed. "How do you feel?"

"Bruised, but pretty good, all things considered."

"I heard you had quite a knock on the head. Are you sure you're all right to be working?" Johnson asked. "I know Steve gave you as much time off as you need." His light brown eyes searched her face and Ana thought that he might actually be worried about her. Plus it couldn't help his department that she'd been kidnapped; the sales guys would have trouble getting prospects to actually talk about the product.

In his early forties, Johnson still had boyish cheeks, but any resemblance to the child he had once been ended there. His silk shirt accentuated the hard lines and angles of his chest and the thick muscles in his upper arms. He made Ana uncomfortable because he seemed so disciplined and at the same time his gaze always followed her through a room at company events as if he couldn't help himself.

"The doctor said it was a mild concussion," she told him. "I'm not dizzy or anything, I actually feel pretty good, and I'll go nuts if I have to stay home all week."

"Perhaps you'll join us for lunch," Drake said. "I know it wouldn't make up for what my brother put you through, but I must start somewhere."

"Thank you but I'd rather stay here," Ana said. "I have a lot to catch up on and I'm trying to stay available to help the police as much as I can."

"Some other time, then." He turned to Johnson. "Do you know where my next meeting is?"

"Follow me," he said.

Johnson and Drake walked away through the cubicles and Ana watched until they were out of sight.

"Bad shit," Detlefsen muttered loudly. "When you're settled, come see me."

Ana looked around the familiar cubicle. The stack of papers she'd been working on beside her computer was now on top of the magazines a foot away. Considering the care with which Drake replaced the photograph, the fact that he'd moved other parts of her desk around meant that he was trying to unsettle her.

She sat and stared at the changed landscape of her desk. How had Helen first connected with these men? If she could figure that out, maybe she could trace the path all the way to their identities.

She moved the picture of Gunnar, refusing to leave it where Drake put it, and picked up the phone.

"Yeah?" Gunnar said.

"You working?" she asked.

"Yep."

"Can you do me a favor later this week? It's…well, I need to get into an apartment and look around a bit."

"Friend?" he asked.

"Yes, and my boss, or she was. I mean, someone killed her."

"Ana?"

"I'm okay but it's not something I can explain, I just think she has some information I need. Will you do this?"

"Friday morning."

"That would be perfect. I'll text you the address."

She hung up before he could ask her anything else. She'd have to find a way to explain some of this to him without the part about demons but with the part where he had to be extra careful with himself. Maybe Lily or Sabel could help her come up with a cover story that would convince Gunnar he had to watch out. If anything happened to him, she couldn't bear it. She'd already fucked up his life enough when they were kids and instead of siding with him, she'd lumped him in with Mack and attacked them both.

Ana decided to go the long way around the floor to Detlefsen's office so the rest of MarComm wouldn't all descend on her. She stuck close to the outer wall, cut through the customer service bullpen and then past shipping, which brought her to his office from the back. His door was open and he sat back in his chair glowering at the pages spread out on his desk.

Of all the people in her office, he was definitely the safest to be around. He couldn't possibly be one of the demon summoners. His body was too distinctive to have hidden under any of those dark robes and, despite his gruff manners, Ana pegged him as a person who could be trusted. His yelling and swearing were a smokescreen so the people who worked under him wouldn't see how much he cared about them. Ana had seen enough kinds of yelling to recognize that under his bluster he was solid.

He saw her standing in the doorway and waved her in, saying, "Shut the door behind you. How are you really?"

"Pissed," she said.

"Sons of bitches. You didn't get a look at 'em? That's a shame." One rough hand, dotted across the back with spots of brown and wiry white hairs, slid over the other.

"What's up with Simon Drake?" she asked.

"Drake Investments wants to buy us," he said. "Nathan was in town to soften us up for the deal. Like I'd throw us in the shitter with that lot."

Ana glanced at the closed door. "Some of the executives want a sale?"

He didn't answer at first and kept rubbing one hand over the other. He wasn't wringing them, just sliding the fingers across the back of the other as if testing for something.

"It's a lot of money," he said.

"Why does Drake want to buy us?"

"We're poised for growth, we're working on the next generation of our software, but we don't have the capital to go after the growth we could have. With the right investment, this company could triple in a year or it could fall on its ass. I'd rather grow organically, but the other VPs see profits, bonuses, raises."

He leaned back in his chair, only a few inches from leaning forward, but his weight shifted and settled, and then he went on talking. "I have to wonder what that fucker Nathan was doing screwing around with Helen. She didn't seem the type to be interested in that kind of flashy crap."

"I don't think Nathan Drake was Helen's lover," Ana said.

His thick brows shot up, "Why not? The cops found her goddamned toothbrush at his place."

That was easy evidence to plant, Ana thought. But she couldn't tell Detlefsen that Drake hadn't been human. She put her suspicions together into reasons she could voice. "Drake talked to me after he grabbed me, when he was driving, and the way he sounded...well I found an email in Helen's account from the person I think was her lover and it didn't sound like Drake. I think her lover might have been someone who works here."

"And Drake killed her, so maybe the lover set Drake up? Ratted him out to the cops 'cause he was pissed?" Detlefsen asked.

"Something like that, yes."

His hands rubbed the arms of his chair. Those hands hadn't stopped moving the whole time Ana spoke. "You're going to send that email of Helen's to me and the cops, right?"

"I already forwarded them to the police, I'm sorry I didn't send them to you."

He stabbed the air with his finger. "You've got good instincts about people. You think something else is going on, I want to hear about it. You send me anything else you find. There's dirty business going on here and I'll be damned if I can't nail these rat bastards before they make us sell."

"I will," she said. "Thank you."

She stood up to leave. When she had her hand on the doorknob he cleared his throat. "Don't go anywhere by yourself," he said. "Call me if no one's around."

She walked a little distance from his office, back toward shipping, and then paused to talk to Abraxas.

How much in danger am I? Do you think Drake will try to grab me from the office like Sabel said?

He sensed me in you as I sensed his demon nature, so yes, he will be making a plan to capture us. However, if he seeks to buy this company, he won't do it in any way that connects him to your disappearance.

So don't go anywhere alone? Ana asked and looked into shipping where she could see four people moving around between the boxes. They were close enough to hear her if she yelled, but not so close that they could overhear her talking in a whisper so she switched to spoken words with Abraxas. She preferred speaking out loud, it made the whole voice in her head experience just a fraction less creepy.

"Why would he want to buy this company anyway?" she asked.

To channel resources to his human servants.

"Money?"

Yes, and status.

Detlefsen had mentioned bonuses as one of the reasons the VPs wanted to sell the company and she suspected they also stood to make a lot of money off the sale of their stock. Even Ana owned a little stock in the company. They got some every year. The people in leadership positions probably had a ton more shares than she did. Of course that suggested that some of Drake's summoners worked at Roth.

"How are we going to get him?" she asked.

First, we're going to make it harder for him to get you, Abraxas said. *I have been thinking about how to teach you to be unpossessable. Demons cannot possess human consciousness.*

"But I have been possessed," Ana said. "I felt it. I couldn't move or anything until you pushed him into my left side."

The demon didn't possess your consciousness. He possessed your identity, the self map that your body carries. By activating your painful memories, a demon can trap you in your small defensive self and command your body, but he does not actually overtake your consciousness and that's an important difference. You must learn to separate your consciousness from the self-defined identity. Otherwise these demons will overtake you again and I will have to fight from the inside. I don't know if you could withstand that.

That sobered her. "How do I separate from my own identity?"

Begin by simply being aware of it. You must learn to sense that the pain and fear you feel is not really you. That will spread to include other sensations, which also are not you. I'll help you.

Ana had another question in mind that she didn't really want to ask. Actually, when she thought about it, she had a lot of questions she didn't want to ask. But this one came out first, "So what is thinking? Is it really a sense organ?" That had been bothering her since he first asked her in the desert days ago.

I don't presume to say what things are, only what they could be said to be. To name a thing is to give it a certain power, but also to limit it. It is useful to think of the mind the same way you think of your other senses—as a filter through which the world comes to you.

"If I think my brain is like my ears, what good does that do me?"

What do you know about the limitations of your ears?

"The limitations? Well, there are sounds I can't hear, like those ultra-high dog whistles. And I don't have great pitch, I'd never make a good singer."

Your ears do not allow all sounds through equally, as you pointed out—human ears can't hear certain sounds. The brain is even more strict as a filter, ruling out a great deal. But as you remain unaware of the filter you think that you are actually having an experience of reality.

"Are you saying I'm out of touch with reality?"

Yes. You are in touch only with your own mind.

She almost didn't want to ask, "Can I get in touch with reality?"

Maybe. Start by learning to see the mind working. Learn to listen to the speaking of your thoughts.

She laughed. "I am getting used to hearing voices in my head." She imagined that he smiled at that.

Use your experiences with me to guide your understanding. Listen to your thinking the same way you listen to my voice.

She tried to do what he said, to listen to her thinking. What thinking? she thought. Oh, is that my thinking? I'm listening to myself thinking about listening to my thinking? Wait, I'm talking myself in circles.

Yes, you're hearing your own thinking. Tell me how often it speaks to you.

Ana listened to herself think about that. How often? It was always there. She was always talking to herself in the back of her mind, only it had never sounded like talking before, it was just there. It was thinking. Everyone thought. Was there something wrong with that? Was she supposed to learn to stop thinking? She didn't know how she could do that. Even as she wondered about it, she knew she was thinking about thinking, and then thinking about thinking about thinking. It went on endlessly.

"All the time," she said. "I'm always talking to myself in my head. I can't stop."

Then tell me, who is listening?

For a split second, Ana heard a silence she had never experienced before. Her inner ear turned on itself and heard only the sound of its own listening, which was non-sound. The back of her head and throat opened into vastness.

It's so big, she thought and the vast, open feeling vanished and left her standing alone in a hallway of Roth Software with what she could only assume was a stupid grin on her face.

* * *

When Sabel had told Josefene she was ready to take the leash, Josefene insisted that they wait a day and let Sabel catch up on her sleep. On Wednesday night as Josefene fitted the woven energy inside her body, Sabel understood why.

The process took about three hours and she slipped in and out of consciousness a few times as it went on. This wasn't a simple matter of just tossing a few cords of energy around her: the loops of the leash connected to the energy system of her body in dozens of places and allowed for varying degrees of constriction. The human energy body extended beyond the physical body in most cases, usually by a few feet, and crossed multiple fields of magic, so applying a specific set of constraints to it wasn't easy. Depending on the kind of demon magic and its nearness, the leash could close off her throat and prevent her from speaking or could begin to constrict her chest to warn her to get away, in addition to simply knocking her out.

It went around her body in three bands: one band just below her breasts that covered her solar plexus, one above her breasts that covered her heart, and one around her throat. It was invisible and intangible to others. It felt like it rested just under her skin and she would only feel it if demon magic triggered it.

"There," Josefene said. The leash flared for a moment and she felt a painful tightness around her chest. She opened her mouth and found she couldn't speak. After a moment, it loosened and she couldn't feel it at all. Josefene went on speaking, "If a demon seeks to possess you, it will render you unconscious instantly and only release when the threat is well past. If you're in too close proximity to demon magic, it will begin to tighten more slowly so you have time to get to safety if you can."

"How do I cause it to loosen?"

"Return here and try to relax. It should reset itself and if not I will come reset it."

"What if I can't get back here?"

"I'll try to find you or, given enough time, it should reset itself unless the demon magic is still near you."

"So if it knocks me out in a hotbed of demon magic, how long could I be out?" Sabel asked.

Josefene didn't answer.

"I'd be out until someone finds me, wouldn't I?"

"That's the most likely scenario."

"What's the worst case?"

"If the summoners capture you and try to break the leash, eventually it would kill you."

"Oh, great."

"I told you, they cannot take your Voice into their dominion. The leash can slow your breathing and heart rate. If the magic is too strong or you're in it for too long, it will kill you to protect us all."

"You didn't want to tell me that before you put it on me?" Sabel asked.

"As if it would have changed your mind," Josefene said with a bare hint of lightness in her voice. "This woman, Ana, you won't let her cloud your judgment."

"No," she said evenly.

"That wasn't a question," Josefene told her. "Now, I have the name you want and his address. We've done all we can to bias him toward accepting you as a new recruit. We planted some information for him about your abilities and implied that you knew Helen from a group for magically gifted seekers."

"Thank you," Sabel said.

The ghost of a touch fell on her shoulder. "Survive this," Josefene said.

* * *

The name and address Josefene gave her led Sabel to an investment fund manager named Gabriel Leonard, working out of the financial district downtown. Sabel went on Thursday after her class. She expected to take the elevator up to a marble-paved lobby, but the offices looked shabby for downtown. The carpet was an old taupe and the walls seemed dusty. Outside the elevator was a tarp and ladder with a young man taking down an old sign with the firm's name on it.

"Big changes," Sabel asked.

"We're redoing the whole floor," the kid answered with a grin.

The reception desk might be paneled with faded wood, but the receptionist's computer was top-of-the-line. Sabel told her that she was just in the area and had been recommended to Gabriel Leonard, was it possible to see him? After a few minutes of waiting, she was shown back to the man's office.

Here the signs of renovation were more evident. Leonard sat behind a new desk of shining walnut in a mesh chair that probably cost more than all of Sabel's office furniture combined. Leonard looked to be in his late thirties, with his brown hair cut in a deliberately messy style. He was just starting to put on an inactivity gut and the weight only showed at his belt line and in his face. She couldn't be sure that he was the man who'd lain unconscious over Ana's legs the night of the rescue, but his frame looked familiar. She forced herself not to stare. He shook Sabel's hand and sat back down.

"What can I do for you?" Leonard asked.

"You look like you've been very successful recently," Sabel said. "I'd like to share a bit of that success."

"How much are you thinking you'd like to invest?"

"I got your name from Helen Reed. My investment would be in knowledge and abilities you might find useful."

"How is Helen?" he asked smoothly, but his face was paler than it had been when she came in.

Sabel settled back in her chair and crossed her legs. "I think we both know she's dead."

"That doesn't trouble you?" he asked.

"I don't make the same mistakes other people do," she said.

"And what do you think I can do for you?"

"I hear you're a man of knowledge," Sabel said. "And you work with a group of men who are good at certain things that I might be able to help with and benefit from."

Leonard's gaze flicked to the door, making sure it was shut all the way. "Where did you hear this?"

"What I want to know is whether or not I'm wasting my time here. There's a group of men in the city that I want to be a part of. Do you know what I'm talking about?"

"I think I do," Leonard said. "Tell me again in plain English."

"There are spirits you can call and bind to do things for you. This group knows how to do that."

"And you know how to do that too?"

"I'm just not powerful enough on my own."

"What you think you do know is probably wrong. Why do you think people call spirits, provided that's even possible? To curse people or even to kill them? You just saw something in the paper, didn't you, and thought it looked like fun?"

"If I really needed to kill someone I could hire it out. You don't use demons to kill people, you use them to get information." She was reaching now into the depths of her memory, frantically pulling together shreds of reading she'd done over the years. Automatically she slipped into her lecturing voice, smooth words rolling out of her mouth. "Since ancient times, demons have come at the bidding of magicians to offer knowledge, glimpses into the future, higher magics, curses on your enemies. A demon isn't a blunt weapon. These are highly intelligent creatures who are only bound by people of strong will and then usually at great cost. There are people in this city who are willing to chance the danger that a demon brings."

"Are you one of them?" Leonard asked.

"I am," she said, hoping that lying about such matters wouldn't come back to haunt her in an awful occult way. "Are you?"

Leonard shrugged. "I don't know what you're talking about," he said.

Sabel pushed herself smoothly up from the chair and leaned for a moment over the desk. She hadn't been planning for this so her shirt wasn't adequately low-cut, but it would have to do. She picked up Leonard's notepad and pen and wrote down her name and phone number. Then she walked out.

CHAPTER ELEVEN

For the eighth day in a row Ana woke before dawn. She wondered if she was developing insomnia from the trauma of the kidnapping, but Abraxas assured her that she needed less sleep with his energy in her body. Gunnar said early morning was a good time to break into a place, so they decided to meet at Helen's at six a.m. She'd waited with poor patience through two days at work that seemed ridiculously boring compared to everything going on in her life.

Now that it was the day of the big break-in, she still had an hour until she was due to meet him at Helen's. She checked the street for strange cars and then, seeing nothing out of the ordinary, went for a short run. Her usual two-mile jog seemed effortless.

"You're changing me, aren't you?" she asked Abraxas. "Will this reverse when you leave me?"

You'll need more sleep again, he answered. *Do you want me to put the rest of your body's systems back the way they were?*

She sprinted up the street toward her house and it felt good. There should be some trade-off for the fact that she couldn't kiss Sabel without Abraxas experiencing it as well.

"As long as my eternal soul isn't in jeopardy, I think I'll stay like this," she told him.

Showered and dressed in her best breaking-and-entering clothes, she drove over to Helen's building and waited around the corner. She'd gone business casual for this with gray slacks and a light cashmere sweater. In this neighborhood, no one would look twice at a woman in that outfit.

Her phone rang and Gunnar said simply, "I'm in front."

Shaking her head, Ana got out of her car and walked around to the front of Helen's apartment building. The day she heard her brother put together more than a few words at a time would be a miracle. But she shouldn't complain, he'd driven out here to pick a lock for her, not something an ordinary brother would do. Nothing about their relationship was ordinary, and she just wished that most of it weren't quite so broken, and that she hadn't been the one who broke it.

He stood by the front door like a stone statue wrapped in rumpled and stained denim, ending in enormous boots. His tool belt hung low on his waist. Somehow he managed to bring South Dakota with him all the way to San Francisco, except in this city his farm-boy hands and rough demeanor seemed more charming than threatening. Ana smiled at him and watched the lines around his mouth deepen in what passed for expression on his face. He held open the door for her.

"Seen better security in a 7-11," Gunnar said as they walked up the central stairs together.

"Nothing you would want in there or here," she replied.

He made an eloquent grunt, indicating that he agreed, he'd never bother to break in to a place like this, this was a favor for his little sister, and even if there was something worth stealing, he was long past that now.

Faced with the locked door to Helen's apartment, crossed with police tape, Gunnar raised one side of his lip. From out of his tool belt came a slim black case, and from the case a couple of tiny silver rods. Ana didn't know how he could maneuver them into the dark opening above the doorknob, but he did. She watched his little movements in awe. Her brother had finally pulled his life together enough to marry a very decent woman, and now made his living as a silversmith on the art show circuit. The few times she went to his workroom it amazed her to see her tall, lean brother turn a tiny pair of earrings between his blunt fingers. She loved the idea of him working on women's jewelry, but she didn't visit often because most times she would see the scar that ran across his left hand and feel the hot pain in her belly and the pressure in her head to not cry. A few years ago, when he moved to the city where she lived, Ana didn't even know if she'd be able to see him at all. Now she just limited their time together.

It was Mack's fault, she wanted to believe that, but that idea just never took root in her. Mack wasn't that much older than either of them, but he was a lot stronger. She knew as young as eight that something wasn't right between Mack and Gunnar. Two years later, Mack started hitting her too. It should have brought her and Gunnar together. If they'd been allies, maybe they could have stopped Mack, but she was never sure back then how much she could trust him or anyone. They rarely spoke to each other. If they had, how would it have been different?

Gunnar's hands made tiny motions as he rotated his tools in the lock, and Ana saw clearly the ridged white scar across the back of his hand. He had smaller but longer scars on his chest and one thick scar across his thigh.

The image came up suddenly of her fingers curled white around the handle of a knife. The motion of the blade through the air, cutting white cotton and skin, blood dripping between the fingers of Gunnar's left hand as his right hand reached for the knife. He'd been the one between her and the door when he and Mack came into her room that night. And he'd been the one holding the knife, though she knew that Mack made him do it.

Her sin had been bringing a boy home, never mind that once she kissed him, it turned out not to be nearly as cool as the girls at school made it sound. The house had been empty when they arrived, though she was still an idiot for bringing him home at all, and then they were too wrapped up in their exploration to hear Mack sneak in. He'd seen the boy's bike outside and he came in silently and got a hunting knife out of his room, then collected Gunnar from the front porch. He didn't share his plan with Gunnar, but Ana knew the moment she saw him in the thrown-open doorway of her room that Mack planned to rape her and make Gunnar his unwilling ally. His mistake was giving Gunnar the knife. Though it satisfied his personal sense of sadism to turn Gunnar into an abuser, Gunnar could only stand still and hold it halfheartedly.

Ana had snatched it from his hand and slashed him from rib to collarbone. He was the one between her and the door. When Mack closed on them, Ana went for his face but cut his ear instead. She slashed furiously at him and Gunnar, but it was Gunnar who tried to grab the knife from her and that's when she put it through his hand.

She ran, meaning to get away to anywhere, but she was thirteen and in a T-shirt and jeans, barefoot with no cash, so later that night she returned home. Mack told their parents it was an accident, a game gone wrong. The hospital staff barely believed that story and Ana ended up with a few months of surprisingly helpful anger management counseling. Gunnar avoided her after that and Mack's harassment lessened to the level of cruel jokes and an occasional hard shove.

She and Gunnar didn't talk about the past. Their conversations were all about silver and public relations, and who would have a baby first. But every time she saw him it was all there in front of her again.

The door clicked open, bringing Ana out of her reverie. She paused at the threshold and then stepped into the suite of rooms that had been Helen's home until the previous week. The police had obviously been through everything. Ana had been here once before to borrow a book from Helen and knew the apartment had been relatively neat before men rifled through all the drawers and closets. She didn't know what she could find that they would have missed, but she had to look.

"Kitchen," Gunnar said, inclining his head in that direction and then following with his feet. Ana nodded to his retreating back. She picked the bedroom to start with because of her suspicion that Helen had been sexually involved with her killer.

A half hour later she had been through every drawer, under the bed, up and down the closet and found nothing useful. Gunnar poked his head through the door, looked pointedly at her and said, "Try the desk." As she traversed the short hall, she heard him in the guest bedroom opening the closet door.

She sat down at the desk and opened the file drawer. There were gaps in Helen's filing, and Ana assumed the police had taken anything that seemed suspicious. That left a bulk of folders from work that Ana was tempted to skip. But she started through the files, thumbing old press release drafts, company statements, contact lists and clippings.

Two-thirds of the way through the drawer, a folder brought her up short. It was titled simply "Clippings" which wasn't so strange in and of itself, except that Helen tended to be more precise in her organizing. When Ana held it open, its contents perplexed her. Most of the media clippings that interested Roth's public relations group were from national technology magazines, but these were all stories from local papers in California and Nevada. Some of the stories had to do with Roth software executive promotions, but there were other clippings from out-of-the-way papers that seemed to have nothing at all to do with the company.

Ana spread them out across the top of the desk and started grouping them by location to see if Helen had been working on some kind of map. But the various geographies had no logical connection. Not all of the stories were about technology or business. The stories got older toward the back of the file, dating back two years. As she looked at them, she saw the same names repeated over and over again. Why would Helen keep stories about a dozen men...

The pattern connected in front of her eyes: all the stories featured people succeeding or gaining wealth. Here were short promotion announcements, awards, patents, changes in local real estate, a wedding announcement, in one case a winner of a small, local lottery, another was the sale of a small company to Drake Investments. Helen had kept track of a dozen men who when put together would seem to have extraordinary luck—or extraordinary help.

You said demons confer money and power, right? Ana asked Abraxas silently. Her brother didn't need to think she'd started speaking to herself, and he certainly didn't need to hear the word "demon" if he was listening.

I think you've found it. Helen knew enough to be watching and these are men that she either knows or suspects were in this group.

Why did they kill her?

I'm not certain they intended to. Many unexpected events can happen during a summoning. I saw her standing between life and death. She refused their demon.

Ana stacked the clippings and slid them into the folder. This was Helen's backup. She'd been collecting information about the identities of all the summoners in case she needed leverage against them, and because she worked in PR and her files abounded with news clippings, they would never have suspected that this was her way of tracking them. She whispered a quiet, "Thank you" to Helen's departed soul.

"Gunnar!" she called softly and he came noiselessly out of the back rooms. "Let's go," she said. "I've got it."

She let him walk her down to her car. He gave her a rough hug, the steel edge of his shoulder hard against her cheek, and then opened her car door for her. The desire to talk to him, to reach out, came over her. Would he understand if she told him about the demons, about Abraxas riding around in her own mind? He would probably think she was being metaphoric, speaking about the "demons" they both brought with them from South Dakota.

While she thought this through, he shut her door and walked to his truck, his left shoulder a fraction lower than his right. He always cradled that side of his body and Ana wished she could reach across the gulf between them and straighten him up again, as if none of it had ever happened. He waited by the door of his truck, his mouth turned down. When she pulled away down the street he was still standing there watching her.

* * *

The day's schedule was clear of appointments, as Fridays often were, and so Lily had spread her materials over the back table. She was trying to work backward from certain mentions in the texts in order to find out exactly how big this vessel was going to need to be. The sound of the bell on the door jerked her upright. Very few of her regulars would understand what she was trying to do and if it was one of them she intended to keep them away from this area. All the rare books that made up her retail business lined the walls at the front of the store. This area was for marketing clients.

"Lily," Ana's voice called back at the same time Lily spotted the other woman's ruddy blond-brown hair around the bookshelf that separated the sales area from this meeting space.

"Back here," she said and sat back down on the couch. "There's hot water in the pot if you want."

A short bookshelf held an electric kettle, mugs and a variety of teas and cocoas. Ana got herself a steaming mug and brought it to the table.

"I'm making progress on finding another vessel for Abraxas," Lily said. "But these texts are deliberately obscure and when I asked Abraxas the other day, I got the impression he was obfuscating."

Ana rolled her eyes. "Get over it," she grumbled quietly, and then to Lily, "Not you."

Lily smiled. For a woman surprised with a demon passenger a week previous, Ana had adapted better than she'd expected. She didn't even react as Lily lit a candle and set it on the side table so Abraxas could form himself a temporary extension of body from its flame.

The problem with moving Abraxas was that Lily couldn't just dump him into an amulet or statue and let it be. Working with demons for decades, Lily had seen tremendous variation, but never one as elegant as Abraxas. She imagined it was his centuries on the paths of the dead that wore away the arrogance or grandiosity so many of the older ones developed. Abraxas had the attentive gentleness of the truly ancient beings. She wanted to create a vessel that honored and protected what he was.

It would have to amplify his power, draw him into himself faster, and give him some mobility. That was the problem that occupied her this morning. If she put him in an amulet or token, he'd be squeezed in, limited to one or two abilities.

"What kind of vessel would you like?" Lily asked him.

The face he made himself became more detailed every time she saw him. Now his full lips pressed together briefly and then opened in a breathless sigh. "Unbreakable," his voice whispered out. Without a real mouth or lungs, he wasn't actually speaking but causing the illusion of words, much as he did inside Ana's mind. He could have spoken only to Lily, but she guessed he was too polite to exclude Ana. "A pendant or a ring, maybe stone. No bottles or lanterns, if you please."

"We can't go too small," Lily told him. "I'm not sure what the limits are, but according to these authors..." she couldn't resist the joke, "size matters."

Ana choked on her tea and nearly spit it back into the cup.

"Then perhaps you should transfer me into a standing stone," Abraxas replied.

Lily laughed. "You'd like that? Some massive lingam?"

"Do demons have relationships?" Ana asked. "I know Drake said he was involved with Helen, but I think she was really with someone else in the circle, another human."

"It depends on the demon," Abraxas said. "We are each unique."

"And human lives are so short," Lily said, watching his face. He looked up and met her eyes. Instead of pupils, he had candle flames and for a moment they held steady without flickering.

"I don't mind that," he said. "We are all eternal."

Ana looked up from the table and stared back and forth between the two of them. Lily felt her cheeks coloring and went to get more tea. Yes, he was mightily compelling, but the man didn't even have a body. This was beyond the pale even for her history of doomed attempts at relationships.

"I found something at Helen's," Ana said hastily and Lily returned to the table with relief. She pushed together some of her papers to make a place for Ana to set down the thick file folder she pulled out of her bag.

As Ana explained the purpose of the clippings, Lily made a list of the men's names. She could give this to Asilal and see what he could discern about these men. Ana volunteered to send a copy of the list to a reporter friend of hers to see if he'd heard anything about these men. They needed more solid proof to involve the police, but it was a better lead than Lily had hoped for.

Lily looked over her research with fresh eyes. Maybe she could put Abraxas into a small standing stone, perhaps even in lingam stone meant for a fountain. It would serve him right. Smiling she went up to her library for more books.

* * *

Lily set another mug of hot tea next to Ana on her way to close out the register and Ana curled her hand around it feeling spoiled. It was almost time for the shop to close but she didn't want to go home.

The chimes on the front door jingled and Lily asked, "May I help you?"

"I hear you have a remarkable rare books collection."

That was Sabel's voice. Ana jumped up off the couch wondering how Sabel managed to track her down here when she'd never given her the address. Seeing the slender woman standing just inside the front of the store in a long, charcoal skirt and lighter blue jacket, Ana realized Sabel hadn't expected to see her at all; Ana had only called this place "Lily's store," she'd never used its real name. Sabel must have stayed late at the university and come here because she really was looking for books. Apparently Ana wasn't the only one who learned that if you needed to know more about demons, this was the place to be.

"I was going to call you," Ana said and then realized how stupid that sounded. "I mean, I got some leads, a list of names."

"You know her?" Lily asked as the two of them walked from the front of the store to the area where Ana had been sitting.

"Lily, this is Dr. Sabel Young from SFSU, she helped me get away from the summoners."

"You were recommended to me," Sabel said to Lily. Then to Ana, "What names?"

"I, um, got into Helen's place this morning and went through her files because I thought the police might have missed something since they think the case is closed and anyway they weren't looking for demons, you know. I found this file folder of clippings of stories about men who've been accruing a lot of power in the last few years."

Sabel sat carefully on the far end of the couch. Ana handed her the folder and she began to page through it.

"Gabriel Leonard, good," she said.

"You know him?"

"He's on my list too."

"You have a list?" Ana asked.

"I wasn't going to leave you to deal with this all by yourself. I have an idea for finding the identities of the summoners."

"Oh?" Ana asked and Lily arched her eyebrows with a similar, unspoken question.

"I talked to Leonard yesterday about joining the group," Sabel said without looking up from the folder.

"Do you have any idea how dangerous that is?" Lily asked.

"Less dangerous than Ana walking around in a city where they all know her face and have already come after her," Sabel said.

"But you're the one who wanted me to stay home," Ana pointed out. "You're the one who yelled at me about going to my office."

"You know I have more resources to protect myself than you do," Sabel said. She set the folder down and stood up from the couch, but that did nothing to back up her point. Lily raised her eyebrows. Standing next to Sabel she looked like a cat next to a bird. Lily was shorter, but solid, almost weighty in her thick boots, even though she wasn't a heavy woman.

"Perhaps we should spend more time comparing notes," Lily said. "Neither of you should go rushing after these men. They still have at least one powerful demon with them and you," she looked at Sabel, "look pretty human to me. Do you even know how to bind or banish a demon?"

"I've never tried."

"But you think you can defend against them? Because at least Ana has Abraxas and he's growing in strength—"

She stopped abruptly because Ana was vigorously shaking her head, but it was too late. Ana circled a couple of steps around Sabel to get between her and the door so she wouldn't rush out.

"Abraxas?" Sabel sounded out the name. "As in the Gnostic deity? How are you under his protection?"

"He's not a god, he's a spirit," Ana said. "I mean a Sangkesh or whatever."

"You mean a demon," Sabel said and the word "demon" crackled with accusation. "And you put yourself under his protection?"

"Um, not really. I mean, I didn't have much choice."

"You didn't tell her?" Lily asked Ana, which didn't help the situation.

"Hey, I'm still getting used to this! Last week as far as I knew demons were made up and now there's one talking to me inside my own head and pardon me if I didn't want to broadcast that!"

Sabel stood up and turned on Lily, "You didn't banish him?"

"He's too weak."

"*He* is? That's why they're coming after Ana and you're going to let that happen because *he's* weak? You're lecturing me about danger?"

On the table nearest where Ana stood, a candle's flame leaned sideways and traced filaments of fire on the air. The head and torso of a man formed and Abraxas's wind-soft voice blew through the store.

"I protect her while she hosts me," he said.

Ana saw Sabel draw a breath and raised a hand to stop her, but it was too late. The words that leapt from Sabel's mouth had the force of a landslide behind them.

"*Demon, out of her!*"

Pain lanced across her skin and for a split second she felt Abraxas thrown out of her and out of the store entirely by the power of the words. But although he was out, he was not unconnected from her. A thick energy bond stretched between them. The bond jerked her off her feet and she was falling backward through the air. She struck one of the windows and felt it pop out of its old, wooden frame. It shattered on the pavement and then she hit two surfaces nearly simultaneously. The first was warm and yielding and it lessened the impact of the second, which was asphalt.

Thank you, she offered silently to Abraxas, who'd done all he could as she fell through his insubstantial body. He was fully inside her again and already working to repair the damage from hitting the window and the street. At least she'd missed striking the light post or landing in the shimmer of shattered glass left by the window.

She was on her feet before she realized it and vaulting through the now empty window frame. Lily had wrestled Sabel to her knees and had her subdued with her arm across her throat. Sabel's eyes were half-closed from lack of oxygen and in another moment she'd be unconscious.

"Not in my house, witch," Lily snarled at her.

"Lily, don't," Ana said. "Let her talk. She won't do that again."

Lily paused for a moment and then said quietly to Sabel, "*Maarevas*, I know you now. If you use that voice again against Ana, or Abraxas, or me—there won't be a place in this city that's safe for you."

She moved her arm and Sabel gasped.

"Sorry," Sabel said breathily, still sucking in more air. "Not supposed to happen like that."

"He's connected to my body. When you threw him out the connection dragged me with him."

"Hurt?" Sabel asked.

"Less than you'd think." Ana struggled with what to say next, but Lily cut in.

"She's using you," Lily told Ana. "The witches always do."

Sabel rose gingerly to her feet. "Oh and you're not beholden to anyone? You work entirely for yourself then?"

"The Sangkesh protect this city and they'll do everything they can for Ana," Lily said loudly.

Sabel raised the volume of her words to match Lily's, "The Sangkesh would go after a fly in a china shop with a baseball bat and damn the humans too stupid to duck—you call that protection?"

"Are you using me?" Ana asked of no one in particular. The other women both turned to look at her.

"The other witches assigned me to watch Helen," Sabel said. "That's why I found your phone and knew you were in trouble. I came after you on my own. But yes, I'm a Hecatine witch and I report to our governing body and I keep them updated about what's going on here."

It made sense, but it stung. Sabel found her not because she'd started out watching over Ana, but because she was checking up on Helen. And she reported to some other group of witches—which made Ana feel angrily self-conscious.

"Do you tell them everything?" Ana asked.

Sabel dropped her gaze. "Not everything," she said quietly.

"And you?" she asked Lily. "Are you lying about how hard it is to remove Abraxas just because you're fascinated by him?"

Lily's eyes narrowed. "I'll have him out of you within a week, maybe less. Do you really want him out so badly you'd kill him to do it?"

"No," Ana admitted.

"And hasn't he already protected you?"

"Yes."

"There," Lily said decisively. "And now if you'll pardon me, I have to call the glass company." She stomped to the front of the store with more force than her boots warranted.

"You didn't tell me," Sabel said.

Ana noticed that she took the chair furthest from the couch. Instead of sitting, Ana paced, careful to never get closer to Sabel than the far end of the couch. If Sabel didn't want anything to do with her now that she knew about Abraxas, then fuck it. She wasn't sure how pissed she should be about the fact that some governing body of witches were behind Sabel following her in the first place.

"I have a fucking demon in me." She spat the words. "What was I going to say? I'm sorry I can't make out with you 'cause there's a fucking demon in me?"

"You went to the Sangkesh rather than ask me for help." She gestured toward the front of the store where Lily was facing away from them, the phone held to her ear.

"I'm not part of your politics. I was in pain. I went to someone who could help."

Sabel turned to look at the broken-out window and then ducked her head in acquiescence.

Ana wanted to shake her and demand that she explain herself. Why did she look so defeated? She sat down on the edge of the couch close to Sabel and leaned toward her.

"Sabel..."

She was still trying to figure out what to say or to ask when Lily walked back to them.

"Excuse me," Lily said to Ana. "I need to reinforce the protection on the store now and I would like to do it without the witch here."

"We're on the same team here," Ana told her. "As far as I'm concerned, it's Team Ana and you two have to set aside whatever bullshit politics you have going on."

"A thousand-year conflict probably counts as more than 'bullshit politics,'" Sabel said quietly without looking up, but Ana heard the smile in her voice. "And I should be going anyway." She got to her feet and smoothly pulled a card out of her purse, offering it to Lily. "Please send me the bill for the window."

The lines around Lily's scowl softened a little and she took the card. "Can you tell me the Hecatines' interest in this matter?" she asked in a neutral tone.

"It's my interest," Sabel said. "I asked for permission to help track the summoners and to protect Ana. The others don't want to get involved."

"Good. Will you let me know what you plan to report back to them?"

"It's enough to have to report to one authority," Sabel said. "How about I just let you know if I plan to tell them anything about the Sangkesh in this city? Not that they don't already know. Will that satisfy you?"

Lily nodded.

"And I'd appreciate it if you'd let me know your plans for Abraxas."

"I expect Ana will keep you up-to-date on that," Lily said, a note of tension creeping back into her voice.

"You know what would be great," Ana said, fed up with their terse back and forth. "Someone should really set up a diversity training seminar for the witches and the Sangkesh demons."

Lily's dark expression didn't change, but Ana was rewarded with a suppressed smile from Sabel.

CHAPTER TWELVE

Ruben's agent finally came through with a small part for him and he wanted to fly down to LA on Saturday and party there for the weekend. Although Ana had only known Lily for a week, she called and asked if she'd consider staying at the house with her for a few days. She usually liked being alone, but if the summoners came back, she wanted backup. Plus, she hoped that having Lily around to work on moving Abraxas to an appropriate vessel would speed things up.

She had trouble thinking of anyone else she'd rather have stay in the house with her, other than Sabel. The two friends she'd stayed close with from college were both in committed relationships and it would be weird to ask them over. She hadn't even called them about the whole kidnapping and demon summoning situation because she hadn't a clue where to begin.

Lily showed up on Saturday evening with carryout Indian food and a stack of books. After eating, they settled in the living room with tea. The file from Helen's apartment was open on the table and Ana worked on filling in her matrix of information from the articles: who they featured, where the story was from, what success had been detailed. She felt Lily watching her and looked up.

Lily raised an eyebrow, and Ana was taken aback by the structure of her face. In the bookstore, she thought she was imagining it, but Lily's features had shifted from rather good-looking to plainly beautiful. She had thick, bow-shaped lips in an oval face. Her dark eyes, set close together, augmented each other in a singular obsidian stare emphasized by thick, gracefully curved brows and light olive skin. Her high round cheeks disappeared under the smiles that came slowly but filled her face. Ana blinked and wiped a hand across her eyes. She appreciated any beautiful woman, but she didn't usually fixate on the straight ones—there wasn't any point.

"Cut that out," she muttered to Abraxas.

"What is he doing?" Lily asked in the curious tone of a scholar. Even her throaty voice sounded good to Ana.

"I'm pretty sure he's sweet on you. Every time I look at you, you get more attractive."

Lily laughed and reached across the space between them, holding her fingertips toward Ana. She felt her own arm tremble and then her hand lifted itself and reached toward Lily. When their fingers met, a cloud slowly blossomed up from the touch. Lily slid her fingers across Ana's hand, the pads of skin soft against the warm palm. The cloud between them became thicker, rising up like a plume of smoke, wavering but not dissipating. In it, Ana could begin to see features, a man's chest and the beginning of arms, a trunk that hinted at legs. She strained to see the face but could not make out features, only the darkness of a mouth and two smaller hollows that evoked eyes.

"Not bad," Lily said. "Think you'll be able to do it on your own soon without flame to draw from?"

"Maybe," Abraxas's voice came very softly from the heart of the cloud.

"Can you come into me?" Lily asked. She closed the book she'd been reading and set it on the coffee table.

"Hold on to Ana," Abraxas told Lily.

Lily's fingers closed firmly around her hand and she felt a rush of wind go out of her. Lily's dark eyes flicked shut, leaving Ana sitting on the edge of her seat, hand extended, achingly alone. With her free hand she reached up and touched her forehead. She wanted to call Abraxas's name, to see if he would answer her, but she was afraid either that he wouldn't or that he would come back from Lily to her.

She felt deflated, less of herself. Having Abraxas in her head seemed like such a bother at times, but she missed knowing that there was another voice she could call on, a wise companion who could give opinions without judging who she was. She'd not seen so clearly before how amazing it was that Abraxas could live in her head, hear her thoughts, and still try to teach her everything he was teaching her. She didn't deserve it. She'd been a jerk to him, trying to get rid of him, shutting him out.

There had been an ever-present sense that she'd never noticed until now that she was all right with him. Perhaps it came from knowing his mind while he knew hers. She couldn't exactly read his thoughts, but they shared the same mental space. He couldn't lie to her or hide from her. With every other person in her life, she knew they kept something hidden away from her, away from other people, and with Abraxas she had nothing hidden.

"Abraxas," she said quietly.

Lily opened her eyes and Ana, through the connection of Lily's hand, could feel Abraxas looking at her.

I'm here, he said, once again inside her head with her.

"Incredible," Lily said aloud as Abraxas streamed between them, back into Ana's body.

Lily shook her head and dropped Ana's hand abruptly, running her palm thoughtfully across her own thigh. Ana rubbed her thumb over the tips of her fingers as if she could feel traces of Abraxas's path back into her body. Her skin was a half-degree warmer than usual, but otherwise no different.

"Why me?" Ana asked. "And why you? Would this work for any two people?"

"It took enormously powerful magic to put Abraxas in you. I've been thinking about it and I think that Helen's death had to be a significant factor. That's mainly why it's so hard to get him out of you. But he can visit me because of my demon blood."

"You?" Ana started and then didn't know what to ask.

"I'll show you," Lily said. "Provided you don't tell the witch."

Ana shook her head. That didn't sound like a good idea. She was still processing the altercation at the bookstore.

"She already knows you're part demon," Ana said. "After the fight, she said you were too strong."

"You'll find it hard to talk with her about this anyway, and even harder to tell people who don't understand magic," Lily said. "This world that we share, the material world, it resists change by magic because…well, that's a very long story. There are other worlds where magic is very natural, the Unseen World as they're called in the aggregate, but not when you're dealing with material substances. But there have been rare times when a fundamental shift occurs in what is possible here."

She reached down and began unlacing one of her boots. The few times Ana had seen her, Lily was wearing heavy boots as was the style of the day. Maybe a little heavier than a small frame like hers would support, but not outside the bounds of taste, though Ana had wondered why a woman in her mid-forties who owned a business was wearing Goth-girl boots. As Lily unlaced one and started to pull it off, Ana saw that she wore some kind of very thick cotton sock, and just below the edge of the sock, as it folded down in the removal process, her skin became thick and very brown, creased almost like the skin of a crocodile.

Lily pulled the sock all the way off and flexed her foot. A little yelp escaped Ana's mouth before she got her hand over it. Lily had three thick toes that extended most of the length of the foot, ending in talons that looked like small horns. A tiny toe extended off the heel of the foot. It looked almost like a bird's foot, only the toes were much thicker.

"What the hell?" Ana said under her breath.

"Two thousand nine hundred and seventy-four years ago, with the building of the Temple, King Solomon altered the material world so that demons could take physical form," Lily told her. "There's great debate about whether he understood that this would allow them to breed with humans. I like to think that he did because it meant the Sangkesh, the protectors, literally have skin in the game."

"But it means that the bad ones do too, right?"

"They can but, as you saw with Drake, a lot of them prefer to steal their bodies. The Sangkesh are much better at working with half-breeds like me."

"One of your parents was actually a demon?"

"My mother. Demons reproduce in a couple of ways. There are those who have manifest forms very unlike humans; their bodies consist of elements like fire, water, sand, stone, and so on, and they produce other demons like Abraxas. Usually when those demons reproduce like that it weakens them, so they tend not to do it very often. Then there are the demons who are closer to humans in appearance that can actually, more or less, interbreed with humans. That's where I come from. You know, you have some demon blood too. You'd have to in order to be able to host Abraxas and get through everything you've been through."

Ana got up from the couch and stared at her hands. "But I'm not..." she gestured at Lily's feet.

"You need to be at least one-quarter demon to have any real physical signs, useful as they can be." Lily lifted one leg and curled the toes of the foot together. "For you, one-sixteenth probably means you've got a temper and you tend not to live the life that people expect you to live."

The idea of having a demon relative felt frightening and exciting at the same time. She never did want to live the life others expected of her. She loved freedom and she had always craved something she couldn't name that wasn't provided in her normal life. It felt like a longing for a deep, resonating connection to life itself. Was that from the demon blood?

She also loved the physical strength, energy and endurance that Abraxas brought her, but she kept wondering if there was a cost. Being raised with the ideas of demons as lying, evil creatures was hard to shake.

Demon blood is strong, passionate, disruptive. Do these not describe you? It is not evil, Abraxas told her. After a moment, he added: *Ask her how old she is.*

"He wants me to ask how old you are," Ana said, perplexed.

"Ninety-two," Lily said.

"Oh," Ana heard herself say in a small voice. She stared at the faint lines by Lily's eyes, the smooth, creamy skin firm over her high cheeks. "You don't look much over forty."

"Demons are long-lived," Lily said. "If I keep my nose out of trouble, I plan to make close to two hundred. You don't have enough demon blood for that, but I suspect you'll be pretty spry in your eighties and nineties."

"If I make it that long," Ana said.

"Allying with that witch won't help," Lily said.

"Shit, what do you two have against each other anyway? You never even met before yesterday. Is the whole demons and witches thing that serious?"

"It's over a thousand years of serious," Lily said. Ana made a circular motion with her finger to show that Lily should keep talking and she did. "We look after things. For millennia the Sangkesh have hunted the harmful demons and protected humanity. I won't bore you with hundreds of years of history. The Hecatines intervene when it suits them and they haven't hesitated to kill Sangkesh and even side with the Shaidans if that favors their goals. They perverted the magic of Solomon to create their own creatures to serve them, the way Solomon gave the demons form. They will bend anything to suit their ends."

Ana thought about Drake's eyes as he stood in her cubicle. He saw her as a tool or an obstacle, not a person. She knew that Sabel could never be like that, but what about the people she worked for? What were they using Sabel for and did she know?

* * *

Gabriel Leonard, the investor turned demon-summoner, called and invited Sabel to "meet his friends." It wasn't her idea of a thrilling Saturday night, but Ana had that Sangkesh demon bookstore owner at her place and Sabel didn't relish spending time around her.

The details about the meeting seemed fairly safe on the surface. These men had no reason to suspect that she was connected to Ana, and the meeting was in a public place. Plus Sabel was straight up angry now that she knew the Sangkesh were mucking around in Ana's life. This was their city, they should have this handled already. How hard could it be to shut down one demon and send another back where he belonged? She had the impression that they were toying with Ana or using her as some kind of experiment. The sooner she could wrap this up, the sooner she could be back to the part about suggesting that she and Ana have a drink together and laugh about all of this. She loved hearing Ana laugh.

It was already late on Saturday and she sent Ana an email rather than a text telling her that she was going to meet the summoners. Ideally, Ana would check her email in the morning and Sabel would have sent a second message by then telling her that everything was okay. No point in worrying her now when she couldn't do anything to help.

Sabel went downtown for the meeting dressed in one of her most conservative gray pantsuits and wearing the little pearls that were both beautiful and lightly magicked. Leonard waited for her outside the door to the restaurant. They were close to his office building and she wondered if he'd come from there. He was also in a suit.

"Ms. Young," he said. "We're going around the corner."

She paused. If they did have a relatively powerful demon with them, they wouldn't need her consent to abduct her. He could just knock her out or try to possess her and trigger the leash, which would have the same effect. After all, the leash wasn't for her protection—it was to protect the other witches from her. Technically a clever demon could possess her and get her to use the Voice on herself to make her tell them everything she knew about the Hecatines. The leash made that impossible.

"Dr. Young," she corrected him and followed him around the corner to a building of loft apartments. They took the elevator up to a studio where three men in dark masks waited. The effect was ominous, no matter how Sabel tried to minimize it by telling herself they looked ridiculous with the dark hoods coming down to the collars of their suits. The hoods had one very practical purpose—even if she was accepted into the group, Sabel would not know the identities of the other members, aside from Leonard.

She didn't care about most of them because they'd be the ones mentioned in the clippings Helen had. She only wanted the identity of the one man she was certain Helen hadn't collected information on—the one she called Jacob in the emails Ana found. As Helen's lover, the leader of the group had an extra level of immunity because she wouldn't want him caught. That was the man Sabel needed to find here and identify tonight. Until they knew his name, it was too soon to move against this group.

She was also betting that his house was the place they'd taken Ana and that his hidden basement was the location where the police would find traces of Helen and be able to connect all of these men to her death in a way that would stick legally. Sabel had no other recourse. Maybe the Sangkesh of the city had stronger magic to deal with demons, but witches didn't interfere in that way. The only way to protect Ana was to find rock solid evidence to send all of these men to jail.

"Welcome," one of the hooded men said. His voice was deep and sandpaper rough. Likely he was tightening his vocal cords to disguise his normal speaking voice. "I'm Jacob and these are Night and Crow."

"Sabel," she said simply. "But you know that." She didn't like that they could see her face and knew her full name, but when the police got involved none of that would matter.

He gestured to a folded robe on a chair. "Did you want to change or did you plan ahead and wear no metal?"

She walked over to the room and put her purse on the chair on top of the robe. "Outside of the keys in my purse, the only metal is my gold jewelry and I've magicked it myself."

"Good, we'll see how well your magic holds." Real approval sounded in his voice. Apparently not all of his recruits knew that demons could often draw themselves into metal, including belt buckles and keys. Her pants were a woven Eileen Fisher with an elastic waistband, the buttons on the jacket were bone, and she'd worn a sports bra to avoid even the tiny metal hooks. If a demon tried to touch the white gold of her necklace, it would be in for a harsh surprise.

In the back half of the studio there was a thick cloth rolled out on the floor that had been painted with an array of symbols. At its center was a circle and there were five smaller circles around it.

"We're going to test your resolve and ability," Jacob said. "Normally there's a period of study of a year or more, but with your background we're going to assume you've done that work and let you demonstrate what you know."

The men each took a circle so Sabel stood in the empty one. Jacob sat and the other men followed, so she settled down into a cross-legged sit in her circle.

"We'll begin with meditation and then with your assistance you'll call a lesser demon and ask it for information."

Sabel tried to calm down enough to meditate, but her heart and mind raced. What if they called a demon and it triggered the leash? Could she pretend it was a medical condition or would they taste the magic on her and know her for a witch?

After a long silence, Jacob started chanting quietly and the other two men joined in. Sabel couldn't quite make out the words. It wasn't one of the languages she knew. She had read about rituals like this but certainly never attended one. The Hecatines never used demons directly, but she knew from their history that if they saw demon affairs pushing events in the direction they wanted, they would use that facilitation.

For the Hecatines there was a rigorously choreographed dance between ends and means. No end was ever an end in itself and no means were ever separate from their ends. They could be called highly manipulative, but they were always driving toward a life-affirming end and of all the people Sabel had ever met, the Hecatines were the clearest about tracking the big picture. She wondered what ends Josefene saw that had her grant Sabel permission to be involved at this level with demons.

A charge came into the air. It was the same charge she could feel during religious ceremonies, political demonstrations, championship football games, and her college days of spin-the-bottle: pure energy ready to be discharged for one use or another.

"Now," Jacob said. "We have called power for you. Use it."

Sabel was glad for her obsessive rereading of everything she had on the topic of demon summoning. Start in her mother tongue, she remembered that, because you didn't want to misspeak anything during a conjuration. Conjure the spirits by their obedience to the patriarchs, she remembered. It was all so Western, old white male that she almost couldn't bring herself to do it. Technically it was old Middle Eastern male, but it still reeked of patriarchal pomp. Only her nerves made her keep a sneer out of her voice.

"I invoke, conjure and command you, spirit, to appear and show yourself visibly to me, before this Circle, in fair and comely shape, without any deformity or torturosity, by your name and in the name which Adam heard and spoke..." and on it went through a recitation of most of the primary stories of the Hebrew Bible, peppered with names for God.

"...and by the dreadful Judgment of God; and by the uncertain sea of glass: which is before the face of the divine Majesty, who is mighty and most powerful. And by the four beasts before the throne, having eyes before and behind, and by the fire round about the throne...

"I command that you make true and faithful answers to all my demands, and to perform all my desires so far as in office you are capable to perform therefore come you peaceably, visible and affable now without delay, to manifest what I desire speaking with a perfect and clear voice, intelligible unto my understanding." The words rolled off her tongue easily enough, but absolutely nothing was happening. What would they do to her if she failed at this?

Say your will, a voice quivered through the room.

Sabel was used to hearing unspoken voices, but this one chilled her. In a spoken voice, an edge of malice came across only as a sound, but she felt this creature's hate like an oil on her skin. She couldn't see much in the central circle except for a dark smoke form about as big as a medium-sized dog. The smoke seemed to be massing on the side of the circle nearest Jacob. That couldn't be good.

"Here," Sabel said. "I called you. Attend to me."

Her heart fluttered between her ears like a trapped bird. How close could it come to her without shutting her down?

Say your will, the voice repeated.

"What demon came through to this world eight nights ago in this city?" Jacob asked before Sabel could speak.

Not the one you called, it said. *A prince who has forgotten his name.*

"But these are the men calling for a demon of power?" Sabel asked.

Yes, and the woman who did not live.

"Why did they call it?" she asked.

To control the minds of their enemies, for greed and gain.

"Where is that demon now?" Jacob asked.

It is where you know it to be, the creature said. Then it turned again to Sabel, *I have answered, release me.*

"Tell me the names of these men," she said.

"No," Jacob countered. "Our energy called you, you'll keep our secret."

"Tell me his name," Sabel said, pointing across the circle at Jacob. She prayed that these men didn't have a gun, because if they did, they would probably shoot her as soon as this was done.

Johnson, the demon said and the name held a strange number of syllables in its accent. *Release me into your world that I may serve you.*

Before she could say the devocation, Jacob stood and cut a hole in the air with his hand. "Get out," he commanded and Sabel watched the cloudy demon flee through that invisible opening, laughing. Great, another demon loose in the city, but she had more immediate concerns. Jacob, who she now also knew as Johnson, stalked around the circle to stop inches from Sabel.

"Why did you ask my name?" he growled.

"You know my name," Sabel said. "I don't like that being a one-way proposition."

"Secrecy is important to us."

"Names are power," Sabel said evenly.

"Indeed." Jacob held out his hand and Sabel stared at it for a moment, trying to figure out why the man didn't just hit her. Then she realized she was supposed to shake hands.

"Welcome," Jacob said, exerting an iron squeeze to Sabel's hand. "Go home and get some sleep, we will need you again soon."

Could it have been pure dumb luck that Jacob took her name question as a power-hungry stunt? But more importantly, wasn't Johnson the name of a VP at Ana's company? She remembered meeting a man by that name at the anniversary party and he'd been the right size to be this man Jacob. Of course there had to be thousands of men named Johnson in the city. She would tell Ana before she went back to work on Monday, but first she wanted to think everything through.

Sabel pulled into her driveway with a throbbing headache and nausea in the pit of her stomach. All she wanted to do was fall into bed and sleep, but first she sent Ana a quick email saying she was home safe. Then she made herself write out the account of the night while eating a hastily compiled sandwich. She left it in the meditation room where Josefene could read it.

When she got into bed, she lay on her back and stared at the ceiling. Men didn't usually bother her. She was used to them in university politics and global politics and she'd seen her share of violent and short-sighted women as well—but something about an organized and secret group of men coming together to amass power that allowed them to control the minds of others—that scared her down to her marrow. She grabbed the extra pillow and rolled on her side, holding it tightly to her chest. She wanted to feel Ana's arms around her blocking out everything, but how likely was it that a woman she'd essentially thrown through a window wanted to be with her?

CHAPTER THIRTEEN

Ana dreamed of shimmering fabrics and the smell of night-blooming jasmine on the warm wind. She stood in the sand outside a tent, the walls puffing lightly in the air's breath, and everything shining like cut glass, or stars inside of crystals. Then she saw a hand come up to push aside the tent flap. From the angle it should have been hers, but it was red-orange and marbled with gold and she knew she was in Abraxas's dream, if demons dreamed, or his memory.

Inside the tent, a bed dominated, surrounded by intricately woven carpets whose threads swam with colored light. Tasseled pillows and thick blankets made a mountain of silk and linen on the bed. All those blankets looked strange in a desert tent, but she could feel the cold bite of the air—on what skin she didn't know, since Abraxas seemed to be made of fire. A shape heaped the blankets and she approached it in Abraxas's dreamed body.

It felt dizzyingly strange to be riding around in him: the way he flowed across the floor without seeming to walk and the glimmer of energy through his body rather than the familiar pulse of blood. Any other dream and she wouldn't have found it unusual to inhabit another body and not be in control of her own actions, but from the days of having him in the back of her mind she now marveled at the reversal and the sensation of sitting back from the eyes and hands, simply watching. Was this how it felt for him?

His hand spread itself on the blanket and the figure beneath stirred and rolled over, pushing back the heavy cloth and brushing the dark hair out of her eyes. Lily looked like she belonged here, surrounded by rich fabrics of bright colors, the low lamplight darkening the color of her skin and the blackness of her hair and eyes. She smiled, eyes half-lidded.

"Am I dreaming?" she asked.

"In a sense," Abraxas said. "We can be together here."

"You brought me into your dream?"

"Basically," he said. His voice sounded rich and warm, not the whisper he used through Ana, but a full man's voice, liquid and accented. "You had some questions for me?"

"And they're best answered in a bed?" she quipped, then paused and opened her eyes wide. "That's why you wouldn't tell me! Of course! You'd think I'd know better at this point. I guess I'm kind of shy around you."

"If you don't—" he started, then paused. "Shy?"

"I've been with men centuries older than me, but not millennia. You're like a force of nature, which, I should add, is what I like about you. I should be the one asking you if you want this." She pushed up on her elbows and the blanket slid off her bare shoulders.

"Beautiful." Abraxas's hand cradled her cheek and Lily's eyes turned to look at him again.

Her arms came up around his neck, pulling him down to her mouth for a kiss that lay them both out on the bed. Ana experienced this from the back of Abraxas's mind and alongside his sensations she felt her own longing unfold like a night-blooming flower—but it wasn't a desire for Lily. She wanted this to be her pressing down on Sabel as they sank together into the bed.

Lily pushed the blankets to one side without breaking the kiss, and helped Abraxas to get under them with her. Ana felt hands on silky skin, the spreading pressure of breasts against a flat, muscular chest. So this is what it's like, some part of her thought, while another wriggled in alarm to feel an erection filling out against Lily's thigh.

Lily's fingers wove themselves into Abraxas's hair, her body small and rounded inside his muscled arms. He felt a little like the body Ana was used to, most of the same basic parts like a head and arms, except that from the knees down she became a million tingling particles running in streamers out into the world, mixing with the fabric of the bed and the very strange outline of Lily's own feet. It had to be a dream, nowhere else could she imagine the sensation of caressing from all directions legs that ended in clawed feet. The actual contact felt interesting, but the idea of it was disgusting enough that Ana turned her attention upward again.

She had wondered what a man's body felt like from the inside. Abraxas had broad shoulders but a narrow waist that made his body into a long plank with its square chest and slim hips. But Ana was surprised to find his nipples were almost as sensitive as hers and hardened against the softness of Lily's breasts.

Again her mind filled with thoughts of Sabel. Her breasts were fuller than Lily's, though not quite as heavy as Ana's own. A pang of need went through her at the memory of kissing Sabel—how exquisite it would be to press together like that without clothing in the way as Abraxas and Lily did now.

Abraxas's long fingers reached up Lily's ribs to cover her breast and stroke in shrinking circles to caress and tug at the nipple. His other hand rubbed down the small of her back, pressing her against his manhood where it lay along her inner thigh. Lily groaned, her lips against his throat, and rolled her hips so that he was rubbing into the warmth between her thigh and her mound. All attention went there. What a wonder to have that desire fill out a length of him, to throb against Lily.

Lily's hands trailed down his back to cup his ass and pull him further on top of her while her lips kneaded the front of his throat. His skin wasn't as solid as human skin and he could feel her lips the moment before she touched him and then experience not only the surface of them, but slightly around the concave sides of them so that he was kissed into as much as kissed upon. He could have been less solid if he wanted, Ana realized, but no more solid than this. He'd done his best in this dream to touch Lily as completely as he could, and for her to have all of him as a physical presence. Lily's skin felt like the wind underneath him. He explored her neck and ears with his lips and the fiery tip of his tongue and edged down to kiss her breasts, but she held him tightly and wouldn't let him.

"You're driving me crazy," she said.

He didn't understand the words but he absorbed the sense of them and flushed with relief to not be holding himself back from the one thing he wanted most. With one hand he spread her lips and felt the thick liquid that pooled there, spreading it liberally around the opening. Then he stroked up and down with his fingertips, circling the areas that would give her the most pleasure, until her head rocked back with a groan. Ana found a moment to wonder that a demon would know about a woman's clitoris, her attention riveted to the tips of his fingers and the slick satin of Lily's labia.

A spectator who kept fighting with herself to look away while unable to remove her attention in the least, she felt Abraxas's hand reach for his aching member, rubbing the tip with Lily's wetness. It really did ache, not like pain but a fullness, a heavy longing. As he guided the tip against Lily, liquid fire ran down the insides of his thighs, up the inside of his belly to his throat. Lily's lips parted over him and he slid an inch into her. She anchored her hands on his ass and worked herself down over him, the most sensitive part of his body being slowly enfolded in hot wet silk. No wonder men could come so quickly, Ana thought. But Abraxas didn't, though she could feel the pressure building in his pelvis, he took a deep breath and slid halfway out of Lily and then deeper. Each time he pushed back into her, electric currents of delight shot up through him, settling in his gut in a swelling pool of pleasure and increasing desire.

Lily had her legs all the way open to his hips, her calves curling around the back of his thighs to pull him closer when he thrust in. Her arms came around his sides to clutch at his back and shoulder blades as he rocked against her. She had been moaning as he went into her, but now her voice rose in pitch until she yelled and bucked against him. He brought his hands from around her shoulders to grasp her hips and thrust into her quickly until the electric mass between his hips exploded out into her, his muscles clenching like a fist, jerking inside her, hot and liquid.

Wild joy fireworked through Ana, exploding in her belly, center, heart, throat, head. She heard her own voice yell and came alive in her own body, sitting up, dizzy, room spinning, sheets under her hands.

She was on her feet in an instant and then she didn't know where to go. She stared around the room and settled on her jeans and T-shirt thrown over a chair. She put those on and went down two flights of stairs and got into her car. Then she realized that not only was she barefoot, but she could hardly drive over to Sabel's place and pound on the door and...what?

Hoping that she was far enough from the second floor that the sound wouldn't wake Lily where she slept in Ruben's room, she beat the heels of her hands against the steering wheel and yelled in wordless frustration.

* * *

Ana woke up in the early morning light, still in jeans and T-shirt and facedown on her bed where she'd thrown herself after coming back up from yelling in the car. She remembered the dream created by Abraxas and the barely banked coals of desire warmed in her gut. She thought about Sabel and the moments when her tightly wound discipline cracked open. She was always beautiful, but it was her surprised laughter or unguarded emotion that made Ana's heart clench and want to hold that moment close. What excuse could she come up with to see her again this weekend?

That question opened up a can of worms because as soon as her brain heard "weekend," it wanted to remind her of everything she meant to get done in these two days. She sighed, rolled over and sat up.

"Abraxas, make it shut up, my mind is really obnoxious," she whispered.

Says who?

"My mind says it. Oh. Can I ever say anything outside my mind?"

That's an answer for another day.

"How do I shut it off?"

You don't. Stop paying attention to it.

That was like asking her to stop listening to a radio playing in her ear. The dream of the night before returned in its entirety and she blushed even though she was alone in her room. Was it easier for Abraxas to bring Lily into his dream because she stayed in the same house?

"Abraxas, last night...?"

He seemed to shift around and then settle into a mass of silence even though he spoke. *You were in the dream? I didn't intend that, I apologize.*

She thought about telling him not to worry about it; she'd sort of enjoyed the experience. But he was so quiet she thought that saying anything at all about it might worry him more rather than less. She got out of bed, brewed tea, put in a load of laundry and then stood in the living room looking around herself. The peace was nice, but boring.

Ana decided she did have some nagging questions. "Abraxas, can you take me back to the desert?" she asked.

Come here yourself.

Ana closed her eyes and tried to remember what it looked like, the long curving dunes and the hot white light over everything. The picture that formed in her mind was small, a memory, not something she could step into, not the place where Abraxas brought her. Why wouldn't he help her and just take her there as he'd done before? Was this another one of his teacherly riffs? Ana craved what he knew and resented him for awakening that desire in her when he seemed determined to be so obtuse about fulfilling it.

She let the heat of anger ripple through her, just under her skin like fire, like the heat of the sun. She stopped trying to picture the desert and let that heat rise up in her, rippling over her from the inside out until she felt it beating down on her.

When she opened her eyes, she was standing on the dune. In the distance she saw round tents, tassels off the tops flopping limply in the hint of a breeze.

You'll learn to walk outside your body yet, his voice said from beside her.

As usual, he stood just outside her range of vision, a wavering heat at the edge of the seen. But his voice tickled the side of her ear with its warming breath. Everything here was hot today and she wiped the back of her hand across her sweating forehead.

"Why is it so hot?"

You chose midday. The heat is a function of the way you came.

"You have a really amazing habit of answering my questions in a way that isn't an answer at all."

And you have an amazing habit of listening to my answers in a way that ceases to make them answers.

Ana knew she didn't have to voice her annoyance at that comment for him to perceive it. It still galled her that he was privy to every one of her thoughts. And for someone with access to her innermost thoughts, he didn't criticize her nearly as much as she expected. She was waiting for a wave of rebuke to crash over her from him, unconsciously holding still for the time he could no longer stand to be in her head another minute and would come exploding out of her with bruisingly accurate recriminations. The longer he stayed in her without that, the more anxious she felt.

With that realization she had to look at him, to see the creature who could be so frustrating to her, so intimate, so upsetting. She couldn't stand that he would know her so well and she had never even looked in his face. She didn't care what he looked like, horned or barbed, made of animal parts or decayed flesh. It would be better if he was awful, then she'd have something to hold over him.

Ana whirled on her heel. He moved back a step under the force of her glare. His body rose up from the ground like a pillar of flame, but the tongues of fire licked around the outlines of shoulders and long arms with the rise of lean muscle, a broad flat chest, and a face: a face in the flame that looked at her with thick lips open in surprise.

"You're not awful," she said.

Did you want me to be?

"Sort of. You get to see everything about me and now you're actually good-looking. I thought I'd have something on you."

He looked down and so did she to see that he had no feet. Instead he had something like a cloud of electricity, snakes of fire and light that cut the air between the ground and place mid-calf where he began to be constituted of fire.

"Those aren't so bad," she said, still trying to figure out what they were made out of.

I'm glad you think so, he said.

"You're not really what I expected from a demon," she told him. "You're kind of a good guy, unless you're the prince of lies or something."

He folded his arms across his chest in a gesture that actually made him look a little like a genie from a bottle. On impulse, Ana stepped forward and touched his arm. It was hot, like liquid satin. Her fingers sank a little way into the flame and then struck a solid surface. His fire on her skin didn't feel any hotter than the air around them and she ran her fingers across the top of his forearm and arm to his shoulder. The longer she looked at him the clearer his face became. A narrow, square jaw, aquiline nose, slightly almond eyes and thick lips all painted in ruddy flame that danced less and consolidated itself into a mass very much like skin only marbled with fire colors.

"You're beautiful," she said.

He smiled. "It takes your eyes to see me this way. Some people would be terrified, some see me as a consuming fire, or a storm, to others I look darker, like an angel of death."

"What do you mean? Can you tell me and actually make sense?"

He tipped his head back, laughing, a throaty sound that reverberated with the moods she'd felt from him inside her mind. "I'll talk, you make sense," he said. "You're seeing me with your beauty, and I see you with mine."

"Wow, I must look great."

"You do. You have been so afraid that I will criticize you, that I will have seen the truth about you and will bring horrors into the light. You think that you are dangerous, harmful, uncivilized, brutal, disgusting, but that is your own warped vision of yourself. You think that because you once took a knife to your brother in anger that you are that child forever. You have been frozen inside yourself as the girl who hurt her brother, the girl who was beaten, the girl who is afraid she deserved it by being monstrous. You have been blind to your own majesty. Let me show you what I see."

Stunned, Ana nodded. His fingers lifted her chin and he lay his lips along hers; unlike any human kiss, when his lips covered hers a wind pressed her on all sides and she fell out of herself, landing in the sand. She looked up at herself.

A whirlwind of colors and patterns shot through with gold ribbons trailed out into the air like a dye dropped in water. A bit of radiance and rage had shaped a life of pain and struggle, then formed all that into this person who would stand against killers. An indomitable spirit in which every petty anger and judgment shone like a jewel, not because she operated in spite of these limitations, not in condemnation of them, but because of them, because each little piece made her who she was: cheating on a math test in fifth grade, stealing from her parents, lying to men and women she slept with, driving a knife through her brother's hand: every large and small moment, every drop of hatred, anger and fear was deeply loved.

She couldn't understand it. She could hardly watch it. All those years she'd hated herself for things she had done and now

Abraxas could look on all of them and love her. Abraxas who had lived thousands of years and had traveled in the realm of the dead, who trafficked with angels and devils and wise men of the ages—he loved this mess of a woman because of the mess. That mess had been created by the same source that created the sunrise, the oceans, music and mathematics and all culture, and it was no less beautiful to him. To his eyes, it wasn't even a mess, it was a pattern with purpose and intention. Everything she thought was a mistake was a beautiful swirl in the pattern, a new creation.

Ana felt herself falling apart; the world she knew shredding around her. His lips still on hers, Abraxas inhaled and she was drawn up into herself again. Her knees buckled and he caught her against his chest. Ana rested her cheek on his shoulder while his arms encircled her waist. Patterns of electricity and heat coursed through her.

"Oh my God," she said. "It's like that?"

"Yes," he said.

"Because of who you are?"

"That's the love of the divine for creation. Anyone who has eyes to see can look through that love."

Ana couldn't say anything. She shut her eyes and rested against Abraxas's chest, thinking she might just stay there forever regardless of what happened in the rest of the world.

At some point the desert slipped away, and the feel of Abraxas's body with it, and the couch rose under her again. When she opened her eyes on her living room, lying in a sunbeam, she felt as peaceful as she could ever remember feeling. Even the inside of her head sounded quiet. Nothing familiar looked the same. She went from room to room staring in wonder at the graceful arc of a lamp, the sheen on the floor tiles, the pleasure of a refrigerator to keep food cold and an oven to cook it, the miracle of the kitchen tap, the beauty of window glass and then outside the almost unbearable glory of trees.

* * *

When Sabel woke, it was already well into Sunday morning and she had two text messages from Ana, the first checking in and the second suggesting they meet for lunch. She gave her a quick call to pick a time and a place. On the phone, Ana sounded distracted, but when Sabel walked into the restaurant for lunch, she looked attentive, much more so than Sabel felt. Her dreams had been restless and leapt back and forth from demons to Ana.

"I ordered us an appetizer, I hope that's okay," Ana said as Sabel sat down. "I've been starving lately. I think Abraxas revs up my metabolism. How was the thing last night?"

"They took me up to a studio apartment and asked me to do a summoning with them." Sabel looked around at the neighboring tables but Ana had positioned them well and it was unlikely that the other chatty diners would hear them. Of course if anyone did overhear, they'd probably think the two women were chatting about a book or movie. "The, um, demon confirmed that they're right to think the other guy is with you."

"Well that's no worse."

"I asked for the name of the leader."

Ana sat forward. "And?"

"Johnson."

She hit the table with her right palm. "Charles Johnson, it has to be!"

"There are a lot of people named Johnson in the world," Sabel cautioned. "But I thought the same thing."

"I wondered if Helen was involved with someone at the company. Kerry said she thought Helen originally got promoted because she was hooking up with an executive. I took it for sour grapes, but over time it seemed to ring true. Plus Johnson has been trying to get Detlefsen to agree to sell and there's a lot of money in it if he does. It has to be him."

It was hard for Sabel to gauge how impetuous Ana could be with this information. At times Ana seemed to understand the kind of information they needed to get before they could turn the summoners over to the police, and other times it looked like she was about to charge in with guns blazing.

"We can't do anything until we have proof," Sabel said.

The server arrived with a large, shallow, white bowl filled with mussels and steaming with the scents of wine and garlic.

"An appetizer?" Sabel said to Ana with a smile. She thought, but didn't add aloud, *More like sex on a plate*. Muscles across her midback loosened up a bit and she leaned against the chair and let the small tense places she hadn't been aware of slowly give up their death grip.

Ana grinned back and picked up a mussel. Sabel tried not to watch the strong line of her jaw as she tipped her head up and ate it.

"I like them better than oysters," Ana said.

"You're in a good mood."

Ana's cheeks colored and she glanced away. "I guess I'm getting used to all this a little. He's not a bad guy for a…spirit, demon, whatever. I always felt like there was more to life, you know, and now this is all starting to make some kind of sense. When did you come out as a witch?"

"It's hard to say," Sabel said and then paused. This was the first time she'd been in public with someone to whom she could tell some of the real stories of her life. In the past, with other women, this was the point where she talked about discovering Wicca and other goddess religions and practicing them in secret during her last few years of high school. It was in the neighborhood of the truth, but it never felt really satisfying to talk about because she didn't get to say: yes, magic is real and I can do it and maybe you could too.

Ana was waiting for her to say more and she smiled a little. "I don't usually get to tell people the truth," she said. "I don't know where to start."

"Maybe at the beginning?" Ana suggested.

"I'm not sure where that is. When I was quite young, I came back in time from an older age to prepare myself for what I would learn when I met the Hecatine witches. We work in a field of magic that deals with time and information, so the beginning is both before and after I met them."

"You can time travel?"

"Not physically, but with my consciousness, yes. The easiest way is to connect with yourself through time, younger and older selves. Actually quite a few people do it without ever realizing it. When I hear stories of people who say that at a dark time in their lives they suddenly knew it was going to get better or they felt like some force was taking care of them—sometimes that's their future self reaching back. When I was a kid and I needed help, that opened me up to having my own self come to me with aid. The only unusual part of my story is that when I was seventeen, I realized it was me who had been coming to help me and I started to use that power intentionally."

"Did you ever cheat on tests by telling yourself the answers?" Ana asked with a mischievous grin.

"Once," Sabel told her. "But it wasn't very useful because I still had to learn all the answers and I like to learn. Mostly I gave myself spiritual practices to study and lots of reassuring talks until I could get to college."

"Rough home life?"

"Not like yours," Sabel said and then added, "I'm sorry, I shouldn't have said that. I mean that mine was just restrictive. Magic was the only thing my parents didn't control because they didn't understand it…they didn't see it as real."

She didn't know how to describe it to Ana. Her household hadn't been strictly regimented but the expectations were so high and clear that there was little room for variance. The trap wasn't obvious because she'd been born inside of it. Her parents always told her she could be anything she wanted, but they meant anything inside of a very narrow range of possibilities. Disappoint the family and she'd find herself a bright kid with no wage earning skills and no money—that was always clear.

"And yet you didn't grow up to be a party animal." Ana tried to keep her tone light, but Sabel saw the tightness around her eyes and kicked herself for bringing up Ana's childhood.

"You just missed my midtwenties," Sabel told her. "You'd be surprised."

"Maybe you can take me back in time and show me."

Sabel laughed. "I can't time travel physically, though I wonder…"

"What do you do with magic?" Ana asked.

"I can stutter time a little, but that just looks like me moving quickly or anticipating what's going to happen because I have more conscious time than you're seeing. And if the temporal weather is just right I can do a few fancier tricks like slowing or speeding time in an area, like a room, or even stepping out of the timestream completely."

"But Lily still got you in a headlock," Ana pointed out.

"I was distracted by the part where you went through a window. Plus she's pretty fast as a crossbreed."

Sabel didn't add that the magic triggered in Lily's store when Ana went through the window also started the leash constricting in her chest. Some of her shortness of breath hadn't been from Lily's choke hold.

"You knew that about her?" Ana asked.

"Not until she had me in the headlock, but then it was obvious. She's pretty strong for a plain human of her size."

Sabel ate another mussel. They were incredibly good with the base layer of salty flavor from the mussels themselves overlaid with sweet tomato, pungent garlic and acidic wine.

"Should we skip entrees and get a second bowl of these?" she asked.

"I love the way you think," Ana said and then turned away quickly looking for their server.

Sabel couldn't hide her smile, but she transmuted it into a smaller gesture than the huge grin she felt. It just wasn't the time, but she hoped there would be a time...

"So you can give yourself information from one time to another? Can't you just tell yourself who the summoners are?" Ana asked when she had their order in and returned her attention to the table.

"I can only pass information that doesn't change what already happened. I can't change the timestream. So, for example, I couldn't tell myself of a few weeks ago that you were going to be kidnapped because then I would have stopped something that, from our perspective now, has already happened. But I could tell myself that I was going to learn magic because I had already learned magic in the future to be able to tell myself that I was going to learn it."

"That made almost no sense to me."

Sabel laughed quietly. "It rarely does. I may not be able to tell myself who the summoners are because in the future I don't know, but it's equally possible that I do know and I can't communicate back to this time. Not all times are equally easy to reach."

"Do you know when you'll die?" Ana asked. "That would be really creepy."

Sabel shook her head. "No, a person's death is a time that's almost impossible to bridge into."

"But if you talk to your future self and she's like sixty, then you know you'll live that long."

"You can't see the future clearly from your present. My future self can give me information but I don't see her or know how old she is. And I think if I tried to tell myself about my death, the information simply wouldn't pass. The timestream is very powerful and obeys its own rules."

"Oh." Ana sounded disappointed.

"If you keep asking me questions about time magic, we're going to have to initiate you as a Hecatine witch."

They finished the second plate of mussels while keeping the conversation to light topics, then split the bill and walked out of the restaurant into the shopping arcade to which it was attached.

"We need a way to get the police to search Johnson's house," Ana said as they wandered slowly down the colonnade. "I wonder if we could do an anonymous call or something."

"It would be helpful to know exactly where he's hiding the summoning stuff, otherwise we just tip him off. And if it's not him or not at his house…"

"I could try talking to him on Monday, maybe drop some hints."

"Dangerous."

"But if it is him, he already knows I have Abraxas. Oooh, look at those boots."

Ana stopped in front of a shop window and Sabel paused next to her. They were nice boots, but what she really noticed was that after a moment Ana leaned close enough that their shoulders touched. Then Ana's fingers touched her palm and slid down until their fingers interlaced. Sabel squeezed her hand to show that the contact was more than welcome.

Their shoulders were already touching, Ana's slightly higher than hers. She leaned into Ana and a days-old tension flowed out of her body. Then she felt the band across her chest start to constrict. She ignored it. The stupid leash and its hair-trigger sensor. Had it gone off when Abraxas stepped out of Ana in the bookstore? No, because she was standing at least five feet away from Sabel. But now this simple touch put Sabel close enough to the threatening power of a demon that the stupid thing decided it was a danger.

She dropped Ana's hand and stepped away from her. The second band of the leash was beginning to close around her upper chest. The pain was blunt and diffused through her chest, but it already stopped her from taking full breaths.

"Can Abraxas protect you?" Sabel asked, trying to ignore the building pressure.

Ana paused and then answered, "He says he can, plus there will be people around."

"Let's think about it."

She gestured to Ana to come with her and started walking in the direction of her car. All three bands were pressing on her now. Stepping away from Ana slowed the compression, but it wouldn't stop and reverse until she could get home and apply the right magic, or until she passed out and some time elapsed, but she didn't really want to collapse in the middle of a mall. How long did she have until she couldn't talk?

She stopped outside the elevator to the parking garage. Her chest felt like someone was standing on it. From her lower ribs up to her throat, she ached and she was starting to fear she wouldn't be able to keep the pain from showing on her face for much longer.

"Thanks for suggesting the mussels," she managed. "I had a good time."

"Me too." Ana looked confused. "I'll see you…?"

"Call me."

She stepped into the elevator before Ana could try to hug her. When the doors closed, she put a hand to the wall to support herself. She was gasping in shallow breaths. If she had more air, she'd have cursed Josefene and this truly stupid magic.

* * *

When it came down to actually walking through the halls to Johnson's office on Monday morning, all the bravado Ana had been building up over the course of Sunday leaked away. As soon as Sabel had said his name, Ana knew she wanted to confront him, but now with her heart pounding, she wondered if maybe Sabel had been right that they should have come up with a more circumspect plan. Sabel had tried to talk her out of it when she called her Sunday evening to see when they would meet up again.

Ana wanted to look Johnson in the eyes. On the bright side, the fact that he was Jacob made it even clearer that she could fully trust Detlefsen, which she'd wanted to do but had held herself back just in case.

Charles Johnson had a corner office in the sales department that he oversaw. It was about the same size as Detlefsen's, but positioned on a wall of the building with more windows, so it looked larger. He had the same executive furniture as every other VP in the company, a U-shaped, cherry wood desk with a hutch on the wall-facing side, and a five-shelf bookcase. Detlefsen's held books, Johnson's held sales awards. He also had a small round table in his office with four chairs around it, plus two chairs facing his desk. He clearly liked to hold meetings in his office.

When he saw her in his doorway he gestured her into a chair. "Are you feeling better?" he asked.

"Yes, much better. Thanks for asking." She paused, not knowing what to say next, though she'd practiced the conversation in her head a hundred times. "I think I have something you lost," she said finally.

He moved a stack of papers from the front of his desk to the back, muscles shifting under the brushed cotton of his shirt as he spun in his chair to set the papers down, then turned back to Ana. Three more piles sat on the front surface of his desk and a couple on the back.

"I can't imagine what," he said.

"Then perhaps you should call your friend Drake and ask him if he's lost something."

He leaned back in his chair casually, but his face had lost its color. "You want to return the item?" he asked.

"Let me ask you something," Ana said, feeling stronger in the face of his fear. "What did you want this demon for in the first place? Was it worth the price you paid?"

He frowned at her use of the word demon and looked around, as if he could see through the walls. Maybe he could. He shouldn't have anything to worry about—anyone who overheard them would only think they were nuts, or role-playing geeks. She could see he was considering whether or not to answer the question, so she prodded. "Look Johnson, I'm eager to get out of this and once I'm out I don't intend to ever think about it again. And frankly, anyone I did mention it to would think I'd lost my mind."

"Then you probably shouldn't talk about it." He stood up from his desk and crossed his office to shut the door. "Ana, it wasn't my choice to involve you in this, but I think I can help you out." As he turned back around, he reached under his shirt and pulled out a large, flat amulet. It had squiggly words all around it and symbols in the center and he held it out, speaking a word that reverberated in the air like a shot. Ana opened her mouth to comment, but Abraxas shushed her.

Act paralyzed, he said. *I want to see what he does.*

Ana froze, wishing she'd shut her mouth first, but it was too late. Johnson smiled and touched his palm to the top of her head like a father patting a startled child.

I hope you know what you're doing, she told Abraxas. *Because this is uncomfortable.*

Abraxas ran through her nerves and muscles, holding her motionless in a way that she never could by herself.

Johnson picked up his phone and dialed. "Ana's in my office with the prize," he said. "She's immobilized." Then he paused and listened for a minute. "All right," he said. "No problem, we'll be there in ten minutes."

He opened his file drawer and pulled out a large, green bottle, uncorking it while saying a few words Ana didn't understand.

Do these demons all ride around in bottles? she asked Abraxas. *I don't want to do this again.*

I would like to test this one, see what I can learn from him.

Ana gave a prolonged mental sigh. At least it would be an opportunity to try the lessons Abraxas had been giving her. A thin vapor streamed out of the top of the bottle, across the desk to her.

This time, since she expected the pain, she thought it might hurt less, but it didn't. Abraxas's immobilization prevented her from screaming as the pain ripped down her throat into her lungs. From there, ribbons of agony rolled out her limbs. But this time, under the sheer repulsion of it, she actually felt curiosity. She could experience her mind thrashing around and still have a little awareness left over to voluntarily touch the pain and explore the size of it, the dimensions. It had edges, it didn't engulf her whole body as she first thought; the parts of her that hurt were limited. Her skin didn't hurt, nor did her head, just her muscles and lungs, and then her belly. Her nose felt fine, she thought and was almost able to smile about it.

As she examined the edges of her pain, it started to recede. It shrank inside her until it localized behind her left lung, pressing hard against her back, but bearable. Abraxas held her up during the attack but he no longer immobilized her and she lifted her head to smile at Johnson.

As her mouth turned up, the smug satisfaction on Johnson's face vanished. He pressed his lips together so tightly they wrinkled and whitened. He looked sick.

Abraxas extended out from her, tickling her skin, his cloudy form enshrouding her body. When he spoke, his voice came from somewhere above her head.

Tell your master he can't hope to take me. If I come at all, it will be willingly. If he makes a good offer.

Then he swirled back down into her. Ana pushed off the chair and stepped toward the door, more slowly than she intended because of the stabbing pain in the area of her left kidney.

"Ana?" Johnson asked. "What do you think you're doing?"

She turned and glared at him. "I really don't appreciate being possessed," she said. "And I wasn't well-disposed to begin with, so maybe we'd better drop this for now."

"You don't know what kind of deal you're making. You can't just go around in life with that...thing in you."

"Watch me."

She opened the door and stalked, as best she could, into the hallway. From her cubicle she grabbed her purse and beelined for the elevator before Johnson could recover himself and come after her.

In the elevator, she let herself sag against the wall. "Shit that hurts."

You did very well, Abraxas said.

"I never could have done it without you," she told him, wondering if there was a camera in the elevator through which someone could see her talking to herself.

Practice, he said in his smiling tone.

"Just get me to my car."

CHAPTER FOURTEEN

She called Sabel on her cell phone on the way and told her it had gone well and that Johnson had called someone when he thought he had her immobilized. Sabel volunteered to talk to her police contact and see if she could find out who. Ana didn't notice until she'd pulled up in front of Lily's store the familiar truck that had been following her. Despite the shooting pain, she jumped out of the driver's seat and spun around to it before the driver could get out.

"Gunnar, what the hell?"

"Followed you," he said.

"Why?"

"You're in trouble."

"I'm fine," she insisted.

"I see that." He was out of the truck now, leaning against the door, his baggy jeans riding low on his hips and bunching around the ankles of his work boots.

Ana found herself looking at him for what seemed like the first time. In the past all she'd seen was his sloping left shoulder and the scars, visible and otherwise, that she'd cut into his body. She hadn't noticed that his weathered face was good-looking, from his solid jaw to the way his eyes crinkled when he tried not to smile. He had his thumbs hooked into the pockets of his jeans, long-fingers splayed on his narrow thighs. Absent the burning memories of her own guilt, she could see how he'd grown up into a careful, introspective man. She'd taken his silence as a reprimand to her and everyone else living, but now she wondered if he was just shy or didn't believe in talking much. He looked comfortable in his body. He'd told her three months back that his wife was expecting, and she could imagine those hands around a baby—what a father he would be, strong and tender. Somehow he had erased from himself the traces of their childhood, before she could erase them from herself.

Ana blinked away the tears in her eyes. "Gunnar, want to come in? Meet a friend?"

He shrugged, but she caught the corner of his mouth turning up. "Sure."

She took the steps slowly and Gunnar reached out to cradle her elbow. "Someone hurt you?" he asked.

"More complicated than that. Actually, it's all kind of weird."

"You always were," he said.

Ana laughed, which made her grab her side with a gasp at the pain. He opened the door for her and Lily looked up from the counter. Ana made quick introductions and then got to the heart of the thing. "Johnson tried to get us with a demon but Abraxas seems to have it trapped in my left kidney, which I'd like to add hurts like a bitch, so if you could get it out I'd be a lot happier."

Pain doesn't prevent happiness, Abraxas said.

Okay, okay, she shot back. *I get it, Little Buddha. But can we get this thing out?*

Lily ushered them to the back of the store and then disappeared even further back.

"Demon?" Gunnar asked.

"It's a long story," Ana said. Lily saved her from having to tell any of it by returning with a stone box.

"Let's try this one. Ana, just lie back and shut your eyes, Abraxas and I will do the heavy lifting. With the ban on summoning in the city, they should be running out of these little guys."

Ana closed her eyes, grateful for the rest. She felt a stab in her left side and then another, and took a moment to enjoy the irony that she was sitting here with Gunnar who had a curving scar that ran up from his lower rib on that side, which she had given him, and now she got to feel that pain. It made those scattered bits of her life make more sense. As the little demon was torn out of her body, she opened her eyes.

Gunnar sat forward in his chair, hands clasped between his knees, his mouth in a single, straight line. "Demon," he said when he saw Ana looking at him. "Never saw one before."

She laughed. "Well there are plenty around, apparently." Then she looked at Lily who was sitting on the table, one boot resting on the seat of a chair across from her. "What are we going to do next? Sabel's trying to trace the call that Johnson made, but I want another way to find out who he's working with."

"I could follow him when he leaves your building," Lily suggested.

Gunnar looked so confused by this interchange that Ana quickly summarized the background information about Helen having been killed by a group of demon summoners of which Johnson was the leader. He nodded as she spoke and didn't seem nearly as startled by the demon summoning part as he should have been.

When she finished, he said, "Following's dangerous. Criminals develop good paranoia."

"Could we track him with magic?" Ana asked. "Don't you and Abraxas have some woo-woo thing that would do the trick?"

"He'd probably know what it was," Lily said. "He's not new to this."

"Transmitter," Gunnar said.

They both looked at him. He smiled, a sort of lopsided, bashful affair that raised the left side of his mouth and lowered his eyes. "Made a few as a joke last Christmas. Nothing James Bond. Good to about a hundred and fifty yards. You can follow out of sight. Don't know how you'll get it on him, though, it's not small."

"How big is it?" Lily asked.

"Cell phone sized."

"Hmm, we could maybe disguise it as a large amulet and tell Johnson we've put Abraxas in it," Lily said. "We could even use that small demon he used to make it look animated, but I think he'd figure out pretty quickly that it was the wrong one. But maybe he'd have to take it to wherever he does magic and then we could tip off the police."

"Why don't I just slip it into his briefcase?" Ana suggested.

Gunnar looked at Lily who shrugged.

"If you can do it without being seen, it's less risky than the amulet ploy," she said.

"His admin likes me. I'm sure I could just find out when he has a meeting and slip into his office. When can you get us the tracker?"

"A day," Gunnar said. "I've got an old one around. Have to tune it up."

"Bring it by here and show me how to use it," Lily said. "Once it's in place, I can follow him for a day or two and we'll have a good idea of all the possible locations. Ana, can you stop by tomorrow for that other project we're working on?"

She meant the project to remove Abraxas from her body to another, more fitting, vessel. Ana agreed readily.

Gunnar walked her out to her car. She hugged him hard, smelling the leather and soap scent of his neck. He thumped her back with the ball of his hand. "Gonna be okay," he said.

Again he watched her drive away. He was scared for her, she realized, and almost turned the car around to go reassure him, except that she couldn't think of anything really reassuring to say.

* * *

The next day, Ana called in sick. That afternoon Lily took her to the second floor over the bookstore. Instead of going to the sunporch she'd used for banishing the small demon the day she and Ana met, Lily moved to the center of the room and picked up the coffee table, which looked far too heavy for her slim frame to heft.

Here in her own home she didn't wear her boots and Ana couldn't help watching those inhuman feet move across the rug. With each step, the first segment of the three forward digits and the one backward-facing all curled down a fraction to grip the carpet below them. Lily carried the coffee table to a wall of the dining room, each step impressively solid. Then she picked up a smaller end table and put it in the eastern part of the living room. Ana realized that on any surface she could grip, Lily would be much harder to knock over than a person with regular feet. That didn't make her feet attractive, but Ana could be open to appreciating them.

"Sit down," she told Ana. "It'll take me a little while to set up."

Ana settled into a golden armchair while Lily stepped lightly into the kitchen. Ana realized she was used to the clomp of Lily's boots. Barefoot, Lily seemed to float above the smooth motion of her legs.

Lily had called the previous evening, after Ana got off the phone from bringing Sabel up to date on Gunnar's plan, and explained that she was set up for the ritual that would draw Abraxas out of Ana and into another vessel. She hadn't wanted to get into all that in front of Gunnar, but it was time to give this a try. Ana felt a pang of loss at the thought of Abraxas no longer existing inside her, but ignored it because this was clearly the best option for all of them. The summoners would have much less reason to hunt her. Plus Lily could take him and run away until he grew more powerful and could take on these demon-summoning men on his own. Johnson might try to come after her, but clearly his people wanted Abraxas. If Ana could prove she didn't have him and demonstrate that she could expose them if they came after her, maybe they would leave her alone.

Plus there was Sabel and if she no longer had Abraxas in her head with her...assuming Sabel was still interested. Sabel was hard to read and the last time they saw each other, one moment she was holding hands and getting close and then she was walking away again so abruptly that Ana couldn't put a finger on what had changed.

Are you looking forward to this? she asked Abraxas.

His answer surprised her. *No.*

I thought you wanted to get out of me.

He didn't say anything and Ana wondered what the deal was. Had Lily picked another vessel he didn't like? Or did it spring from her visit to him in the desert? When he held her, did he feel the same connection with her? Ana didn't want to think about what it would be like to live without him now, but she would manage. Just a few days ago she couldn't wait to get rid of him. She tried to call back that feeling now, but it didn't come.

Lily set out items on the little table: a stone box, a pendant, a cup, a blade, a censer of incense smoking with juniper, a bowl of sand, and a stone. Ana watched her place each one carefully in relationship with the others and wanted to ask what they were all for, but Lily seemed so intent on the creation of the table that she didn't dare.

Finally Lily motioned her forward and sat down, cross-legged on the carpet. "Face me," she said.

Ana bent down to sit across from her, trying to ignore the way Lily's finger-long, scaled toes stuck out from under her knees. Occasionally one foot would flex unconsciously and it took all of Ana's willpower not to stare.

Oblivious, Lily reached out with her left hand and touched the table, then settled that hand back in her lap.

"What do we do?" Ana asked.

"Just listen to the sound of my voice," Lily said.

That didn't seem hard. Lily had a great voice, low and throaty, and now she started a chant at the bass of her register, rising and falling like a boat on water. It sounded so different from the chant Johnson had used to call the demon. His voice had been imploring and demanding, power overlaying anger. Lily's words were calm and certain, but they held another quality to them, a reverence. She was praying.

Slowly, Lily reached over to the table and picked up the stone box, setting it in front of Ana. Then she lifted the amulet and placed it inside the box, with the lid resting at the side of the box.

"Stand up," Lily said. "Step back." Ana did so, facing Lily across six feet of space with the box on the floor between them. Lily continued to chant and Ana could hear Abraxas mentioned regularly.

He began flowing off her like mist over water, accompanied by a undercurrent of grief. *Don't,* she told herself, *this is best for everyone, don't bother wishing otherwise. Do you really want to be inhabited by a demon?* Days ago the answer seemed obvious. She remembered the first time she met Lily in the bookstore, how the woman had said this was an opportunity, and Ana had begun to understand how that could be true. Now that she had acclimated to the alien sensations, she enjoyed Abraxas's thoughts in her mind, his running commentary at points in her life, the level of intimacy she never believed could exist outside of an intimate relationship. But what would she lose if she kept that?

Ana watched him form in the middle of the floor. He didn't look as indistinct as he had even two days ago. Perhaps it was because she had seen him in the desert as the full man carved out of flame. The cloudy mass of him came together into a solid, dense form the color of a thundercloud with ripples of red fire underneath the gray skin. His eyes were defined, dark-lidded, almond-shaped orbs of golden fire. Only his feet remained indistinct, serpents of lightning running into the floor.

"Abraxas," she said without thinking.

He turned and met her gaze, heat running under her skin from the blaze in those flaming eyes. She cast her vision away from him, to the chair, the window, and then the altar. The strangest fingers touched the middle of her chest over her heart, like being touched by smoke concentrated with the heat of a fire, but without burning, soft as a cloud but completely unyielding. Ana looked up to see Abraxas's eyes searching her face.

"You can touch me," she said.

"Apparently." His voice still wasn't human, but it lost the whispering quality. Its tones sounded strong and clear, too many different sounds to be a man's voice, but close.

She reached out a hand for his chest, but her fingertips passed through him. Disappointed, she dropped her hand.

"The box," she said and shook her head, trying to sort out the words she wanted to use.

"You don't want me to go?"

"Does it matter what I want? I'm supposed to be aware but not caught up in my stuff and all that, right?"

His thundercloud lips smiled. "Not right now," he said. "Do you want me to stay within you?"

She knew the answer the moment he asked the question but she made herself stop and consider. This choice could cost her not only her safety but her life as she knew it. And yet, she could work it all out, couldn't she? Maybe he could go somewhere when Sabel was around—into a dream with Lily even. Maybe she could make him stand outside the bedroom door if it ever got that far.

Did she really want Abraxas enough to go on sharing her body with him? But it wasn't just Abraxas himself; since he'd come into her life, she had been terrified, in pain, upset, furious, but brilliantly alive. Was life about sitting in a cubicle sending out news releases on new technology? Not Ana's life.

Her eyes flicked across the room to Lily. Would it be better for her if Ana told Abraxas to go into the box? Certainly that made the relationships clear and easy, but Ana realized she didn't care about easy. She wasn't willing to sacrifice her relationship with Abraxas for comfort or safety, any of those qualities. He had asked her if she knew the desires of her soul and—although she couldn't understand how she did—she knew that she had already chosen him. If she told him she didn't want him to stay with her, that would be the crowning lie of her life that would reinforce every other lie she had ever told. But if she spoke the truth...

"Yes," she said. "Stay with me. Teach me. I choose you."

"It won't be easy. I'll need more from you. I will demand and disrupt your life."

"Do I get the same from you?" she asked.

"Always," he said. "I cannot give you anything else."

Ana found herself smiling. "I may not know what I'm getting myself into," she said. "But neither do you."

His eyes flickered at her and the black lips pulled back in a smile to show teeth of golden fire. "You're right."

"What do I do?"

"Open your mouth," he said.

She did.

His fingers on her chest, his face, his torso, everything swirled into a funnel cloud that poured itself into her mouth. Fire ran down her throat into her chest, swirling behind her breasts and down into her belly pooling between her hips, and up through her nasal cavities, filling her head and bringing tears to her eyes. The sensations hurt a little, but she let the pain come over her and pass through. It swept her like a shudder and was gone.

All that remained was the living room, the box on the floor and Lily rising to her feet, staring at her, asking angrily, "What did you do?"

Ana swallowed, her throat very dry. "I took him back in," she said.

"Why? The whole point was to put him in the box and he's back inside you, why did we even bother...What did he say to you?"

"He asked if I wanted him back. I said yes. You couldn't hear that?"

At first Ana couldn't place the look in Lily's eyes as she picked up the box and amulet and set them back on the altar. It was a cool look, distant, examining her, and then suddenly she realized it was respect. She touched Lily's shoulder.

"Thank you for setting this up. It's different now."

"You chose him," Lily said, her mouth set like a line in stone.

"You don't like that? You think it's a danger?"

"I'm not sure it's a danger, I just don't like it."

"Why?"

Lily shrugged Ana's hand off her shoulder and walked into the kitchen. Ana followed her.

"Is it bad magic?" She directed her question at Lily's back.

"No, you're more powerful than a box," Lily replied, her words clipped and angry.

Ana thought about Abraxas's dream with Lily in the tent. If he lived here in a stone box, could they do that all the time? Is that what Lily wanted?

"You care for him?" she asked.

"So do you," Lily said.

"Not the same way," Ana said. She didn't know how to describe it, but she struggled out the words. "First of all, he's still a guy and I'm so not into that, and then he's also not really a guy. He's sort of like having a really talkative conscience. There's no way it's ever going to be sexual between us, not like it is for you two."

Lily turned and sat against the sink, raising her eyebrows at Ana. "How do you know?"

"Aside from the fantastic sex dream? Because I've been attracted to you ever since early last week and you're not really my type." She grinned. "When Abraxas and I agreed to share my senses, I think I started to see some of how he sees the world. Does that sound weird?"

"To a girl with clawed feet? Hardly."

Abraxas pushed at Ana's hands and feet—not so strongly as to actually move them, but she understood what he wanted. Now that she'd accepted him in her body, he wanted her to give him a little time at the controls. She moved to the back of herself and he came forward.

Abraxas closed the distance between Ana and Lily and kissed her. The foremost sensation wasn't Lily's lips on hers, but Abraxas himself crowding up to the front of her body to meet Lily. Even a few hours ago she'd have fought him out of reflex, but now there was so much more space inside of her. Everything had changed.

He was happy and her body flooded with a light euphoria. She let him take her hand and tangle it in Lily's long, thick hair, pushing their mouths together. She couldn't shut out the sensations, but she tried not to give it her full attention. It was like kissing someone she wasn't particularly interested in, but at the same time she felt the echo of Abraxas's desire for Lily. As with the dream, it made her long to kiss Sabel again.

Okay, she said to him after a minute, *enough*.

He let go of Lily and they stepped back. Lily was staring at Ana, her mouth half-open. Ana had to smile to see the expression of delight, shock and suspicion on her face.

"Awkward?" Ana asked, just to make sure. It was strange for her to see Lily with the just-kissed look and know that her body had done that and yet she hadn't really.

"Oddly, not as much as I'd expect," Lily said breathlessly. "I can tell it's not you, if that makes sense."

Good thing you didn't pick some straight girl, Ana thought silently at Abraxas.

I have discerning taste, he replied.

I'm not clear on your plan for timesharing the body. Do you think it's as simple as you getting time with your girl and me getting time with mine?

You plan to kiss the witch again? He sounded dismayed.

Shut it, bodiless wonder.

Shut what?

Lily watched her, no doubt aware by now that she was having a conversation in her head.

"We're going to need more practice," Ana said to Lily. "I get the impression it's going to take some time to work out the details here. You're really okay with this?"

Lily sketched a shape in the air with her hands that was bigger than Ana herself. "When he touches me through you, it doesn't just feel like your body. It's like your body focuses the sensation, but it's bigger than you."

"That is so weird."

"You two go home before you stir up any more trouble," Lily said. "I'll be curious to hear how it turns out."

Ana nodded and walked out of the kitchen. Before she passed the doorway, she saw Lily turn and put her palms against the rim of the sink, bracing herself up as her head bent down. She looked like a runner trying to catch her breath. Ana kept walking through the living room and out the door. She thought perhaps she should be worried about all of this, but all she could feel was a wild joy in her blood.

CHAPTER FIFTEEN

When the sales meeting adjourned, Johnson sat by himself in the conference room for a few extra minutes to look over his notes. The symbols in the margin were his shorthand to himself as he thought through how to turn around the few remaining execs who were holding out against the sale of the company. He would have tried to steamroll them except that they had the ear of the CEO, who wasn't yet persuaded that this sale was in the best interest of Roth. He was right, of course, but that wasn't the point. What was a small, unknown software company compared to the facility that Johnson could build with the money from the sale?

Could he get Detlefsen to either change his mind or simply admit to being worn down and take an early retirement? The second was more likely. How to do it, though, when he didn't have the authority to make that offer, that was the question.

Another set of notations was to remind him of the three members of the coven he wanted to talk to about his backup plan. Drake was unpredictable and at some point he would become more of a liability than an asset. As long as the deal was on the table with Drake Industries, Johnson didn't really need Drake himself. He couldn't risk letting Drake absorb the power of whatever demon was hiding in Ana—not when he could bind it to himself.

The two men he was sure of, he knew he could buy them with a mixture of money and guilt. They'd seen Helen's death and they were afraid of what Drake could do. But he needed to find out where the new woman's loyalties lay. He knew her full name, Sabel Young, even as she didn't know his—given how common a surname "Johnson" was. That meant he could find leverage over her if he needed it. With any luck, she'd be easy to buy. Once this deal went through, he wouldn't lack for money.

Yes, it would probably eventually crush the company to have that much money siphoned through it without actually being invested, but who cared about one more little software company? A handful of competitors had similar products on the market. Roth's loss wouldn't be felt by anyone except its sentimental founders. And once he had his first billion, he could build a state-of-the-art hospital with research that helped kids never have to face what he had.

He went down the hall to his office. His admin wasn't at her desk, again. She had this habit of afternoon coffee breaks that could stretch out to nearly an hour and he'd encouraged it in the past so that he could use her to keep tabs on the currents of gossip in the office, but now it was bordering on the annoying.

In his office, he slid his netbook into his briefcase and penned a short note: "If Joe calls, forward it to my cell." This he left on his admin's desk. There was no expected call from anyone named Joe, but the lack of surname on the note would make her spend the last half hour of her workday worried that she'd missed the call by not being at her desk or that she'd forward the wrong Joe to his cell. That should lay the groundwork for her staying at her post more often.

He drove to the wine bar where Drake waited for him at a small table by the window. They didn't worry about being seen together; after all, Johnson was just wining and dining the potential buyer of his company.

"How is the girl?" Drake asked.

"As you'd expect. I've been thinking that we should find a way to lure her to us."

"Ah, and here I was out hiring thugs to just grab her. What's your subtle plan?"

"She has a brother," Johnson said. "He keeps to himself and would be pretty easy for your thugs to grab. I believe she might trade her newfound friend for her brother's safety."

"I like it."

In his briefcase, Johnson's phone buzzed. He pulled it out and looked at the faceplate in case it was one of the other company execs, but it was no one important. Probably his fool admin decided to send every call to his cell so that he wouldn't miss the one from the fictitious Joe. He should have seen that coming. He sighed and set the phone heavily down on the table.

Drake looked at it and then raised his head like a dog scenting the air. "What did you buy? Another phone?"

"No."

"There's a device in your bag, what does it do?"

Johnson shook his head. "It's just my netbook. A computer. They're all over the modern world, you know."

Drake looked exasperated. "Give me your bag."

Johnson obeyed. He'd learned long ago that one key to keeping secrets from the demon was to never carry anything incriminating on his person—or in his mind, if he could help it.

Drake went through the main section and then started unzipping side compartments. From an inner pocket he pulled out a small, dark rectangle that looked like a phone with no numbers. He sniffed it.

"Do they have peach soap in your executive men's room?"

"Absolutely not."

Drake grinned. "Then it's from the girl. Oh I do like her."

Johnson held out his hand for the device and turned it over looking for signs of a microphone. All it had was an on-off switch and a small antenna. Was it some kind of bug or transmitter? What did the signal do?

"Let's go ask her what it does," Drake said.

"You have to stay out of sight."

"Of course, but I'm bringing in the hired men, just in case we have an opportunity to grab her."

"It's too obvious," Johnson said, but he knew Drake wasn't listening to him.

The man was already up from the table and moving for the door, leaving Johnson to snatch up his briefcase and follow in his wake.

* * *

Ana spent the rest of the afternoon trying to get work done and failing. She caught herself reading back through all the news stories about Roth Software, starting with the report of the company struggling to grow and people working all hours, then Helen's murder, her own kidnapping, and a follow-up about the potential sale for which she'd written a statement. Drake Industries had leaked the story, but the statement from the Roth CEO made it clear that it was hardly a done deal.

Lily called again at six p.m. "You still at work?" she asked.

"Just finishing up. What's up?"

"What time do people usually leave your office?"

"Four thirty to five thirty."

"I'm tracking Johnson. He went about a mile away but now he's coming back. I can't be sure, but it looks like there are two other cars with him."

"Oh crap."

"Move!"

Ana grabbed her purse, left her computer running and hurried down the hall from her cubicle. It could be that Johnson was only coming back to chat, but far more likely she was about to be in big trouble. There were plenty of places to hide, but no place where she wouldn't be found eventually. Anyone after her would check the women's bathrooms, the cafeteria, and the other departments. With the workday ending, Johnson and anyone he brought back with him could have hours to look for her without interruption. There was only one set of elevators so she couldn't get past them if he'd posted a guard there and at the bottom of the stairs.

She made it to the end of her department and looked around. Detlefsen's light was on and she bolted for his office as she heard the ding of the elevator.

He raised his eyebrows at her breathless entrance. "I hope it's worth your hurry," he said.

"It is," Ana gasped. "Remember when you said you trust my instincts?"

He nodded.

"I need to talk to you and I need your help getting out of the building, but I don't think we should stay here. There are some guys coming up on the elevator that I don't want to run into."

He pushed himself up from his chair. "They connected to the fuckers who kidnapped you?" he asked.

She nodded.

"I'll make sure you get out safe."

He picked his jacket off the hook by the door and stepped into the hallway. His posture was no longer the usual bear-roused-from-slumber. He moved ahead of her in complete silence and she realized suddenly how much his loud, clumsy manner was an affectation.

"Thank you," she whispered.

Down the hall, Ana could see two men walking to her cubicle. They wore suits but moved like they were used to heavy physical activity.

Abraxas welled up in the back of her mind. *The humans are not alone. They are here to take you willing or not and your friend may come to harm.*

Ana reached out and touched Detlefsen's shoulder. It felt like a rock under her hand, but he turned immediately. She motioned toward her cubicle where the tops of two heads showed over the tan walls and shook her head.

"Weapons?" he asked. The word carried on a barely audible breath.

"The ones who kidnapped me had Tazers."

He paused, looking over the dividers as the heads turned toward them. Ana could see him thinking it through and remembered the times he'd told her about his years as a wrestler and then in the military. She imagined his calculus: could he take two men? A moment later he seemed to arrive at the same conclusion she already had, maybe he could take two men unarmed, but not with weapons. He motioned for Ana to follow him and ambled silently down the hallway away from the goons.

Lily says there are at least six of them in the building, Abraxas said. *They left one at the door.*

"Great," Ana muttered, and then in a louder whisper to Detlefsen, "They've left a man at the door."

He led her through the engineering department and then across the back of the building. Now that it was after six and late summer, this area was empty. The engineers who would stay to work late had been dragged off on family vacations.

"How do you know?" he asked.

It was a good question. She wasn't sure what allowed Abraxas and Lily to communicate over short distances, but if she had to guess it probably had something to do with the time he'd spent in Lily's body. The short answer was, "Magic," but she couldn't say that to Detlefsen.

"The guys who kidnapped me—there were a dozen of them and they'd be smart enough to leave someone at the door. We've got to find a safe place to hide and then call the police."

They stopped at a plain gray door in the back wall. "Access stair," Detlefsen said.

He pulled a thick roll of keys out of his jacket pocket. The first one didn't fit into the lock, but the second clicked it open. Ana shut the door behind her, hoping it locked itself again automatically. They padded up the stairs to another gray door, this one locked. Detlefsen shook his head and gestured up the stairs with his chin.

"Only have keys for our floor and the roof," he said.

They went up each flight and tried the door. Ana wondered what would happen if none of them opened. How safe was the roof?

Abraxas, can you ask Lily to call the police?

She's not in a position to do that now. She will as soon as she can.

The third door she and Detlefsen came to had been wedged open with a piece of cardboard inserted between the frame and the catch of the lock. Detlefsen grunted. "Smokers using the back way to go up to the roof." He pushed through the door and let the cardboard square fall to the floor so it would lock behind them.

Now they faced a long, dim hallway. Light from far windows shone through the glass of office doors, illuminating a path for them in the unlit interior of the building. Most if not all of the people who worked on this floor had left for the day.

Detlefsen put out one hand and trailed it along the wall as they walked. This was a floor of smaller offices. Lawyers and graphic designers, Ana guessed from the names and shapes that appeared through narrow interior windows as they drew close. Detlefsen tried each door as they came to it. At the end of the winding hall, they reached the elevators. Ana could see the elevator cars had stopped on the third and sixth floors. As she watched, the elevator on the third floor moved up to the fourth. The men were systematically searching all the floors of the building. They knew that Ana hadn't left yet.

"Don't you have a cell phone?" Ana asked, realizing hers was still sitting in her cubicle.

"Left it at home trying to get my daughter to fix it," Detlefsen said. "Never can get that damn thing to work right."

"They're searching all the floors," she said. It seemed so strange, like a detective movie, but she could imagine them moving casually down the halls, greeting co-workers, looking nonthreatening. When they came to Ana and Detlefsen, it would only take them a moment to pull the vials out of their pockets and possess them. Then she and Detlefsen could be made to walk calmly out of the building with no one the wiser. If only the guys coming after her had guns instead of demons, this escape would be so much simpler.

Detlefsen nodded to Ana and motioned her away from the elevators, back down the hallway. When he stopped, it was in front of an office door that seemed flimsy. Many had solid oak doors, especially the lawyers, but this office had been carved out as an afterthought, with a thin wooden door separating it from the hallway. Detlefsen stepped back and kicked it, grunting as his foot smacked into the wood and cracked the doorframe. Ana wanted to stop him, but she didn't have a better plan to offer. Their best bet was to get to a telephone. He rocked back and kicked the door again. This time it cracked open and he stepped into the office. Ana followed and gently shut the door behind them, hoping that in the dusky slanting light of early evening the goons wouldn't notice the gap between the door and the cracked frame.

This office consisted of one moderately sized room with two single-occupant offices. Both had closed doors. Detlefsen went to the reception desk and picked up the phone. He called the police and explained that they were being pursued inside their office building by godless thugs and needed an escort out. He told them the office number they were in, grunted assent a few times and hung up. Then he settled himself into one of two padded chairs in the reception area.

"We have a few minutes, tell me about these men who are after you."

Ana looked at the dim window on the far wall. It was hard to know where to begin, but she knew that Detlefsen had his own suspicions about what was going on with the company.

"There are some men at Roth who are involved in a variety of illegal activities. I'm not sure about everything they're doing, but Helen was starting to collect information about it and I think that's what got her killed."

"How do you know this?"

Ana cleared her throat. Telling the truth could lose her a job, but lying to a man like Detlefsen didn't go over well when she needed his help. "I broke in to Helen's apartment and found some notes the police overlooked."

He laughed. "You broke in to Helen's apartment? Well, you've got balls. What did you find?"

"Newspaper stories that point to people having more money and influence than they should rightly have." She held her breath. It was slender proof when she had to leave out the part about demons, but he was nodding.

"That makes sense. Someone's using our company to launder money."

"What?" Ana asked at the same time Abraxas said to her, *Of course*.

"With what you're telling me, it's starting to make sense. There's a group involved in shady dealings, drugs probably, and they're making a lot of money." He rubbed his fingers along the arm of the chair. "But the IRS gets suspicious if a person suddenly gets fifty thousand dollars from nowhere, even if they pay taxes on it. A few months ago I found out that Roth has some moderately large accounts selling software to companies that would have no need of our software. Those companies aren't buying our product, they're dummies funneling money into Roth. Then the people involved in this scam use that money in their expense accounts and through phony bonuses. It appears they're earning it legitimately and because we're a private company no one is looking at the whole picture and connecting the fake income to the bogus payments. I've been able to see the pattern, but I'm still trying to track down the responsible parties. There has to be a connection at the executive level and someone who's been with the company for a long time."

"It's Johnson," Ana said. "Helen was having an affair with him. That's why she started to suspect something was happening."

He slapped a hand down on the arm of the chair. "Of course! Johnson's been trying to sell the company for an inflated price. The other executives are behind it because it would mean a lot of money for all of us individually, but it will destroy the company within a few years."

"Johnson wants the money," Ana said. "He's involved with this group of men who all want as much status and power as they can grab. He would make a lot on that sale, wouldn't he?"

"Loads. He's set himself up as the broker so he not only gets his stock value but a commission on the sale itself. That alone is worth millions."

"And the only bid on the table is from Drake?" Ana asked and Detlefsen nodded.

He's looking for a simple way to pass a lot of money to his human servants, Abraxas offered.

"Johnson knows you found him out?" Detlefsen asked. "That's why these guys are after you?"

"My clever surveillance plan backfired."

He shook his head. "You need to turn over the evidence you have and let the police handle it."

Ana had no trouble agreeing with him.

The elevator dinged on the floor below them. Detlefsen's head came up like an animal's, sniffing the air. "Let's go back down."

"What?" Ana looked at him in concern.

"Back to our floor. They won't look for you there, not until they've gone all through the rest of the floors. They don't know you're with me, so they don't know you have the keys to get back onto our floor."

He surged out of the chair and padded like a bear to the office door. They retraced their steps to the back stairwell. Detlefsen eased the door open and held it for Ana. A voice called out from a level above them, "The doors are all locked!"

Detlefsen put his finger to his lips, smiling, and started down the stairs. For a man of his size, it surprised Ana that he could move along in perfect silence. She kicked off her shoes and carried them.

At the level of Roth's offices, Detlefsen pulled the keys out of his pocket and slid one into the lock, clicking the door open. He shut it gently behind them, and skirted the back way around all the offices until they were standing in the finance department. In one cubicle, Ana picked up the phone and dialed 911 again.

"State the nature of your emergency."

"We've already called once, we're trapped in an office building in Soho." She gave the address. "In the offices of Roth Software in suite 700, and there are men with guns trying to find us. Do you understand? I'm afraid for my life here."

"Two officers already reported to that location and found nothing amiss."

"Send them back," Ana said. "Tell them not to leave until they've spoken to Ana Khoury and Stephen Detlefsen. Whoever told them there wasn't trouble here is one of the guys trying to find us."

"All right," the woman sounded resigned. "I'll send them back."

Ana wasn't sure her plea would help. Whatever Jedi mind trick they'd used to dissuade the cops the first time might work a second time.

"Why aren't the damn cops here yet?" Detlefsen asked when she hung up.

"They came and apparently someone told them there was no problem." She hoped that was enough of an explanation without having to resort to the supernatural reasons, though it sounded thin to her ears that the cops would just turn around and leave.

"Damn fools."

The elevator chimed on their floor, Ana heard it faintly in the distance. She was never aware of that sound on an ordinary day, but then noise always filled the office and the short, clarion tone wouldn't stand out. Men's voices, too dim to hear the words, came through the halls.

"I'm getting really sick of this," Detlefsen said. He picked up an empty vase from the top of a bookshelf. "Did they have guns the last time they came after you?"

Ana looked at the stout man hefting a ceramic vase. He looked both threatening and comical. "No," she said. "Just Tazers."

"Let's go fuck up these sons of bitches."

Ana wasn't clear about the wisdom of that idea, but she had started to feel like a rat trapped in a maze with no cheese and no way out. If there were only two men, it was possible she and Detlefsen could take them. All six of them couldn't have demons with them, could they? Lily said they would be running out of the small demons Drake liked to use. And they didn't know that Detlefsen was with her. If they could knock them out before any demons got involved, they had a chance. Even if she had to host yet another little demon in her body, it would be worth it if it meant getting out of the building.

Together they crept back around the gray bulks of the cubicles toward the elevators. Detlefsen motioned, directing her eyes toward two heads barely visible over the dividers. He lifted the vase above his shoulder and headed in their direction. Ana prayed those weren't the cops.

Ana waited for Detlefsen to put on a surprising burst of speed, as Gunnar could when moved to action, but instead he kept his ambling bear's pace, rounded the edge of the cubicle and brought the vase smashing down on one man's head. Then he let his momentum carry him into the cover of a cubicle. This forced the standing man to turn toward Detlefsen, placing his back to Ana. She struggled to remember all of six months of karate she'd taken in college and aimed a shaky side kick at the small of his back. He staggered and then turned, pointing a vial at her.

Detlefsen's arm came around his throat and the two men went down in a struggle. The vial rolled out of the man's hand and Ana grabbed it, stuffing it into her pocket and out of sight. A moment later, Detlefsen pushed himself stiffly up from the carpet.

"Sleeper hold," he said with a smile.

"We should have done this sooner," Ana joked.

"Not possible. They'd gotten careless thinking you weren't here. And they don't really mean to kill us. Well, you at least. He'd have gone for you after that kick if he did." He dusted his hands on his pants as the elevator bell sounded again. "We're not going to be able to take out all of them," he warned.

Ana heard the elevator ding open again and saw two people with blue uniformed shoulders visible over the field of cubicles.

"I think we finally have our cops," she said.

Detlefsen snorted and walked toward them, his rocking gait slightly slower than before. Had he hurt himself taking down that man? She could feel the tightness in her hip from overextending it before impact. Ahead Detlefsen was introducing himself with all the angry bluster of an executive whose sacred office had been violated. He waved toward the two unconscious men and then motioned for Ana to join him.

"I appreciate everything you told me tonight," he said. "I'm going to make that bastard hurt. I'll need the information you got from Helen's apartment—when can you bring it to me?"

She opened her mouth to tell him she'd go right home for it, but another voice interrupted her from the direction of the elevator. It was Johnson.

"Ana, Steve, thank God you're all right. Men came after you? In our offices?" Charles Johnson asked with a shocked tone that Ana knew had to be fake. He held a file folder in his hand and his normally neat shirt was crumpled and untucked from his belt. He looked at Ana. "I'm sorry you got caught up in this. I'm sure it's doubly difficult after your recent experiences. And I'm afraid it was me they were after."

"What?" she asked, incredulous. It was true that he'd been coming toward her desk when the men showed up—could they really have been after him? Had Drake double-crossed him somehow?

Johnson turned to Detlefsen. "We have employees who've been using our company to launder drug money. It's a terrible mess. I've been trying to figure it out for months and it turns out the root is in our IT department, which is why it's so easy for them to hide their activities, but I have the proof right here." He handed Detlefsen the folder.

Detlefsen opened the folder, his jaw tight. As his eyes scanned the page, he grunted assent a few times. "Looks terrible," he said. "This is really going to hurt the company."

"I'm certain the IRS will give us time to sort it out," Johnson offered.

Ana took a step away from them, looking from one to the other. Could Johnson be telling the truth? Her gut said no, but she had no way to prove it. Clearly he had just handed Detlefsen a wealth of evidence. She could only hope that the articles from Helen's apartment still held some persuasive power against whatever Detlefsen read from the folder in his hand.

Detlefsen was shaking his head. "Fuck it all, Chuck, maybe it's time to sell and walk away from this crap. You think Drake would still take us?"

Ana's heart dropped into her belly with a sickening lurch. She'd lose her job if he agreed to sell the company, and more importantly she'd also lose her best access to proving that Johnson had killed Helen.

Johnson shrugged. "I can ask. We'll be awfully lucky if Simon says yes, but he does believe in our product."

"Stick around, I need to talk to you more. No one's getting much sleep tonight and I want you to walk me through this," Detlefsen said, gesturing with the folder toward Johnson. "I'm going to escort Ana to her car. She's been through enough."

"Of course," Johnson said. "If you want, I'll go. You look like you hurt yourself."

Detlefsen laughed dryly, no real humor in the sound. "Pulled something, or a few somethings, but I really need to walk it out or I won't be able to move in the morning. You look like hell too. Go take a load off in my office. I'll be back in a few minutes."

He walked toward the elevators, leaving Ana to match his pace. When the doors closed he said, without looking at her, "You've done a great job, I think you should take a few days off considering everything you've been through."

"But the publicity..." Ana meant to protest everything Johnson had just said, but those were the only words she could get out of her mouth.

Detlefsen smiled and put a hand on her elbow, guiding her out of the elevator and through the lobby without replying. When they got to her car, he looked back at the building.

"I'm going to kill that son of a bitch. Do you have information to fry his ass?"

"Not enough," Ana had to admit. "What I have is a start. I thought you believed him up there."

"Fuck no. He set it up as an exit strategy and some punk kid in IT is going to take the heat for him unless I can tie it back to Chuck. Where are you safest?"

"Home probably, or a friend's house," Ana said, thinking of Lily's store.

"Go there and keep your phone on. If you find anything on him, call me, but don't endanger yourself." He shook her arm lightly. "I'm serious, Ana. These guys think you know enough that they're willing to come after you in a building with people in it, don't assume you're safe. We're talking about millions of dollars potentially and that makes people plenty stupid."

"I'll be extra careful."

"Good girl."

"Are you going to sell the company?"

He sighed, his massive shoulders drooping. "I might have to. This shit makes us look like clowns in the marketplace and I'm going to have days worth of calls from pissed-off customers on my hands. It's more than we can handle and I doubt we have the capital to hire the people we'll need to clean this up. I need you to bring me those articles you took from Helen's place."

She nodded. "I'll drop them off tomorrow morning."

"Make copies," he said. "Two or three sets. And then write down everything you know or suspect, okay? Do you think Johnson set you up for that kidnapping?"

"Absolutely," Ana said. "Drake was the one who kidnapped me, but I have no proof other than my word. Johnson works for him, for both of them. I think Simon had his brother killed."

Detlefsen gave a low whistle. "That's bad shit. Anything else you come across, call me. As soon as I get my hands on my cell phone it's not leaving my grip."

He stepped back and watched her get into her car and turn it on. Then he turned and walked, haltingly, back into the building.

* * *

Sabel had wanted to run over to Ana's on Tuesday. Ana had arranged to spend the afternoon at Lily's shop getting Abraxas transferred to another vessel and that meant Sabel would actually be able to touch her again. After Sunday's doomed minute of hand-holding, Sabel had persuaded Josefene to alter the sensitivity of the leash slightly and make it easier for Sabel to reverse the constricting process if a demon wasn't immediately pressing on her, but it wouldn't come off until this whole business with the summoners was resolved to Josefene's satisfaction.

Unfortunately, Leonard called her toward the end of her workday and told her to join them that evening to practice the ritual they planned to use to pull Abraxas out of Ana. She could hardly tell him it wouldn't be necessary, so she ate a hasty dinner at a restaurant near campus and went to meet them. Wednesday night had been no better—the summoners wanted still more practice and Ana was tied up at Lily's shop planning how they'd give Johnson the tracking amulet and then follow him.

Thursday found her pacing her living room waiting to hear how it turned out. She'd left it to Lily and Gunnar to do the tracking because of the frequency with which this group of crazies pulled out little demon servants. She'd be worse than useless if they tried to possess her.

The call that came in surprised her. The number was blocked, but she recognized the husky, barely disguised voice of Jacob who was Johnson.

"Do you have afternoon classes tomorrow?" he asked.

Doubly surprising was the fact that he posed it as a question and not a command to clear her schedule.

"Only a meeting, but I can postpone it. Is it important?"

"Very," he said. "I have a task for you and if this goes well you might never have to teach another class again."

She paused to make sure she could keep her voice positive and without the hint of disgust she felt. Let him assume she taught for money; let him believe she was motivated for the same reason he was.

"What is it?" she asked.

"Tomorrow," he said. "Wait for my call." He disconnected.

Was that a good sign? He had called her directly rather than telling Leonard to do it. That could mean he was keeping something secret from other group members and picked her as a new person without firm loyalty to anyone yet. Of course it could also mean he was setting her up to get rid of her.

She looked at the clock. It was after seven. Ana should have given him the tracker hours ago and he was expected to at least lead them to his house or some other magic-testing location. Where had he called from? She dialed Ana's cell phone and got no answer.

That was almost enough to make her call Lily but she just couldn't quite bring herself to do it. Instead she searched for

Gunnar's number online and found a professional listing for Gunnar Khoury, Silversmith—Jewelry Repairs and More. She dialed it, hoping it was a cell phone.

"'Lo," he said.

"I'm a friend of Ana's, is she okay? She told me what she was up to this afternoon."

"You the prof?"

"Yes."

"Didn't work," he said. "They're still inside."

What did that mean? Inside of her office building? Did the whole gambit fail?

"Is she okay?" Sabel repeated.

"Should be. Cops showed up."

"What can I do?"

"Go see her," he said.

"You think I should just go over there?"

"You got time, yeah. Bet you're better to talk to than me." The last sentence was said with a gruff lightness.

"Thank you."

As she drove across town, Sabel wondered what Ana had told her brother about her in addition to her occupation and the fact that she was in on this whole business. He'd clearly heard something that led him to believe Ana would want to see her.

When she arrived at Ana's, lights were on across the first floor. She went up the stairs quickly, trying to remember if Ruben was back from LA and hoping he wasn't.

Ana cracked the door, grinned broadly and removed the chain so she could throw the door wide.

"Hey," she said.

"I heard you might want someone to talk to."

"Gunnar said you called. I'm surprised I beat you back here."

"Parking," Sabel said.

"Oh yeah, you want a beer or something?" Ana waved her into the house, threw the bolt, and reconnected the chain.

"Sounds good." Sabel followed Ana into the kitchen.

"Honey Weiss or this weird oatmeal stout?"

"The weird one."

Ana poured the beer into a tall glass. They went into the living room where Sabel saw that Ana's beer was still in its bottle. What in Ana's mind made her the beer-from-a-glass type? Not that she minded. Ana dropped onto her end of the couch and picked up the sweating bottle for a long swallow.

Sabel took the other end of the couch and sat facing Ana. She sipped the slightly bitter, malty beer and appreciated its lush chocolate bass note. Ruben had good taste.

"Gunnar said police were involved?" she asked.

"I put the tracker in Johnson's briefcase, but he must have found it before he got very far and he came back with a bunch of guys. I ran into Detlefsen's office and we hid out for a bit until we could get the police to show. Apparently the cops came once and someone sent them away."

"It's easy enough for a strong demon to be persuasive like that, particularly if the police didn't want to stay. Drake must have been there."

"I'm sure. But here's the strange thing. After we took out two of the guys—Detlefsen is ex-military—Johnson shows up and says he called the police and he's got this whole file of information about a few guys running some kind of drugs and money thing out of our shipping department. He tells the cops they were really after him and of course they buy it, though Detlefsen believes there's something much bigger going on. Johnson had this backup plan all along to throw suspicion off him."

"He called me tonight," Sabel said. "What time did all this start?"

"Around six."

"He called after that, so he already knew he was going to have to expose this fake drug ring. He didn't say what he wants, but I'm supposed to help him with something tomorrow afternoon."

"That can't be safe!" Ana protested.

"Did you just tell me you just spent hours being chased through your own office building? What's good for the goose is good for the gander."

Ana smirked. "Which one's supposed to be the girl in that saying?"

"The goose."

"Then I'm pretty sure you've got it backward."

"Oh, you think you're the gander?"

"Don't you?" Ana's grin widened and Sabel felt herself start to blush.

Ana moved down the couch toward her and Sabel reached out to weave her fingers through Ana's hair. Ana put a strong hand on the curve of her waist while Ana's other hand curled around the back of her neck to pull her close.

A warning shock of pain lanced up from her breastbone to her throat. She dropped her hand from Ana's hair to her shoulder and pushed at her gently. Ana drew back and gave her a questioning look. Sabel turned her attention inside her own body. Above the heat and desire in her gut, she felt the tug of the leash's three bands across her chest and neck. She put one hand over her heart as if she could stop the painful tightening. What triggered it?

"Did they set a demon on you again?" Sabel asked.

"No."

She stood up and stepped away from the couch. The leash didn't release, but it stopped compressing. She moved back toward Ana and felt it notch tighter, so she stepped away again.

"What's wrong?" Ana asked.

"There's still demon energy around you. Did you leave Abraxas at Lily's after she extracted him?"

Ana looked confused. "No."

"Is he in this room?"

"Yes."

"What did you put him in?" Sabel asked.

She looked around the room to see if there was a statue or stone of some kind near Ana. Or maybe she was wearing him as an amulet under her shirt. She thought Lily said she was going to put Abraxas into a stone box, but who knew what he would pick at the end of the day. He could be in anything that wasn't too small.

"Me," Ana said. "I put him back into me."

"What?"

"I chose him. He makes me stronger and he teaches me things and...I didn't think you were that squeamish about all of this. Why do I have to justify it to you? I can shut him out of my sense if it bothers you and he won't be able to feel what I feel, though I really think he's not paying attention."

"I can't touch you now," Sabel said, biting off the half-strangled words.

She didn't like how tight her voice sounded when she spoke, but with the leash pressing on her throat it was hard to relax the muscles there. She was grinding her teeth all on her own, though.

Ana stared at her, anger and confusion flickering across her features.

"If you didn't want me to keep him—," she started but Sabel cut her off with a gesture.

"The Hecatine witches won't just let me hang around with demons without...countermeasures." She stopped talking because that just sounded stupid.

"They did something to you?" Ana asked.

Sabel nodded.

"In the mall on Sunday when I touched your hand?" Ana asked.

"It hurts," Sabel told her and was horrified to hear how rough her voice sounded and to feel tears burn her eyes. She turned away and struggled to regain some kind of control over herself.

"And now?"

Sabel put her hand over her upper chest. "It's a magical thing. When demonic energy gets close to it, it warns me with pain and then it starts to shut me down. If a demon tried to possess me, I'd be unconscious in seconds. Because Abraxas isn't actively trying to do anything to me, it's slow and I can step back and stop it, but there's so much of his energy in your body now..."

"Why didn't you tell me?"

"You were going to get rid of him. It didn't matter."

"Can you get it off?" Ana asked.

"When all this is over, they'll take it off."

Ana got up slowly and picked up Sabel's glass of beer. She went the long way around the coffee table, so that she wasn't near Sabel at any point in her journey, and set it on the end table next to the armchair furthest from her side of the couch. Then she returned to her spot and sat.

Sabel looked at the glass of beer for a moment as a warmth overrode any of the residual constriction in her chest. She sat down in the chair across the room from Ana and took a sip of the beer.

"I'm sorry," Ana said. "I never want to hurt you."

"I should have told you. I'm not used to having anyone I can talk to about magic."

"Me either. I still don't think you should go do whatever Johnson's got planned tomorrow."

Sabel managed a little grin. "Aren't you the queen of 'don't tell me what to do'?"

"Are you seriously going to keep flirting with me when I can't touch you?"

"Oh no, I'm going to flirt more. You're the one who kept the demon, I think you deserve it."

CHAPTER SIXTEEN

Friday morning Ana took the articles to a copy shop and made three copies. Then she dropped one off with Detlefsen, stepping into his office and handing them to him while he was on the phone with an upset customer. On her way to the bookstore her cell phone rang. It was Andi, the reporter who she'd first called about the kidnapping.

"Drug money?" Andi asked without preamble. "Who launders drug money through a high-tech company?"

"With so many startups here in the last ten years, what agency has time to oversee all of them, and who would think to look for it there?" Ana didn't completely believe that herself, but she said it anyway to hear Andi's reaction.

"Can I quote you on that?" she asked.

"Not on your life! What've you got?"

As she continued, Ana heard her smiling. Andi always smiled when she was on the track of a hot story. "Just the basics. Some guy in your IT department was masterminding this laundering business. They took him down along with a buddy and two of your sales guys who weren't selling software at all, it turns out. They found a few kilos of coke in the shipping area and some crazy financials, but the whole story will take weeks to put together."

It sounded neat and reasonable, and she had no doubt that Johnson had planted enough evidence to come to light in unexpected ways that the police would never suspect they weren't getting the truth. Compared to a tale of demon summoning and ritual murder, who wouldn't rather believe drugs were being sold out of the back office of a software company?

"Andi, are you at your office?" she asked.

"Yeah."

"I'm coming over."

She turned toward downtown, taking a roundabout route in case anyone was following her. Andi was waiting for her in the lobby of the *Chronicle*. She wore jeans and the Polartek zip-front sweatshirt that she always had on, looking more like a ski bum than a reporter. She gave Ana a quick hug and ushered her into a meeting room. Andi's office was a messy cubicle in the newsroom with no privacy other than that afforded by the perpetual loud bustle of activity around it.

Ana handed her a copy of the articles. "I found these in Helen's apartment. Yes, I broke in and no, you can't report that...Andi, it's bigger than drugs."

Andi opened the folder and flipped through the first few articles, pausing on each as her amber eyes scanned a few paragraphs. She was almost a head shorter than Ana and as she read, Ana could watch her progress over the top of the tipped up folder.

"What is all this?" Andi asked.

"I can't tell you except it includes some serious power-brokering and these men are all involved, including Charles Johnson."

"Your VP of Sales? But he called the police last night. He's the one who exposed the—" Andi stopped and ran a hand through her already tousled red-brown hair. "Ana, can you—?"

"No," she said for what felt like the hundredth time. "I can't prove that he's connected to the money, or the drugs, or Helen's death, but he is."

"Those are serious allegations."

"Andi, have you ever known me to make up wild stories?"

She laughed and shook her head. "You should be scared out of your mind. Oh right, Ana doesn't get scared, she gets pissed off. These guys picked the wrong woman to kidnap."

"You can say that again. Look, I'll bring you anything else I can."

"This is already a lot."

"I know, I know, don't put myself in danger. That's all very sweet, but as you said, I'm pissed."

"Okay, just one more thing."

"What?"

"Next time you pick up the phone to call the cops, make the next call to me."

Ana gave her a quick hug before leaving. Andi had once pointed out that only cops, emergency workers and reporters were stupid enough to run into danger rather than away from it, but Ana could see that Andi was also beginning to include her in that esteemed company. She'd said "next time," knowing that Ana wasn't going to stop pursuing these guys, and that understanding warmed her.

Ana drove over to the bookstore, eager to see a person who understood what her life had become. A clean-cut college kid was working at the front register, so Ana went to the back and then up the stairs to Lily's apartment. She paused for a moment at the door, her hand raised but not knocking. She remembered kissing Lily a few days ago in that apartment, and though technically Abraxas was responsible, it was her chest that felt this alien mix of shyness, embarrassment and anticipation. Could she completely separate her feelings from Abraxas's while he lived within her? What if she couldn't?

Abraxas flowed up her hand and knocked for her. *There are many options*, he reassured her. *I won't trap you in my emotions.*

Lily answered the door still in her robe and slippers. Above the tops of them, Ana could see where the scaly skin of her lower calves turned smooth.

"Morning," she said. "Oh, afternoon. I was up late with another possession. I think Jacob's boys are playing with demons they don't know how to control. I keep finding these little lost creatures around the city. Come in, you guys."

Ana settled on the couch and Lily curled herself up on the other end, kicking off her slippers and tucking her feet underneath herself. She had the windows open, and a cool breeze trickled in, smelling of eucalyptus. Ana rubbed her hands over her upper arms, wishing she'd remembered a sweater.

"Quite a night, huh?" Lily asked.

"I can't believe Johnson...okay, I can, but damn we were so close. I wonder if there's anything else we can do to nail him. He was such a smug bastard with his little folder of evidence. I bet he's had that prepared for months. Sabel said he called her yesterday afternoon and he wants her to help him with something today."

Lily shook her head but didn't say anything.

"She'll be okay, won't she?"

"The Hecatines are subtle but powerful when they want to be," Lily said.

Just thinking about Sabel rekindled an ache of longing in Ana's gut. She wanted to tell Lily about the energy leash and the whole situation and how infuriating it was, but she didn't want to give her any more reason to dislike the witches. Still, she couldn't help but remember kissing Sabel and wishing they had had more time together.

Abraxas shifted low in her body and she felt a hot echo of her own desire. He wanted Lily the way she wanted Sabel... well, maybe not exactly the same, but it was in the ballpark. His desire burned fierce and clean while Ana's felt deep and smoldering and complex.

You're thinking at least one of us should be able to get lucky? she asked him silently.

Not in so many words, he said with more than a touch of humor. *It would settle both of us.*

How does this work? Do you just take over my body?

In answer he pushed lightly on the back of her skull and she relaxed back against the couch and let him pour through her nerves like hot wind.

Lily looked up from taking a sip of tea and her eyes widened. "Abraxas?" she asked.

"Yes." The voice that passed Ana's lips wasn't quite hers. It held notes of her voice but also a whispered resonance of a deeper tone.

"Is she still conscious in there?" Lily asked.

"She is."

"Go look in the mirror and show her what you did."

The feeling of her body standing up without her conscious will was dizzying and she couldn't focus on their movement across the room, but when they stopped in front of a mirror she saw what Lily meant. The irises of her eyes were no longer brown but rather a golden fire like the sun, and the copper and gold colors in her hair shimmered and glowed. She looked like an artist's depiction of some ancient sun goddess.

Nice, she told Abraxas.

I thought it would be important to distinguish between us, he said.

No kidding.

He moved them back to the couch and sat next to Lily who smiled and traced their face with her fingers.

"Lucky for you I'm not picky with my genders," she said. "Though you'd do so much better in a man's body, it's almost a shame. Now, where to begin?"

"Perhaps," Abraxas said softly, "you should stop talking."

Lily laughed. "I'm nervous," she said. "You're a little out of my league."

He touched a finger to her lips. Lily leaned forward and kissed him...except to Ana it felt like Lily had leaned forward to kiss her. Now that she wasn't startled, as in the kitchen the

other day, Lily seemed to know everything about kissing. Her
lips were firm and soft, and when she opened them, Ana felt a
tongue that was rough as a cat's. A hot thrill ran from her chest
down to her feet and was met by a pang of loss that this wasn't
Sabel. She wanted Sabel so badly now that it was a physical
pain, but that only reminded her of the leash and the real pain
she inflicted on Sabel.

Do you want me to shut you out of your senses? Abraxas asked.
Would that just put me to sleep?
Yes, or I can send you out of your body for a walk.
Can I try that?

In the next instant she was standing by the near wall of the
room watching herself and Lily tangle together on the couch.
She had to pause for a moment and stare at herself. Ruben was
right, she looked fine with a few extra pounds on, softer around
the edges and more filled out. That shirt was the wrong shade
of peach, it made her hair look pale gold rather than ruddy;
she'd have to remember to toss it into the Goodwill pile when
she got home.

Is that how she really looked kissing someone? She could
imagine that same scene with Sabel in Lily's place and picture
their dark and light hair tangling together. When Lily's fingers
started to pull her blouse out of her pants, Ana turned and fell
through the wall and down. She landed on the sidewalk outside
of the store, though there was no impact and she had the
sensation that what stopped her was the idea of the sidewalk,
rather than any actual surface.

She went along the street floating. Something connected her
to her body, like a rubber band that tugged harder the further
away she got. It was the same kind of connection that jerked her
through the window of Lily's store when Sabel cast Abraxas out
of her. But it was thinner and longer so that she could go a lot
further from her body than Abraxas could.

Without her body she could travel much more quickly
than walking. If she looked at the far corner of the street and
thought about being there, she crossed the intervening space in

an instant to be at that corner. She practiced going a block at a time and then a couple of blocks.

People couldn't see her, but she could sense that there were other disembodied creatures in this city and took care to avoid them as best she could. First, she wished she could go look in on Sabel during her meeting with Johnson and make sure that she was okay, but she didn't know where they were or even what time the meeting was. It might not have started yet. Of course if that was the case, then maybe she could go peek in on Sabel showering or something like that. No, it would upset her to have someone look in on her like that, she wasn't going to do it to Sabel.

Then she stopped and smacked her forehead with one insubstantial hand. If she could move through walls and travel unseen, why not return to the house where she'd been taken when she was first kidnapped and look for evidence of Helen's death? She couldn't find the house when navigating by eyes and memory, but without her body the whole world felt different—a map of ideas and feelings. Why hadn't Abraxas suggested this sooner? Maybe he didn't know what it was like to be a human outside a body. If she found the address and the evidence, she could call the police and send them in with a search warrant to get it.

Orienting herself with the sun, as she had never been able to when camping, she leapt across the intervening streets in the direction Drake had driven when he kidnapped her. Soon she could pick up the traces of her own remembered fear, which she followed to the gazebo where she'd hidden. Then she ran backward along the route she'd taken when she first fled that house. In her body, she would have been lost, but all she had to do was orient toward the sensation of terror and she knew she had the right path.

To her eyes all these houses had looked so alike, but now one stood out vibrant with her fear as if it had been this morning that she was kidnapped. She slipped in through the back wall and found herself standing in an expansive, spotless kitchen with glass cupboards and gleaming metal sinks. Moving into the dining room, she spotted a man at his table. He looked up and she froze. It was Charles Johnson. Could he see her? His eyes danced over the wall behind her but found nothing to focus on, even if he could sense a shift in the room.

Ana wasn't sure how much time had passed while she was moving around the city without her body, but probably less than she thought if he hadn't left for his meeting with Sabel yet. Strange that he would be at home and not at work, but he'd likely been up most of the night with Detlefsen, covering his ass. In fact, that shirt was the same one he'd been wearing the day before. He must have stayed at Roth all night and just come home recently. He was finishing a microwaved meal, reading a cooking magazine. She watched as he took the empty tray into the kitchen and put away the magazine neatly in its rack.

Ana smiled to herself and slid out of the room. She went up the stairs. Here at the end of the hallway was the bathroom. Across the hall a door stood open to a huge, fantastic study with a desk that curved around three quarters of the room and held two flat-screen computer monitors, plus a flat-screen television bolted to the wall. The other half of the upstairs held two ornate bedrooms, both with richly appointed king-sized beds. She went back and forth trying to decide which was his.

She decided that he slept in the less gothic of the two rooms. The other had a mission oak dresser that stood empty. This one held a couple of locked chests, a dresser and a walk-in closet filled with business attire. The bed had six pillows, two of them the funny-shaped pillows that chiropractors recommend for neck comfort. If Ana hadn't seen the iron muscles in his arms, she'd have thought Johnson was a real softy. As she smiled at the bed, he ascended the stairs and entered that room.

Unable to resist, Ana watched him strip out of his shirt and slacks. He was a handsome man, standing in nothing but his crisp, white boxer briefs that showed the tan of his skin, tall and lean, but with enough muscle to look strong. If he hadn't been evil, he might have been cute. With the strange out-of-body vision, she could see shadows of his innards, the muscle glowing, and she realized that this body of his had outside help in its formation. Did her body look like that now that Abraxas lived in it and strengthened it?

Looking deeper, she saw the traces of struggle on his bones from a childhood of cancer, the places in him that had been damaged. He had built over these places with a framework so strong that no disease could ever get in or out again. That's what he got from his demons, not just the money to buy his fancy toys and nice clothes. He wanted physical power and the security of knowing he couldn't be hurt ever again.

Ana's hand went to her jaw, though she couldn't actually touch anything. That motivation of his she understood. She'd made a few bad bargains in her own life to get away from physical pain and know she wouldn't ever be beaten again. She'd even slept with a man she had no interest in when she knew he could help her get out of the crushing poverty she'd been born into. But, unlike Johnson, she would never go so far as to kill anyone. Was it so much better to have been willing to sacrifice herself rather than someone else?

He walked into the bathroom. Whatever evidence he might have had from Helen's murder, he wasn't going to keep it in a box in the bedroom, lock or no. She passed back down the stairs and through the kitchen into the basement. In California, the land of no basements, it was a very strange addition to a house. They'd put a concrete foundation under the house, as was usual here, but they'd left a hole in the foundation through which descended a flight of stairs.

It was well disguised and Ana found it only in reverse. She didn't relish the thought of finding herself head-deep in dirt, but probably better to try this without a body than with one. Kneeling as best she could without knees, she stuck her head through the floor. Boards and wiring passed over her and then she was pushing through the concrete and finally looking, upside down, into a large room. She dropped through the floor into the chamber below.

Spotting the staircase she followed it up to a trapdoor. It was set into the bottom of a closet in the back of the house so that no one would find it if they didn't know what to look for. No one in this city would expect that this house carried a basement underneath its slab. The design was insane, but effective.

Now that she knew how to get in, she walked around the room. It had been laid entirely in concrete, like a bomb shelter, but then covered with drywall and painted black. The dimensions of the room were the same as the house, which made it huge. Halfway around she found the black wood chests that held extra robes, various ritual implements that she didn't care to know the purpose of, and the evidence of Helen's murder. The sheet was in there, more like a canvas tarp now that she looked closely at it, about thirty feet to a side and painted with lines of blood. Disgusting.

If the blood was Helen's, it must have come from her days or weeks before her death, since the police didn't find any fresh wounds on her. But even if it wasn't here, Ana knew this was the cloth on which Helen died and it had to have trace elements from her: hair or saliva or tears. Time to call the police.

She wanted to look in on Johnson one more time before she left, to see what he was doing. Eager as she was to call the police, she could spare a few more minutes to let Abraxas and Lily have their time together. Johnson had no idea she'd been in his house, so he wasn't likely to move the evidence when it had already been in his hidden basement for two weeks.

She found him upstairs, coming out of the shower. Ana couldn't help it, she watched. Shouldn't she know the full measure of her enemy? Really, she thought, she just wanted to have this over him, not that it would ever be of any use, but it would make her feel more powerful to know that she'd peered on him in the most bare circumstances. She watched him shave, put on deodorant and select a pair of khakis and a silk shirt. He had just finished dressing when the doorbell rang. She followed him, wondering if it would be Sabel at the door.

The door swung open. Drake stepped past Johnson into the house. His dense presence commanded the front hallway and next to him Johnson looked plain. He turned his head, sniffing like a dog, and fixed his eyes on her.

"Ana!" he said. "What a surprise."

His eyes were two holes of darkness. She snapped back like a kite in a strong wind. Faster than thought, she followed the trail back to her body.

CHAPTER SEVENTEEN

Ana jerked back into her body and was overwhelmed with sensory data: lungs breathing, heart pulsing blood through her veins, bare skin warm on hers. She fought like a fish on a line, trying to move away but unable, prevented by Abraxas's control of her and the floor against her back. Above her, Lily's eyes opened wide and her fingers touched Ana's lips tentatively.

"Stop," Abraxas said with her mouth.

"What's wrong?" Lily asked.

"Ana's back. I'm giving her control again," Abraxas said and then his presence under her skin flared and pulled back.

"Hell of a time," Lily said, rolling off her to lay in the crook of her arm. "We were just going for round two."

Ana found herself looking into Lily's face from a few inches away. She held still, refusing to pull away suddenly. That would be a crappy way to end their time together and the skin contact felt good. It was hard to argue with the pleasure of bare, soft skin along hers.

"Sorry to interrupt," she said. "But I just saw Drake at Johnson's house and he saw me." She pushed up on her elbows and realized she was not only naked, but covered in a thin sheen of sweat. She shivered and grinned. Her body felt satisfied with the lingering relaxation of a good orgasm humming along her nerves. She almost regretted that she hadn't been there for it, but that would be way too awkward. She didn't like Lily that way and now at least she got a few aftereffects without having to do all the work. The pain of her ache for Sabel was slaked for the moment.

Lily pulled the throw blanket off the couch and handed it to her, seeming untouched by the chill in the air. Her dark hair hung in thick tangled threads. Oddly, her feet matched her body better when she was naked, the transition from scales to skin looking natural, and the solid muscles of her calves matched in density by the muscles of her thighs and hips. She had great hips, broad but strong and Ana immediately wanted to lose ten pounds.

"Can he follow her back here?" Lily asked Abraxas.

"Yes," Abraxas said. He leaned forward with Ana's lips and kissed Lily's forehead. "Thank you," he said softly, the end to another conversation.

"I know," Lily said, laughing. "You haven't done that in about a thousand years. It's been a few for me too. Ana, we both really appreciate—"

"Don't mention it," Ana said. "And I mean do *not* mention it."

Lily laughed and pushed off the floor. "We'd better get downstairs, I'd rather face him in the bookstore."

Ana untangled herself from the blanket and started gathering the articles of clothing she could find. Her pants were on the floor by the couch and her shirt draped over the coffee table. She had to hunt around for a few minutes before she found her bra a few feet behind the couch. She wondered what it was like for Abraxas. He seemed like a pretty manly man the few times she'd seen him pull together an image of a body. Was it humbling for him to have sex in the body of a woman?

She also wondered about Lily's parents. Lily had told her that her mother had been the demon parent; apparently their bloodline was matriarchal. She couldn't imagine what a human woman would think of a child with clawed feet, though if she'd slept with a demon she might have expected it. But then what would it be like for a half-human child to be raised by a demon? Was that part of the attraction to Abraxas for Lily? It certainly explained why she wasn't freaked out by the body swapping that had her effectively sleeping with Ana.

Ana wasn't so sure she could say the same for herself. Sometimes she looked forward to Abraxas having a body of his own, but she also felt a thrill at the thought of the whole experience. It was all hopelessly confusing and there were more pressing matters to figure out right at this moment.

The three of them descended the stairs to the back of the shop, and then Ana and Abraxas waited in the back area while Lily went to check on Jason, the kid who was minding the front of the store. The bells jingled as a customer came through the front door.

Should we leave? Ana asked. *He won't hurt Jason at the counter, will he?*

I don't know, came the reply.

We don't have much to fight him with, do we?

Less and more than you think. Very little in this world can resist a pure heart.

That would be great if we were in possession of a pure heart, Ana shot back. *I don't think either one of us is high on the pure scale at the moment.*

Don't judge me on the values of your civilization, he said, laughing. *Some of your morals are more outdated than I am.*

While they talked, the door to the back opened and Jason came in, eyebrows knit with confusion. "Lily said she needs her Modern Demonology book," he said.

"That's at my house," Ana said. "Oh—" Lily knew she'd taken the book home. She wasn't asking for it, she was asking for Ana and Abraxas.

"Shall we?" Ana asked.

"Sure," Jason said.

"I'm not talking to you," she told him.

Let's go have another look at him, Abraxas said.

Tell me you have an escape plan in case this goes horribly wrong, Ana said, remembering not to talk aloud as she walked around the shelves to the front of the store. She could see part of a tall back from between the aisles as she walked up toward the front. He wore a long, black cashmere coat, perfectly tailored for his size. His brown hair curled just past the collar, and looked oddly similar to the first time she'd seen him in his other body, just after he kidnapped her.

* * *

The girl's dark brown eyes held fear as Drake looked into them, but not really as much as he'd hoped for, and utterly absent was the desire that would have been better yet. Ah well, he'd have to kill her, he supposed, though it would be a terrible shame with her body already strengthened and her blood singing to him. Equally interesting was this Lily Cordoba the crossbreed, she must be the ally who'd alerted the city's protectors that he was in their area. He couldn't retaliate against her directly without making more trouble for himself than he wanted, but he'd know to avoid her attention in the future and look for ways to exert control over her. He wasn't a particularly vengeful man when it came down to it, he had so many desires that they took all his energy. But he did like a smooth path to the objects of his desires and he'd do what he could to ensure she wasn't going to be an obstacle.

"Ana, we meet again," he said. "And your guest…who is he? I believe he has caused us both some trouble. Perhaps we can put an end to this simply."

That he still couldn't see the creature in her only made him want it all the more. Small demons could never hide themselves from him like that.

"What did you have in mind?" Ana asked.

"Certainly you don't intend to keep your guest forever," Drake suggested. "You have a little power and you're playing with us because of the unfortunate death of your friend. Will you tell me what would make that right for you?"

"I want to know what really happened first," she said. "Who killed Helen?"

He tilted his head toward her. "No one did, dear girl. Helen volunteered for the ritual. She believed she could pass through the door we opened and go into death with her fully awake consciousness and not the confusion and loss of sense most people experience."

"What went wrong?"

"Helen went back on the bargain. She blocked the door herself but she was already dead on this side."

"She didn't want to let your demon through," Ana said. "Sounds like a real charmer."

He laughed. "If only you could meet her. She would enjoy knowing you."

"I want the men in the circle who arranged this brought to trial and convicted for Helen's murder anyway," Ana said. "You set her up. And I want you...Lily, are there demon courts or something?"

The little, dark woman shook her head. "Not like that. They'll throw him out of the city, which they'd probably do anyway."

"Then you should go to trial as a human too and to jail."

She made him smile. Inventive, vicious, vindictive as she was, maybe he could find a way to keep her with him after this was all over. "So I can be shanked in the yard and come back in another body?" he asked.

"I'm sure that doesn't feel good," she said.

"And if I agree to all these extravagant terms of yours, you let me take your guest as my own? Who is it you have?"

She paused, eyes unfocused, paying attention inward, probably talking to it. "Show me yours and I'll show you mine," she said at last.

"My name is my own," he said. "But I'll give you my title. I am the Ashmedai."

A dark voice whispered through Ana's lips. "For how long?"

So she'd already given this one access to use her body.

Drake raised a finger and shook it as if scolding a child. "Show me yours."

A cloud came out of Ana's body and inside of it the colors of flame formed the shape of a man, tall and slender, muscled like the warriors of old with long, lean strength, and in the place of feet, serpents of fire.

"The Abraxas," Drake said. "The old one who died. How did you return?"

This was so much better than he'd dared wish. Not a mere thousand-year-old princeling, but the former Abraxas, before he'd been tamed by the Gnostics. He had been killed in the desert over nine hundred years ago. Although Drake had risen to power quickly and had the added benefits of his office, Drake as the Ashmedai was just over eight hundred years old; if he could bind this power to him while the creature was weak, he could rule human countries and demon princedoms.

"Helen opened the door for me," Abraxas told him.

"So you could fall into this girl and do what…go shopping? Come with me and we will both gain in power."

"No, it is not for you," he said and sank down again into the body of the girl. Was that all he could sustain? Was he really that weakened? If that was the case, he was a ripe peach nearly falling into Drake's hand. And if he would not come willingly, Drake had an alternative offer he could make. Jacob was right to point out the weak link in the situation was Ana's brother Gunnar who had been trying to watch over her, never realizing the danger that put him in.

He raised a hand dismissively. "Stay out of my business and I will stay out of yours. If you meddle, I will send you back from where you came. Don't doubt that I can do it."

"You're welcome to try," Abraxas said from the girl's mouth.

Let them wonder about that threat, empty as it was. Let them wonder about anything except his real next move. He turned on his heel and stalked out, though he was elated rather than angry. First to call in the group of men whose power and ritual would help extract Abraxas and then pick up the brother.

* * *

Sabel got a call from Gabriel Leonard in the evening, giving her an address of a warehouse where she was to meet with the other summoners in an hour and practice their ritual again. His voice held a high note of excitement and that worried her. He seemed to think that soon they would have Ana in hand and be able to perform this ritual. She thought about calling Ana, but she wanted more information beyond "you're in danger," which they already knew.

Minutes later, Johnson called her. "It's time for that favor," he said. He gave her an address of a coffee shop three blocks from the warehouse and asked her to meet him there. This worried Sabel more than some off-the-beaten-path abandoned warehouse. To his knowledge, she only knew him as the nebulous "Johnson." What could it mean that he was willing to show her his face?

At least there would be people around.

When she arrived, she scanned the place for men sitting alone. She'd met Johnson once in person without a hood and she mostly remembered what he looked like, but she had to pretend she'd never seen his face or he would realize that she knew who he was.

A man with sandy hair raised his hand and beckoned to her. She went to his table. "Can I get you anything?" he asked as if this was a normal meeting between two people in a coffee shop.

"A cup of tea would be nice. White, if they have it, or green."

He got up to order and she looked at his empty chair. His briefcase leaned against the side of it, but there were no other obvious clues about this meeting. When he returned with the tea, she hazarded an opening.

"We've met before," she said. "You work for a company where I did some trainings, I think."

He nodded, "Roth Software."

"And I saw you in the news."

"Unfortunate."

"I gather you didn't ask me here on a date," Sabel said. If he didn't know she was a lesbian, that would confirm that he hadn't connected her with Ana.

Johnson smiled. "Perhaps another time. You haven't dealt with demons before now?" he asked.

Sabel shook her head.

"There is one essential lesson about them: they will always turn on you sooner or later."

Her heart sped up and she sipped the warm tea in an effort to cover any change in her breathing rate. Did that apply to Abraxas too?

"You learn," he went on. "To take countermeasures. Not just with the demons, but with the humans as well. Tonight you'll meet Simon Drake, a demon in a human body. I need your help with him because you're new and don't have strong ties to him, and you need to know that it's better to be on my side than his. He doesn't understand as much about the modern world as he thinks he does."

"I thought you were on the same side."

"Demons are never on the same side as their humans. Not for long."

"If he's a demon, how does he have a human body?" she asked. To keep up the appearance that she knew nothing about Drake, she figured she should ask a question and she was curious.

"He finds empty bodies and inhabits them," Johnson said. "Or half-empty bodies and pushes the human spirit out."

"That's just creepy," Sabel told him and she meant it. Could that happen to Ana someday? If Abraxas stayed in her long enough, could she lose her hold on her own body?

"We need to take him down today. After the ritual, we'll be able to take possession of this other demon, but only if Drake is out of the way."

Sabel made herself smile all the way up to her eyes, forcing the muscles around them to crinkle so that her gesture read as genuine. "We get to do the real ritual?"

"We'll have the girl by tonight," he said and her heart dropped like cement in an icy lake. She kept the smile up. He had to mean Ana, which meant that they had some other plan to grab her. She needed to warn her, but couldn't do anything that would tip off Johnson. If they did grab Ana, the best place for Sabel to be was inside the circle of summoners with her.

"I'm finally going to see powerful magic at work," she said. "But you need something else from me?"

"As soon as the ritual is complete, you need to leave the circle. I'm sure you can come up with a reason. Drake will be distracted with the captured demon. You need to get to his new apartment. Do you have a problem pretending to be his new lover?"

"No."

"Good. Then your excuse is that you returned to claim something you forgot there in the morning. You will look through his closets and in one you'll find a body."

"A real one?" She didn't have to feign alarm at the idea.

"Yes."

"Who did he kill?"

Johnson smiled. "He will have killed the brother of the woman with the other demon, or at least that's how it will appear."

Outwardly, Sabel didn't blink. She kept her breathing slow and cocked her head slightly to one side to suggest curiosity. Inside she was as cold as death and she felt as if a thousand dirty insects crawled over the underside of her skin. They were going to kill Gunnar.

"You want his death on Drake," Sabel said slowly and carefully. "And you've connected it somehow to the news stories about that other woman's death and that kidnapping. You'll show that he's involved in the same sorts of things his brother is, right? But won't he just come after you from prison?"

"He's still new to this Simon Drake body. He'll have to stay near it for years and if the body is in prison, well, then so is he. By the time he can travel enough to come after me, I'll have made an ally of this new demon or maybe I'll take my money and go someplace he can't find me."

"The money," Sabel said.

"When the company sells, I'll see that you get a very generous payment. Maybe I will ask you out on that date then and shower you with gifts. I take you for a woman who likes small diamonds and large houses."

She laughed a little, thinking how wrong he was, and turned it into an affirmative gesture. She wasn't sure if he was offering the date seriously or just as a cover for paying her off.

"Very true," she told him. "So all I have to do is excuse myself at the end of the ritual, talk my way into his apartment since I don't have a key, discover this body and do the screaming woman thing?"

"The men I've selected to take the brother to Drake's apartment will leave the door unlocked for you. You only have to get through the lobby."

"That's easy."

Now it was starting to come together in her mind. Johnson had two men among the summoners that he trusted and they would make sure that Gunnar was taken to Drake's apartment, then kill him there and hide his body for Sabel to find. Johnson needed her because she could play the distressed girlfriend and make the situation look so very incriminating for Drake. That might be the reason she had been accepted into this group so quickly.

After what happened with Helen, the police and media would be quick to believe that Simon Drake was continuing what his brother started. He'd be arrested immediately and as a wealthy flight risk probably held without bail.

"Good. You'll tell the police that he's been acting strangely and going on about this woman Ana and her brother."

Sabel nodded. "Why kill the brother? Why not the woman?"

"She may not survive the ritual, in which case, I'll count on you to help make it look like Drake killed both of them."

Sabel had the impression that by "may not survive" Johnson actually meant that if Ana did make it through the ritual alive, he was willing to kill her himself. She had to warn Ana.

"I need the address," she said.

He pulled out his smartphone, touched the screen and held it up so she could see the address on it. She reached for her phone but he put his hand on her arm and stopped her.

"Memorize it," he said. She did.

He put the phone back into his briefcase and pulled out a flat, square black box with a jeweler's logo on the top.

"Open it."

She looked inside and saw a delicate gold bracelet with two dozen perfect diamonds around it. It wasn't ostentatious, but it was expensive.

"That's your advance," he said. "And your other goad is this: if you try to betray me to Drake, the university will receive electronic files detailing your involvement with the drug smuggling Satanists who killed Helen Reed."

"Payment and threats? You're very thorough."

"We're very similar, you and I," he said.

She was afraid he might be right about that part. She slid the diamond bracelet in its box into her purse. Her fingers brushed her phone. The moment she was alone in her car, she'd call Ana and warn her, though Johnson's paranoia about betrayal made her worry that he'd bugged her somehow.

He stood up from the table. "We'll take my car."

"Won't it be suspicious if we arrive together?"

"He's preoccupied and distracted. I have someone taking photographs of the warehouse for the police later. It's best that they don't see your car."

"How will I get to Drake's apartment after the ritual?"

"I trust you to figure that out," he said.

Sabel followed him out to his car. When they got to the warehouse and started to prepare the ritual, she would have to put her phone in the pile with everyone else's. They couldn't wear any metal while working demon magic. Even if she tried to hide the phone, Drake would sense it and then he'd be tipped off. She had to find a way to get a message out, but her window of opportunity had already slammed shut.

CHAPTER EIGHTEEN

By late evening, Ana was starting to panic. She'd tried calling Sabel multiple times but got no answer. Then she got a worried call from Gunnar's wife because he hadn't come home from work or checked in with her the way he did if he was running errands.

She called the police and told them that she thought Gunnar was in danger from the men who had kidnapped her and they put out a watch for his car. Then she called Detlefsen and gave him the address of the bookstore. He was there a few minutes later. She and Lily brought him up to speed on everything short of the actual existence of demons, though Ana thought he would probably take that in stride along with everything else. He told them the police were still looking through the company's financial records and there would be some arrests later in the week. Unfortunately, he had nothing to tie Johnson to Helen's murder.

At ten her phone rang.

"Ana." Drake's gorgeous voice drew up a seething hate in her. "As you have no doubt discovered, I have your brother, Gunnar. I have arranged for us to trade. You will get in your car, alone and not followed, and drive to the corner of Washington and Fifth Ave. North where you will be met."

"You son of a bitch," she said.

"This doesn't need to be uncivil," he said. "I will make it easy for you. Keep talking to me and walk out to your car. I'm sure you're there with friends trying to figure out what you're going to do about the fact that we have Gunnar. You don't want to get them involved, so just keep talking to me and walk out to your car."

"Fine," Ana said, "I'm walking to my car." She lifted a pen off the table and wrote, "Drake has Gunnar—meet him at N. 5th & Washington. Don't follow."

Lily wrote back, "We'll find you."

Ana continued out the back of the store to her car, still talking into the phone, "Tell me again how exactly this is going to be civil?"

He chuckled. "You'll come to me and offer up my old friend and I'll give you Gunnar. It's simple."

"How do I know you won't just kill both of us?"

"You don't. But you know that Gunnar's life is forfeit if I don't get what I want. And you may have surmised that I'm not completely eager in this day and age to leave a trail of dead bodies."

"But I know who you are."

"Ah, but after tonight you won't. I can take parts of your memory. You will go back to your life as it was. Won't that be nice?"

"Sure," she said. She could see the corner he'd directed her to and there was a car waiting, its lights squinting in the darkness. "I'm here," she said and hung up the phone.

She was glad Drake hadn't made her this offer two weeks ago. Then having her old life back seemed like the perfect answer.

A man in a suit held the door open for her. Every nerve in her body jangled. This was the most stupid thing she could think of, walking right into the arms of her enemy, but she didn't have a better idea. The backseat of the car smelled like new leather and stale alcohol. As soon as she sat, a man reached over and put a blindfold over her eyes.

Abraxas didn't speak, but she felt a shock of dismay from him and sent a questioning feeling in his direction.

They have a way to keep me from talking to Lily, he said. *Not surprising, but unfortunate.*

Was she having any luck?

Before we were cut off, she said Detlefsen had a plan but she's concerned it will take too long.

Any words of wisdom from you? Is this completely stupid?

I would have stopped you if I had any better idea, he said. *We are not lost yet, but definitely at a disadvantage. Drake cannot remove your memories of all this in any exacting way. He's lying to you.*

Will he kill me?

He might, but right now I am strong enough that if he kills you he gives me greater freedom to choose from any nearby body. He will try to take me first. In the process, it will seem like you are going to lose yourself and fall into death, and you will fear this. Only be certain that you will survive. Not a you that you know yourself to be, but the indestructible portion of your Self will come through this fire intact and burnished by the flames.

And everything else is crisped to ash?

Basically, yes.

Including, possibly, my body, my life?

Yes.

She sighed. "Bring it on," she said aloud, with a large measure of sarcasm.

Some part of her looked forward to this confrontation if only because it meant the end of all the fear and waiting. One way or another, tonight would decide whether these men managed to kill her or not. She also felt, though she couldn't explain it to herself, that she had been born for this. Already she knew from her childhood that she could face darkness and it would not destroy her. She could be deluded for a time, she could have her light covered over, but it was still there. Of course that high-minded metaphysical thinking didn't do much for the fact that Drake could pretty easily put a bullet through her head and then her light wasn't going to be able to stick around one way or the other.

It was one thing to experience herself as indestructible at the same time that her heart pounded and her palms drenched themselves in sweat. She didn't want to die and give up this life, not now when she could finally see its beauty. Only a few days ago she'd been able to see her brother clearly for the first time. Would that be the last view she had of him?

The car stopped and her door opened; Ana got out blind. A man's outstretched hand grabbed her elbow to draw her onward. She let herself be led, noticing that the sidewalk seemed even and there were no stairs to the door. Even though the blindfold covered her sight, she would log every detail in case it could help Lily find her. Once she was through the door and down a short hall, they took off the blindfold. She could have been in any one of hundreds of small buildings in the city. This one was being remodeled and looked half-finished, buckets of paint in the halls and spare pieces of drywall leaning up against unfinished studs. Two men flanked her, both wearing hoods and suits instead of their robes, and took her toward the back of the building where the hall stopped at a pair of doors. Through those she found a large room badly in need of updating. Wallpaper peeled on the walls and the tiles covering the floor bulged in places.

They had Gunnar in a chair on the far side of the room, his arms tied behind his back. His face, flushed red with rage, turned a darker color when he spotted her. She felt a pang of sympathy because she knew exactly what it was like to be caught in this situation, followed by guilt for getting him involved. On the heels of that was outright rage at Drake, Johnson and the rest of these men. They stood around in a grotesque re-creation of the first night they'd kidnapped her and all the fury of that night welled up in her, joining with the existing fear into a rush of panic and rage. These men in their black robes and masks, the tarp with circles drawn in blood, the dim lights of the room—she remembered how terrified and powerless she felt the first time she'd come into this group.

Now that she knew who they were, what they had done, and why, she had disgust for them and she leaned on that feeling, hoping for some respite from the feeling that her heart was about to burst. Then she spotted the one figure who stood out as different from the first night: a slender body in a black robe and delicately sewn hood. She didn't dare look at her for long to reassure herself that it was Sabel, but it had to be and she prayed that Sabel had some better plan than she did.

"All right," she said loudly, wanting to say anything before Drake's silken voice could wrap the room in his spell. "Here I am. What do you want?"

He took two steps closer to her and paused, watching. "Please, sit down."

Ana crossed to the chair he indicated and nodded toward Gunnar. "Let him go. He's nothing to you."

"All right," Drake said and gestured to the men closest to Gunnar. They helped him up from the chair, though they didn't untie him. Would they really let him walk out? He didn't go for the door, though, he crossed the room to Ana.

"I'm sorry," he said. "For getting grabbed."

"It's okay. Get out of here. I'll be okay."

"Can't leave you here," he said.

Out of the corner of her vision she saw the cloud coming for him. When it covered him and sank in, his eyes went blank.

Ana jumped to her feet. "No!" But two men had her arms, forcing her back into the chair, binding her hands behind her. They wound a rope tight around her wrists and then tied it to the chair. Automatically she started to work at the rope, praying for it to loosen.

"You have such little faith," Drake said. He fingered the empty vial that had held the small demon now possessing Gunnar. "I really have to get more of these. You two, take him to the bay and let the little one in his mind walk him into the water."

"You fucker!" Ana shouted at him.

Drake grinned at her. "You are such a good vessel. I hope to keep you when we're done with this."

Ana didn't dignify that with a reply, focused on trying to figure out how to get loose and go after Gunnar.

Abraxas, can you break these ropes?

Not these.

Do something!

I am.

Drake stepped into the middle circle of the room, a gray cloud swirling around him like a cloak. "Positions, men, grant me power and I'll get you more than you can imagine." The men formed up in their circles, some sitting and others standing.

How much power does he need? she asked Abraxas.

He's not taking any chances this time, Abraxas told her. *The last time we met, he had demon allies. Now he's on his own aside from those small bottled creatures. He'd like to think he can take me on his own, but he can't.*

If you're more powerful than him, go bash him and let's get out of here.

I can't. He sat you in a binding position in the circles. It will take me at least a few more minutes just to undo that binding. Then we have to get your hands loose and the matter of a dozen men...

Keep working, Ana insisted.

Johnson and then Drake took turns chanting, back and forth to each other, and Ana could feel the power bunching up in the room. It swelled around Drake's feet, ankles, knees, rolling up into him.

Ana struggled against the ropes that bound her wrists and then made herself relax and very slowly return her fingers to the knot to worry it loose. How long could it take Lily to find her? In this city, probably days.

The chanting rose and fell only to rise higher again. Drake moved across the floor toward her, touching her forehead with his hand. Of course it hurt, but Ana was so furious she didn't care. She accepted the pain and kept working at the knot behind her. Her fingers, slick with sweat, slipped off the rope, but she forced them back, the cramp in her hands a welcome relief from the pressure of Drake on her head.

Abraxas had said that Drake couldn't defeat him, but Ana thought that might have been bravado. Worst case if this didn't work for the black hood guys, they could lock her away in Johnson's basement, as they seemed to have had little trouble binding her and Abraxas. How long would it be before she was pleading for them to remove Abraxas? And how long did Gunnar have? With a demon possessing him, he had no chance of surviving a fall into the bay. It could look like an accident or a suicide and there wasn't anything she could do to stop it unless she could get out of these damned ropes.

Drake's touch felt like a vise on her head. If her mouth had any saliva left in it, she would have spit on him. Instead she pressed on another loop of the knot, willing it to loosen. She would not panic and throw herself against her bonds uselessly, she told herself.

The smallest of the hooded, robed figures broke from position and sprinted across the room faster than the eye could track—the way Sabel said she could move when she stuttered time. She crashed into Ana in the chair and they both fell through an invisible wall into a room that simply hadn't been there before.

The ceiling was the same as in the warehouse. Ana blinked hard, took a deep breath and felt the looseness in her arms. As she sat up, she saw they were in a room the size of a walk-in closet with the same walls as the warehouse, but she hadn't been sitting by any door that could lead to a space like this. Her bindings were off and the chair was gone.

Next to her, Sabel sat up. The dark robe and hood weren't there. She was wearing dark pants and a soft, violet shirt.

"This is a time eddy," Sabel answered Ana's unvoiced question.

"You said that like it should make sense."

Ana put her hands against the floor to try to orient herself. She felt off-balance still, not just physically but emotionally from being thrown out of her rage and fear into this empty space. She couldn't hear anything from the warehouse room: not the men, or Drake, or the sound of Gunnar going to his death.

"Remember how I told you the Hecatine witches train in powers related to time? There are eddies that swirl off the timestream. I pushed us into one. For as long as this holds, we're effectively outside of time."

Ana took a deep breath and let it out slowly. It felt good not to be tied up or threatened and to know that wherever Gunnar was, he wasn't getting any closer to the water.

"Do we go back to the same moment we left?" she asked.

"Yes," Sabel said.

"The moment where I'm tied to a chair and you've just given yourself away and we're surrounded by a dozen men and a demon?"

"Well, yes."

"That doesn't seem like the most amazing magical power ever, I'm just saying."

"But now we have time to plan," Sabel said.

"We're going to need more than a plan to save Gunnar."

Ana imagined him frozen in time somewhere on the way to his death. Was he at all conscious inside of his moving body? Did he know what was about to happen to him?

She was surprised to see Sabel smiling broadly.

"I took care of that already," she said.

"How?"

"Johnson is betraying Drake. He called me a few hours ago for help setting him up. Instead of taking Gunnar to the bay, they're going to take him to Drake's apartment to frame Drake for Gunnar's death. I just managed to get a text out with the address while everyone was distracted with Gunnar and you were on your way here. I'm sorry I couldn't warn you sooner, but it took a while to figure out how to stutter time without Drake sensing it and then I had to get over by the phones..."

"You didn't text me, right?"

"Of course not, I sent it to Lily and that reporter friend whose info you gave me. They should be at Drake's place waiting for Gunnar to show up with the guys who are supposed to kill him."

"You really are a time witch," Ana said with some wonder in her voice. She wanted to reach across the small space and hug Sabel but wasn't sure if that would be okay.

"And you're not the queen of foresight, you know that? We really need to plan these things better."

Ana laughed. The news that Gunnar had a rescue waiting for him lifted all the weight off her chest. There wasn't anything that could happen to her now that would be worse than knowing she'd caused the death of her brother just as he started a family of his own. Even if she died in the few minutes after they got out of this eddy, she'd be happy that he was safe.

"Speaking of foresight," she said. "Did you send our whole cavalry to rescue my brother? Who's going to save us?"

"Good thing we're outside of time so we can plan an escape."

"Abraxas is working on the binding circle we're in so he can get free. He said he couldn't untie me but if you can get me loose maybe he can knock some folks down…Abraxas?"

In the space of her mind where he usually answered there was nothing. She asked again in her mind silently, but still got no response and the usual sensation he created of moving under her skin didn't happen either.

"He's not here," she said.

"He didn't come with us?" Sabel asked. "I just assumed… But I never trained to bring a demon along. I didn't think to include him specifically when I pushed you in here. He'll be in your body in the timestream when you get back and I think your idea is good—you just have to make sure you don't go all demoned up until after I get you loose or it'll trigger the…"

Her words trailed off and her eyes opened wide. She touched the area over her own breastbone. Her fingertips traveled up to her throat and then down to the center of her chest.

"Oh my gods," she said. "It's temporal. It didn't come with us either."

"You mean that magical thing that keeps you from touching me isn't here? And Abraxas isn't here?" Ana didn't add the last part aloud: Abraxas isn't here to share my thoughts and feelings about you.

Sabel nodded and her eyes widened with a flash of fear or uncertainty.

"Come here," Ana said. Although Sabel was only a few feet away, she wanted to give Sabel space to refuse if this wasn't what she wanted now that it was possible.

They were both sitting on the bare floor. Sabel slid herself over the few feet to Ana.

"How long does this last?" Ana asked, waving her hand in an arc to indicate the space around them.

"This one's small, we probably have an hour or two before it closes. At least that's what it will feel like to us, technically..."

A few hours was better than what Ana had hoped for. She reminded herself that back where they'd come from, nothing was getting worse. Gunnar was going to be rescued and, from their perspective in here, everyone who wanted to hurt them was frozen in time.

She cupped Sabel's face in her palms and kissed her hard. She wanted Sabel to feel the pent-up pressure of her need all at once. Sabel's lips parted and welcomed the tip of Ana's tongue. Ana put her left hand out to feel the distance of the floor and wrapped her arm around Sabel, lowering her slowly without breaking the kiss.

Right now they had a little place outside of time just for the two of them. There was a real chance they might not survive the next few minutes back in the timestream, so Ana was going to take every stolen minute she had.

This space felt real enough, even if she couldn't understand how it existed. The wood floor rubbed rough on her arm as they stretched out on the floor together. Ana curled her fingers around the back of Sabel's neck. She couldn't touch her enough. She wanted to put her lips everywhere at the same time, but she wasn't the one who could play with the timestream so she had to content herself with what her lips, tongue and fingers could reach.

Sabel's arms were around her back and her hands clenched and unclenched in Ana's shirt as Ana kissed around the line of her jaw and explored the delicate curves of her ear. She bit gently and felt Sabel's back arch.

"We should have imagined a blanket in here," Ana said.

"That's not how it works," Sabel whispered back to her.

Even now, Ana felt bands of tension in Sabel's body that hadn't released. She understood. It was hard to go from being in danger to having this momentary, lovely reprieve. Ana rolled onto her back on the floor and grinned at Sabel.

"Why don't you show me how it works?" she said and started unbuttoning her shirt.

Sabel rose halfway to sitting and arched an eyebrow at her.

"Kiss me here," Ana said and touched her collarbone.

Sabel bent down and her lips brushed the skin running the length of the bone. Ana shivered. She put an arm around Sabel's back and felt her relax.

"Here," Ana said and touched her lips.

They kissed for a long time before Sabel pulled back and looked at her questioningly. Ana traced a line down the center of her chest with her index finger and Sabel followed it with tiny, hot kisses. Ana unbuttoned her shirt just ahead of Sabel's slow progress.

They continued that way across and down her body until they reached the point where Sabel took over removing her clothing and Ana couldn't focus to give any more pointing instructions.

When the waves of pleasure subsided enough for her to think again, Sabel was lying with her cheek pressed above Ana's heart and Ana could feel rather than see her smile. Her body felt completely limber now, almost as relaxed as Ana was.

She wrapped a hand in Sabel's hair and tipped her head up so she could kiss her. Then she rolled them over so she was on top and kissed her harder, pressing Sabel against the floor with the weight of her body. Sabel's hands gripped her shoulders and pulled, indicating that it wasn't too much.

Ana tugged the bottom of Sabel's shirt upward and she shimmied so that the material rose easily up her body and over her head. Before she could pull her arms out of the sleeves, Ana closed her fist around the material and held it to the floor above Sabel's head.

"Your hands stay here," she said.

Sabel nodded, and her eyes smiled back at Ana as much as her lips. Ana moved back far enough to pull off Sabel's shoes and then unbuckle the skinny black belt and remove her pants. Sabel's underpants were small and lacy and the same lustrous black as her hair. Ana wanted to sear this image into her mind of Sabel in only her underpants with her hands raised and tangled in a mass of purple cloth. She ran one finger under the low waistband of the underpants and watched Sabel squirm.

"Pretty. Do you always wear lingerie to a demon summoning turned rescue?"

"You should see my date panties," Sabel said breathlessly.

The idea made the rest of Ana's languor vanish in a flare of ravenous arousal. She pushed Sabel's thighs farther apart and knelt between her legs. Her fingers played under the edges of the panties, particularly between Sabel's legs until she was moaning and her hands around her shirt were white-knuckled fists.

Ana moved forward and kissed her, their bodies pressed together full length and nearly bare. Her hand pushed aside the thin lace and she slid two fingers into Sabel. The lush, wet interior of her burned with an intensity that made everything else fade away. Ana buried her face in the side of Sabel's neck so that she could focus just on being inside her.

"More," Sabel gasped. "Please."

"I want to give you everything," Ana whispered. She pulled her fingers out just enough to tuck the top half of her hand together and push it into her.

Sabel groaned and pushed her hips down to welcome her. Still her hands didn't move from where Ana set them, but her whole body seemed to open and call to her.

"May I?" Sabel asked quietly and at first Ana thought she was asking if she could free her hands. Then Sabel stifled a moan as Ana pushed into her again and Ana realized what Sabel was asking. A blaze of heat rushed down her skin and gathered in her gut like lightning. She thrust hard into Sabel.

"Yes."

She felt the waves of ecstasy crest and break over Sabel and an echoing wave rose in her own body. Her teeth closed lightly over Sabel's shoulder and she was aware only of the wildflower scent of her hair and the entwined peaks of their pleasure.

Slowly the intensity of that sensation rolled away and left Ana with a thick, heavy feeling of joy. She withdrew gently from Sabel so she could hold her in her arms.

"You can let go with your hands," she said and Sabel's hands came loose from her shirt with surprising speed. Her fingers stroked Ana's hair and shoulders and back. Then she wrapped her arms around her and held on to her tightly.

* * *

Sabel wanted to stay in that space for days, with her and Ana holding each other, but a shift in the space nagged at her attention. Her craving for Ana wasn't just because she was an attractive woman, smart, funny—she could always trust her to keep fighting, to face magic and demons and a group of a dozen power-mad men and keep trying. And in the face of all that, in this eddy outside of time, to take delight, to laugh, to kiss Sabel as if she were the only person in the world.

The space around them shifted again, inching inward energetically. Sabel half-untangled herself from Ana and sat up.

"It's closing," she said.

Ana reached for her shirt, but Sabel shook her head. "These are just conscious images of ourselves. We'll be back in our bodies fully dressed."

"But this feels real."

"It is real. It's just not physical."

"So did we really…?"

Sabel smiled at her perplexed look. "Oh, we did. Your body will remember this, even if it wasn't here for it. I can explain how that works later."

"I'd love to hear you explain it," Ana said.

"Listen, we don't have long now. You have to keep Abraxas contained as best you can. Remember, he doesn't know our plan. I'll cut your hands free. You need to get out and get help, okay? Don't stay and try to help me."

"But—"

"I have protection from the witches and I can stutter time, but you're a lot physically stronger than I am. I'm going to try to run too, but you really have to just go. You have the best chance of getting out. Promise me."

Ana's dark eyes held hers. "No," she said. "I can't promise that."

The eddy collapsed.

Sabel was back in her body on the floor beside Ana who remained bound to the chair. There were ten men and a demon in the room against two women and a demon. Shitty odds. The only good news was that none of the men had a gun. Drake could sense metal on any of them so she knew they couldn't be armed.

Although she hadn't been able to bring anything obvious with her, like a gun or even her cell phone, she had a small ceramic knife she'd tucked into her knee-high stocking that escaped both supernatural and human notice. She stuttered time to get it out quickly and sawed against the ropes around Ana's wrists as the room exploded into action.

Ana jumped to her feet the minute the bonds were off and grabbed the chair, holding it in front of her like a lion tamer. Most of the men in the room were in front of her, including Drake. A few were running toward the sides of the room, either to flank them or to escape for themselves, Sabel couldn't be sure. She stepped to one side and slightly in front of Ana so that she was facing most of the men.

"Run," she hissed. "Or get behind me and cover your ears."

She heard the chair drop but didn't turn to look. She drew breath and opened to the Voice.

"*Stop!*" she commanded. Ten men froze in their tracks.

"*Maarevas,*" Drake said with glee. He strode across the room toward her. "Perfect."

"*Sleep!*" Sabel told the men at the same time that Drake made a sweeping gesture of aversion. More than half of the men dropped, but not all of them. Drake's magic protected a few.

"You're mine." Drake's voice was rich with pleasure as he grabbed her shoulders. Ana swung the chair and it hit his back with a solid thud but failed to even slow him down. Sabel felt his power flow into her and the leash clenched in a single painful jerk.

At least this is how it's supposed to work, she thought as she passed out.

CHAPTER NINETEEN

Ana saw Drake sneer as Sabel sagged unconscious in his grip.

"Simple measures, easy to break," he said, but he shoved her unconscious body away and let her fall to the floor rather than try anything. He rounded on Ana. "You first, then there'll be time to break into your friend. Unexpected gifts."

Ana kept the chair between them and circled toward the door. Two of the other hooded men were hesitating, but the third moved decisively to cut her off.

"Johnson, I know that's you, you might as well take that mask off," she called. "I know you killed Helen."

He didn't answer.

"Little good it will do you," Drake said. He reached out and grabbed an arm of the chair. They struggled over it until Ana, still moving sideways and trying to keep as near as she could to both Sabel and the door, saw the little black knife Sabel had dropped. She let go of the chair and snatched it up, backing toward a corner near the door and trying to get both Drake and Johnson in front of her.

"Why did you kill her?" Ana asked.

"It was an accident." That actually came from Johnson.

"She wasn't strong enough," Drake said.

"She was more than strong enough," Johnson spat at him. He pulled his hood off and threw it on the ground. "She was perfect and you pushed the damned ritual. If you hadn't been so stupidly eager, she'd be alive and you'd have your consort."

"Oh, now you want to speak your mind," Drake sneered. "You had more to do with Helen's death than I did. Now this one, she'll make a good vessel."

"Over my dead body," Ana hissed.

"That's an option," Drake said.

He lunged at her and she slashed with the knife, tearing a thin line across his cheek. With a hiss, he stepped back.

"Easy, I like this look," he said.

"Well then take a step back and make me an offer," Ana said.

"You want me to believe I can buy you after all? I don't think so." But he did take a few steps back and paused to look around the room again.

Ana tried to measure the seconds and guess how much time had elapsed already. How much longer did she have to stall until the rest of her plan played out? There were three men and Johnson standing, along with Drake. They could simply rush her, but the men seemed confused by what had happened and by Johnson's anger.

Drake moved a few more steps to his right, which put him next to Sabel's prone body. "How about you drop the knife or I break her neck?"

"I think she's too valuable for you to do that," Ana said. She prayed she was right.

"She's corrupted by the witches," he said. He knelt next to her and ran a strand of her black hair through his fingers. Then he lifted one of her limp hands. "All right, I'll start with her fingers."

He took the little finger in his hands and bent it until a sickening crunch sounded. Ana shouted in wordless alarm, then bit hard on the inside of her cheek in an effort not to show the shock of sick fear that went through her. She just had to stall him a little bit longer—but how long?

He switched to the ring finger of Sabel's hand and stroked it watching Ana's face. She threw herself at him, knife first, but he knocked her out of the air. She rolled and came up next to him, jabbing uselessly at the empty air.

Ana heard the wet snap of another finger breaking. She screamed and charged him again, grabbing with one hand and slashing low and up with the other. His hands caught the wrist of her right hand and twisted. Her fingers went numb and the knife dropped to the floor. She aimed her left fingers at his eyes and, as he twisted to block her, jammed her knee into his crotch. He doubled over with a grunt but when she lunged for the knife, he had enough mobility to shove her away from it.

She staggered into the middle of the room and one of the other men grabbed her from behind, pinning her arms clumsily. Her heel dropped hard onto his instep and his grip went loose, but the only direction she could move to get away from him put her closer to Drake. She stepped away from the man behind her and aimed a tight punch at Drake. He moved to the side and kicked out quickly, hitting her solidly in the gut.

A shattering boom hit the door and then the room flashed with light and smoke. Ana was doubled over from the kick and the smoke made her gasp for air turn into a choking cough.

"Police!" someone yelled. "Keep your hands where we can see them!" Uniformed men and women spilled through the door, guns trained on the various men in the room.

Ana put her hands up and ran, still coughing and bent in half, to where Sabel lay. She dropped to her knees and kept her hands high.

One of the heavily suited officers nodded at her questioning look and she bent down to touch Sabel's face. Her skin felt cold and looked white as ice. Her breathing was shallow and it was slowing down as Ana watched. Did the magic just wear off? Why wasn't she waking up? Ana didn't know what to do.

She pulled the cell phone out of her pocket and closed the open line to 911. When Sabel used the Voice and had the attention of the men in the room, Ana remembered the phone in her pocket. With Drake's attention on Sabel, she had a moment to turn away, dial 911 and slip the open phone back into her pocket. Hopefully they'd recorded Drake and Johnson talking about Helen's death.

Should she call Lily to get help for Sabel? Could Lily do anything?

Abraxas, she asked, *can you get a message to whoever needs to hear it that Sabel needs help?*

I would have to leave your body, but I can try, he replied.

Please.

He rushed out of the back of her body, leaving a vacuum that made her gasp. She prayed he would be fast and find the right person to come help. She didn't like how labored Sabel's breathing looked or the paper-white paleness of her skin. What if the magic they put on her wasn't calibrated for a body going into shock from broken bones?

Next to her, an officer approached Drake with handcuffs. "Hands behind your head, sir," he said. Drake did as he was asked, but his eyes remained on Ana.

"Thank you," Drake said and Ana realized, with horror, that he wasn't talking to the cop. She got to her feet quickly, but already his body was slumping to the ground, empty. He had said she made a great vessel and now she'd sent Abraxas away. Without Abraxas she was a body optimized for demon inhabitation and virtually without protection.

Drake rolled down on her like a thundercloud. His disembodied form poured into her, crushing her, absorbing her, filling her body so completely there was no place for her to be. Ana did the only thing she could think of and leapt sideways out of her body, the way Abraxas had shown her when he borrowed her body. From a few safe feet away, she watched her own head turn toward the police officer.

"My goodness," her voice said lightly. "I didn't take him for the fainting type."

The officer who was checking Drake's pulse looked up and grinned. "It takes all types."

Ana felt the rubber-band-like connection she had to her body narrowing. Drake was squeezing it off and she understood with horror that if she didn't get back in her body soon he would be able to sever her connection to it. Would that make her a ghost or kill her? Could she get back? She didn't want to risk it.

Drake said through her mouth, "Would you mind, sir, if I went outside to sit down? I'm feeling dizzy."

"Sure," the cop said. "Wait on the steps for the paramedics."

"Thank you, I just need to clear my head."

Her body moved toward the door. If he got outside in her skin, he could go anywhere. He couldn't hide her from Abraxas, but he could hide her from Lily and any other help. If Abraxas came back now, Ana felt sure he wouldn't be strong enough to fight Drake from outside of her body. What happened to him if he lost?

And if Drake defeated Abraxas and locked her out of her own body, she would lose everything. Plus, she reminded herself, she'd resolved to kill him. Ana forced herself back toward her body, clawing her way into her skin.

Inside herself was a whirlwind, tearing pieces of her mind apart. He left no space where she could be away from him, but every place her mind brushed up against him burned and tore. He went through her memories with a spinning blade. He plucked out parts of her personality and held them up like bits of glass before crushing them under his heel. The more she resisted the faster he came. A thousand times more invasive than the possessions she'd felt before, he pried through her mind and pulled out every terrible moment of her life. He pawed the good memories and darkened them.

He found the memory about Gunnar and expanded it until it enclosed her: the tight air of her tiny room filled with the smell of young men; Mack's lopsided sneer as he called her a whore and a bitch; the knife in Gunnar's hand. Drake savored her memory. He rolled in it like a dog in grass, repeating it in the theater of her mind. Again and again she felt the terror of knowing her brother was waiting to rape her, being trapped in her own room, the guilty joy of wielding that knife, the raging power that filled her, the desire to take a life, and then later the horror that she'd hurt Gunnar, the brother who loved her.

Drake would keep her here forever watching as she attacked her brothers, the scene played back in detail again and again.

CHAPTER TWENTY

Drake fought to destroy her and he was close to succeeding. Soon she might not be able to remember anything but the worst day of her life. She tried to call on anything Abraxas had taught her that would help. Get outside her identity, sure, but how? How when she felt like sobbing and puking and tearing her own eyes out if only she didn't have to see the knife go into Gunnar again?

But Abraxas had witnessed all of this. He knew her mind and everything she did, and still when she had seen herself through his eyes that afternoon in the desert, he loved her.

He'd taught her to doubt her own thinking and she began to make sense of that. These memories Drake showed her were full of her own beliefs about herself, what had happened, what was right or wrong. She thought she was evil or broken because of these events, but was she?

Drake played the memories again, and this time Ana actually watched them. She saw a terrified girl who was unsafe in her own house, being hit and taunted by Mack, who was in his own way only passing down the violence and neglect that came to him from their father. Yes, that was her, and it had happened very long ago. It wasn't happening now, and she wasn't that girl any longer. Curiosity opened in her and she watched the incidents again. She could see them without the rage and fear. She remembered how she had decided she was broken, dirty, awful—how she decided she must be to blame for Mack's assaults on her—and the steps of her life that led from that decision forward. Those decisions came from the culture she grew up in, the small town, her mother, the girls at school, the people she saw on television; she hadn't come to any of them by her own volition.

Ana had a moment of pride that she'd chosen to fight rather than give in to those feelings of worthlessness, and now she could understand that worthlessness came, not from the abuse itself, but from her belief that it happened because there was something fundamentally wrong with her. Being attacked was terrifying, painful, violating, but it was a wound she could heal physically—it was her belief about herself that carried the damage.

Then, when she attacked Gunnar, it cinched the belief that she was damaged, worthless and evil. Only a messed up, broken kid could knife the brother she loved. Except that now, viewed on the back of Mack's persistent abuse, it made perfect sense. She had refused to remain his victim and she was willing to fight for her freedom. At the time, with the limited understanding she had, she couldn't have done anything else. And she hadn't killed Gunnar, though she condemned herself internally as if she had. She'd seen him in the street days ago, a fully functioning man who was about to become a father, yet she'd clung to the image of herself as a monster. There was no truth to her self-recrimination, only the persistence of her thoughts about these memories. The thoughts weren't real, or true, or worth keeping.

She could choose a new set of meanings about those events. She could choose to believe that she'd been brave and resourceful and willing to stand up for herself. She could forgive the girl she'd been and value her.

Drake must have sensed that his tactic wasn't working because he moved out of her memory to her nerves. Accepting physical pain came easily now, cleansing as it poured through her. She waited, feeling along the surface of her skin, just outside the pain he gave her. Could she contain him? What could she do to this creature inside her body? The relationship had to go both ways. If he was in her, she must be able to influence him too.

She gathered herself at the edge of her body and brought her will inward, squeezing. Her awareness rested beside the pain, opening itself to the experience, and a peace grew in her. The pain didn't mean anything. There had been a time, recently, when she thought she deserved it because of what she'd done, but now she could understand that pain just happened, it was part of being alive.

At worst Drake could stop her heart and she would die and everything would go on. Cars would run, lights change, the sun come up and down. Gunnar was safe and she had to believe that Abraxas would find the right help for Sabel and she would recover. Drake could not destroy the life she had lived, nor could he destroy the essence of herself, the person she now knew herself to be.

Ana felt him squirm in her. She closed more tightly around him. Where there had been anger before, she felt empty. Her emotions had been torn apart when he went through her memories. She couldn't remember what fury felt like, but she knew he had to be contained. That knowing held her together with an iron focus.

He stopped struggling against her and shifted from a broad presence through her body into a narrow thing like a drill. Then he bored straight through her. Ana couldn't hold him. She couldn't hold herself together. The world fell apart.

* * *

Sabel was cold. *That's because Ana isn't here*, her mind told her. Ana should be next to her, holding her, pressing warm skin on hers.

Someone was touching her, but it felt all wrong. The hands were brusque and businesslike. They moved her left arm up and shifted it before putting it down again. She opened her eyes on a white ceiling and a woman's curious face. Her mind quickly registered: nurse, machines, bed with sides—hospital.

"Ana?" she asked.

"Your friend is here too," the woman said.

She took three long, slow breaths. Her chest ached but it was a memory, not any real danger. The leash was reset and dormant, but it was still there.

She glanced around and saw a curtain dividing the middle of the room. She'd been out long enough for them to put her in a room and they'd expected to keep her overnight. Judging by the color of the sky outside the window, it would be dawn soon.

"What happened?" she asked the nurse. "How long was I out?"

"About seven hours. We set your fingers and put you on oxygen, and then your breathing started to improve. Can you tell me what happened to you?"

Sabel looked down at her left hand where the smallest two fingers were set with a splint. Had she fallen on her hand? There was a dull ache but the painkillers were doing their job. She thought about the nurse's question.

Did she mean being attacked by a demon? That couldn't be it. And the leash wasn't visible in any way. Therefore she thought that Sabel had some kind of physiological condition that had been triggered by the other events. What could she say that would allow her to get out of here with the fewest tests?

"I just blacked out," Sabel said. "I don't know if it was the fear or maybe the pain." She held her bandaged and splinted hand up a few inches.

"Have you had breathing difficulties in the past?"

"Allergies and the usual. I can get short of breath if I really exert myself, but my regular doctor never thought it was worth worrying about. She probably didn't expect me to get attacked by a gang of...whatever those guys were. Where is Ana? Is she okay? Can I see her?"

"She's not awake yet," the nurse said.

"But she's all right?"

"We're doing everything we can to make sure that she will be."

"I want to see her."

"Give me a few minutes," the nurse said.

It was more than a few minutes but she came back with a doctor who cleared Sabel not only to walk the halls of the hospital but to go home that morning, provided she agreed to talk to her regular doctor about what he thought was a severe asthma attack. Sabel played along with his concerns and got the discharge papers signed. She changed back into her clothes in the small restroom and went to find Ana's room.

Ana had a two-person room to herself but it was crowded with Lily, Gunnar and Ruben. On the bed, Ana looked sunken and empty. Her consciousness wasn't there.

"Hey," Gunnar said when he saw her. "Heard you rescued me."

She smiled at him. He had dark eyes like Ana's but they were deeper and haunted, and his smile was similar.

"I just tipped off the cavalry."

"I leave town for a week and this is the trouble you get into," Ruben said. He was a hair taller than Gunnar and broader through the shoulders, but seemed less substantial.

"How is she?"

"There's some swelling in her brain and they're worried that she's not waking up," Lily said. "Abraxas is back in her and trying to find her consciousness. He says Drake did something to try to drive her out of her body so he could have it. It didn't work the way he expected and he fled, but she's not in there now either."

Sabel glanced at Ruben but he didn't seem surprised. They must have filled him in on the salient points while she was unconscious.

"You okay?" Gunnar gestured at her bandaged hand.

"Broke two fingers. Falling I guess."

Lily shook her head. "Drake broke them. He was going to work his way through all of them to get Ana to turn herself over to him."

Sabel stared down at the splint on her hand and tried to imagine it. Did Ana fight him? She must have if he ended up inside her body. Sabel put the hand against her belly and held it close.

"You started going into shock," Lily said. "And that witch magic didn't stop. Abraxas said Ana was worried you were going to stop breathing and she sent him to find...help."

"Oh." The word sounded so small to her ears but a hundred thousand words couldn't have expressed what she felt. She stepped up to the side of the bed and touched Ana's hand.

A band tightened in her chest and she winced. There was enough residual demonic energy in Ana's system with Abraxas back in her body to trigger the leash again. Stupid thing. She would demand that Josefene take it off that night, but for now she stepped back so she wouldn't risk passing out again and getting stuck back in the hospital bed.

She picked an empty chair across from the foot of the bed and sat.

* * *

Sand. Ana liked sand. Sand was on beaches and beaches were nice. That feeling on her back, it was warmth. That was a feeling she could have more of.

Ana, someone said.

She didn't know what the word meant.

But sand, that was a good thing. And she had fingers, she remembered that fingers could move and touch the sand, pick it up, run it through them. Blinking in the sunlight. Golden specks in the light.

Look at me, he said.

His voice made her glad, so she did what he asked. A pillar of fire, a handsome face with golden eyes, no smoke, just flames making a chest and arms that reached out to her. She didn't know she could embrace fire, but she did and rested against him.

Ana, he said again, because that was her name after all.

Yes?

You need to come back to your body.

I'm not in my body? She thought she remembered that she could be in the sandy place and her body at the same time, but it did feel different now.

No.

I did have a body, didn't I? Where is it?

It's in the hospital.

Is it sick?

Only if you stay away from it.

Drake got away, she said then, remembering how she'd left her body. *I'm sorry.*

Abraxas laughed. *Let me show you his 'getting away.'* He pointed at the sky and made an image appear some distance away from them like a mirage. Ana saw against the bright blue a blazing comet that arced away and fell to the sand near them, resolving into a lizard-like creature the size of a dog. It was burned badly and whimpering, tail held tight between its legs, limping and running away. She understood that this was only a representation of what had happened to Drake when he fled her body, but it was good enough for her to begin to understand how badly she'd hurt him.

I can't be certain that's the form he took, but it's close, Abraxas told her. *He is over eight hundred years old and you are just thirty. I cannot describe to you the humiliation and limit you placed on him. None of his fellow princes will deign to work with him for a century, none of his former allies will help him. He is as good as banished.*

Abraxas, he hurt me. There are holes in me, blank places. I'm not the same.

I know, he said softly. *Some people would choose to suffer about that, to go away, to be wounded. But not you. You'll come back with me and you'll grow, won't you. You'll use this as an opportunity.*

If I regret that later, can I still be mad at you?

If it helps.

Ana pushed herself away from Abraxas and looked around. She and Abraxas were in a sandy plain between two dunes.

Ana, just come back with me, he repeated.

He held out his burning hand and she wrapped her fingers around his. She expected pain but got none, only a thick feeling like her head was swathed in cotton and her tongue five times too big to fit in her mouth.

Ana opened her eyes, wincing at the bright glare of the lamp. Gunnar was asleep next to her bed, his long body extended like a plank, precariously balanced on edge of the little chair under him. A tiny white glow came from the foot of the bed and as her eyes focused she made out Sabel sitting cross-legged in an armless plastic chair with a book in her lap and a tiny book light illuminating a single page.

"Hey," Ana said. The word came out as a rough breath with hardly any sound to it, but Sabel's head came up immediately.

"Hey yourself," she said quietly. "You got back."

Ana nodded.

Sabel unfolded herself from the chair and set the book down. She picked up a plastic cup with a straw from the table beside the bed, poured water into it and held it out for Ana to sip. She did gratefully. Her mouth felt like she'd been lying facedown in the desert of her dreams.

"How long?" she whispered.

"Just over two days. We've been taking shifts."

Ana reached up and touched the back of Sabel's hand. Sabel put the cup down and took Ana's hand, but Ana saw the muscles around her eyes and jaw tighten.

"Don't hurt yourself," she said.

Sabel shook her head but she dropped Ana's hand and stepped back from the bed. "I haven't been able to get in touch with the others to get it off. Too hard to focus."

"It's okay, we have time."

That made Sabel laugh quietly. "Time," she said.

Seeing the little smile on Sabel's lips reminded her of part of an image: a glimpse of Sabel's body laid out bare on a wooden floor, black lace on pale skin, the feel of the curve of her neck under Ana's lips, the smell of a meadow of wildflowers in the hot sun.

"Sabel," Ana whispered. "When Drake fought me inside my body, he went through my memories. He destroyed some of them. I don't know where all the gaps are yet, but I remember kissing you. That happened, right?"

"Yes, more than once."

"You kissed me back."

"A lot," Sabel said.

"I remember you being...but it doesn't make sense. We were on a floor somewhere and there was more?"

She thought she saw the glimmer of tears gathering above the lower lids of Sabel's eyes, but it was hard to tell in the half-dark room. Sabel turned her face away for a moment.

"Yes, more," Sabel told her in a near whisper.

"When you're free of that thing and I don't feel like I got hit by a truck, will you remind me how that was?"

"I'll remind you of everything," Sabel said.

On the other side of the bed, Gunnar mumbled and tried to turn over in the chair but fell out of it instead. He hit the floor with an "Ooof" and stood up stiffly.

"She's awake," Sabel told him.

"Hey," Ana said as he grinned down at her.

"You feel okay?" he asked.

"Not too shabby, all things considered. You?"

He picked up a newspaper from the broad windowsill. Unfolding it, he held it where she could see the cover photo of the summoners being led out of the warehouse building with their hands cuffed behind them. Johnson looked furious.

"Your reporter friend brought it," he said.

"It's quite the story," Sabel added. "Somehow Andi tied together the drug shipping and money laundering operation at Roth with Drake Industries and a super creepy group of guys who really thought they could get away with Satanic magic, whatever that is. The press is having a field day. Andi brought that teddy bear and chocolates arrangement too—she's pretty thrilled with the story. The summoners are all up on charges including murder, conspiracy to commit murder, kidnapping, drug stuff and a bunch of others. Oh, and she said Drake Industries is getting one hell of an audit right now."

In the half-curtained window beside her bed the sun was warming the sky behind the buildings with a faint orange.

"Do you think they'll let me go home?" Ana asked.

CHAPTER TWENTY-ONE

Back home, Ana savored the simple sensations around her: the nappy weave of the bathroom rug; the cold hardness of the tiles; the motion of air on her skin; Abraxas leaving to talk to Lily and Gunnar who were sitting in the living room; the thousand cotton fingers of the towel on the skin of her back. She could happily stand in the bathroom and just breathe, but someone would probably think she'd gone catatonic.

She'd come home from the hospital in the midmorning after the latest series of tests showed nothing really wrong with her and she promptly fell into a real sleep in her own bed. While she was resting, Ruben invited Lily, Gunnar and Sabel over for dinner. In typical Ruben style, he'd made a salad and picked up the rest of the dinner from a local caterer.

Fresh from the bath, she walked into the bedroom. On the chair next to her dresser was a T-shirt and her black yoga pants. She remembered Sabel borrowing those, remembered being horrified about what she might have seen in the drawer underneath them. She remembered seeing her blood on Sabel's white jacket and being rescued by her when she ran from the summoners, but then there was a gap before that. She remembered running in a dress, but why was she wearing a dress?

She put on the T-shirt and the black yoga pants and went down the stairs. "Sabel, what was I doing the night the summoners kidnapped me?"

Sabel looked at her outfit and blinked, then flashed her a smile. "You were at Roth's fifth anniversary party," she said. "You invited me because you were trying to figure out if I was hitting on you or not. Ruben went with you too and he looked much too fabulous for that group."

Ruben came in from the kitchen and set a tray of drinks on the coffee table. "Oh and you were in that beautiful Armani suit and there was nothing else to look at in that whole room. Ana, your next job needs to have prettier boys." He turned from Ana back to Sabel. "*Were* you hitting on her?"

Sabel's lips quirked up. "I was pre-hitting on her."

"That's a thing?"

"You know, when someone's interesting but you don't know them well enough yet to know if they're really interesting so you're trying to find out—that's pre-hitting on."

Ana grinned and sat on the couch next to Lily. "Ruben doesn't have that phase."

"I do too, it just lasts about as long as it takes me to cross a room."

Lily spoke into the lull after the laughter. "If it's all right to ask, do you know how much memory you lost?"

Standing beside her as a creature made of smoke, Abraxas answered, "Maybe one memory in thirty, but Drake started with some of the more positive ones."

He was getting better at standing outside of her body, not that he could go very far, but it was nice to know she could tell him to sit in the other room if she needed to.

There was one memory that now stood out more clearly than ever, but it lacked the painful emotional signature it carried in the past. She'd lived through it so many times that it became almost pure content without meaning, like a word spoken over and over again until it stopped making sense.

She looked across the room at Gunnar, realizing there were obvious words she'd never spoken to him. "Hey," she said and then didn't know how to continue. "About that time...the knife...I am so sorry. I know I said that before, but I just wanted to tell you again how much I regretted that."

"I know," he said. "I forgave you a long time ago. The whole situation was shit."

She held up a free hand. "Let me finish, I just have to say this. I was so scared. I knew Mack was after me. I avoided him for a year, but that afternoon I knew if I didn't get out of that room, he was going to rape me and I wasn't ever going to let that happen. And you..." She paused as her voice caught. "You were between me and the door. I always loved you and I knew you never wanted what Mack wanted, but I couldn't see any other way to get out, and I'm so sorry for that day, but also that I haven't...haven't said this to you sooner."

He stood up and walked across the room to her, then dropped to his knees. "I couldn't protect you," he said, tears rolling down his face. "God, I couldn't. I grabbed for the blade, I wanted to get cut for what I'd allowed Mack to do to you. It wasn't the knife that hurt. When you were a baby, you used to follow me around all the time, like you were my kid. I've been so afraid to have a baby and not be able to protect her, like with you." He put his arms around her waist and wept. "I couldn't take care of you," he said, the words muffled into her belly.

She held onto his shoulders, lips against his hair while he cried. When his shoulders grew still again and he pulled back from her, wiping tears roughly off his cheeks, she let herself smile.

"You know," she said. "For two fucked-up kids, we turned out pretty well."

He laughed, a light, dry sound. "Sure did."

"You're going to make an amazing dad."

"You think?"

"You make the best toys and anyone who's willing to randomly follow his sister and offer to help when he hears there are demons involved is definitely going to protect the daylights out of any kid he has."

"Yeah," he grinned.

Ana looked around at all of them. Ruben was leaning against the fireplace and blinking hard at the emotion in the room. At the other end of the couch, Lily surreptitiously wiped her eyes. Abraxas hummed in the back of her mind like warm sunlight. And Sabel looked back at her and when their eyes met, Ana saw pride and smoldering desire.

They all had their scars and their demons out in the world, but tonight she wanted nothing more than to sit with these people and enjoy them.

"What do you think we do now?" she asked.

"Ruben and I are going to make popcorn and pick out some movies," Lily said. "And then we're going to sit on the couch for about four hours barely moving."

* * *

By the time the second movie ended, after midnight, Ana looked more at peace than she had since Lily met her.

She'd borrowed Ana's backyard for her late night meeting with Asilal. The day before she'd written to him to let him know that she needed to update him in person.

He came faster this time, perhaps because they'd talked recently and, of the millions of people on his mind, she was in the forefront now. His mind-bendingly large form separated from the skyscrapers and flowed through the buildings up toward her. In the yard he didn't have to shrink to man-sized for her to focus on him, so he stayed next to the old tree, just smaller than its upper branches.

"The human woman ousted the shaidan, the Ashmedai?" he asked without preamble.

"She did."

"Alone? You would have me meet her?"

"Not alone and I do have someone for you to meet," she waved back at the window, though it wasn't really necessary because Abraxas had been watching, and he poured himself down onto the porch. He managed a few strides into the yard before he had to stop, at the limit of his distance from Ana's body.

Asilal bent his enormous head down and sniffed at Abraxas like a giant cat. "You are old and new then," Asilal said.

"I was the Abraxas once, the former one."

"What are you now?"

Abraxas shrugged and the gesture reminded Lily of Ana. "An old man in a young body trying to find my place in this new world."

"You taught the human how to defeat the Ashmedai?"

"I did."

"Do you plan to tell all the humans these tricks?"

"It would harm the Sangkesh none."

Asilal groaned like a tree and Lily heard his laughter in the sound. Abraxas bowed his head and with his eyes on the ground continues, "Protector, I ask permission to reside in your city, in this woman. What is in my purview, I will protect."

"Granted," Asilal said.

"I ask also you close the city to the Ashmedai and any who ally with him so they may not enter and harm anyone within."

"It is done. I cannot reach him outside my city, but any inside this city are safe from him. When he has power again. Do you have anything else to request?"

"That is all."

"Then I do," Asilal's voice dropped to a curious purr. "This woman that you have made interesting, we would like to meet her."

"We?" Lily asked.

"The protectors of the city. We would like to know all of you better. You are helpful."

"Now?" the question squeaked out of her.

He straightened up with another tree-like groan. "We will call for you," he said. He inclined his head once briefly to them and then rolled away down the hill like a landslide.

Abraxas sat down on the edge of the porch, his legs hanging over the side and the lightning of his feet crackling down into the grass. "Simple enough," he said.

"I've never met anyone but him from the city," Lily said.

"You do good work for them, you should have."

"I was overseas for a long time, I've only been here ten years." She walked up the steps and sat next to him. He put his hand over hers. It didn't feel like a hand, more a warm layer of steam on her skin, but the gesture mattered.

"I know more crossbreeds than full demons by far," Lily said.

"How do we demons measure up?"

She grinned at him, "Oh I'm still taking my measure of you."

He laughed. "Then I shall not stop trying to impress you."

The night was cool and dry. A night bird crying from the tree and the sound of cars on a distant street barely filtered through to them. She was tempted to go inside to Ana, just to tell her that she was really safe now that Ashmedai could not come back in the city, but it could wait a little while. She looked at the lit windows and then back to Abraxas's burning eyes.

* * *

As late as it was, Ana only felt a bit tired, probably because she'd slept most of the day. Gunnar had left for home after the first movie and Ruben was upstairs rustling around in the bathroom as he got ready for bed. Lily and Abraxas were in the backyard. Ana still felt Abraxas in her, but it was lighter, as if he could shift his weight a short distance away from her and rest less heavily in her body.

At the far end of the couch, Sabel had her feet tucked under her, which made her look small and delicate, like a little cat.

She had the remote and was clicking through the list of other movies they could watch. During the movies, Ruben had settled himself between them with his arms around both. It wasn't nearly enough connection, but it didn't trigger that energy thing the witches hadn't taken off Sabel yet. The image of Sabel dropping instantly when Drake reached her was still fresh in Ana's mind.

"Abraxas is in the backyard," Ana said. "Could I touch you?"

Sabel put down the remote and crawled down the couch to her. Ana touched the side of her face. This close, she smelled like wildflower honey and the scent gave Ana a half memory of pushing her face through that curtain of dark hair to kiss behind her ear.

"You said you would remind me," Ana told her.

"Do you remember anything?"

"I remember you taking us someplace where we were talking and then it all starts to fall apart and I just have bits and pieces."

Ana trailed her fingers down the side of Sabel's graceful neck and stopped above her collarbone. Sabel shivered and leaned into her so that she was sitting more against Ana than the back of the couch.

"I have one clear memory of kissing you here," she said. "And something funny about a pair of date panties?"

Sabel stretched her legs the length of the couch and turned enough that she could undo the button of her jeans and slide the zipper down. Ana glimpsed a delicate triangle of white lace against Sabel's smooth skin and the cobalt blue demin of her jeans.

"These are the date panties," Sabel said. "Well, one pair."

"How many do you have?"

"That's something you have to discover by experience?" She zipped and buttoned her jeans again.

Ana coughed lightly and tried to get her mouth to form words. "What did we do?" she asked.

"You told me where to kiss you," Sabel said. "I was in a million places in my mind and you focused me here and here and here," she touched Ana's collarbone and then drew a line slowly down the front of Ana's body.

She gasped as Sabel's hand continued below the line of her belt. Her hand clutched white-knuckled at the couch cushion. She wanted to grab Sabel and kiss her so hard that she couldn't breathe, but what happened if Abraxas chose that moment to return?

"Then you held my hands down and told me not to move them and you…" Sabel stopped and shook her head.

Ana could see how quick her breath was by the rapid rise and fall of her chest. She didn't dare move for fear that if she did she wouldn't be able to stop herself.

"Did I take off the non-date panties?" she asked.

"Pushed them to one side."

Dizziness spiraled up Ana's body, traveling around the inside of her legs to gather in her belly.

"I wish I could just show you the memory," Sabel said.

"I *want* you to show me," Ana replied with such fervor that Sabel laughed and kissed the side of her face.

Ana held her tightly, careful of her broken fingers and aware of all the ways she could still accidentally hurt her. After a while, Sabel pulled away just far enough to face Ana again.

"There should be a way to get those memories back," she said. "Drake couldn't really destroy the memory itself, only your ability to retrieve it. If I knew where it was in your consciousness…but I don't know how to access that. Probably Abraxas does."

"I don't particularly want him to find those memories," Ana said. "It's bad enough that I got to ride along with him having sex with Lily."

"You what?"

"He pulled her into a dream so they could get it on and I ended up inside his dream body the way he is inside my physical body," Ana explained.

Then she remembered the other time Abraxas and Lily had sex and that she had let him borrow her body for it, which technically meant that she'd had sex with Lily, or did it? Did it count as having sex with someone if you weren't in your body when it happened? It did count if you were too drunk to remember it, but that wasn't the same as willingly stepping out of your body for someone else. It was so complicated. Was that something she should tell Sabel or not?

Sabel's eyes, distant with thought, were the blue of a deep summer sky. "How long do you plan to keep him?" Sabel asked.

"Until he's strong enough to be on his own, I guess," Ana said. "Once the witches take that energy thing off you, it won't be a problem though, right?"

"They won't like it. Not that they have a say on my dating life."

"Does that mean you're asking me out? Or did I already ask you out and I just don't remember?"

"Formally? You haven't."

"Oh, well then, even though I'm hosting an ancient demon and you're from a group of demon-hating witches, do you want to, like, go out?"

"Yes," Sabel said. She leaned forward and kissed Ana.

Ana put her hand up between them to remind herself not to do any of the things she most wanted to and then let herself forget about everything but Sabel's lips and tongue.

When she felt Abraxas returning from the backyard, she pushed lightly and Sabel broke away from her. They were both breathing hard and Sabel's eyes shone in the low light of the room.

"I wish you could ask the witches to let you spend the night tonight," Ana said.

Sabel laughed. "They'll say: Be patient, it's only a matter of time."

Bella Books, Inc.

Women. Books. Even Better Together.

P.O. Box 10543
Tallahassee, FL 32302

Phone: 800-729-4992
www.bellabooks.com